MW01265339

3 Oct 11

September 27, 2011
To: Joan and Joe;
Enjoy this novel set in
Moultrie County on the
Kaskaskia + Vicksburg.
Ed LeCrone

Fire on the Prairie

by

Ed LeCrone

authorHOUSE®

AuthorHouse™
1663 Liberty Drive
Bloomington, IN 47403
www.authorhouse.com
Phone: 1-800-839-8640

First published by AuthorHouse 2/26/2010

ISBN: 978-1-4490-7554-5 (e)
ISBN: 978-1-4490-7552-1 (sc)
ISBN: 978-1-4490-7553-8 (hc)

Library of Congress Control Number: 2010900953

Printed in the United States of America
Bloomington, Indiana

This book is printed on acid-free paper.

Summary
Fire on the Prairie

THE TURBULENCE OF THE CIVIL WAR swirls throughout the country in the spring of 1861, sucking men and women into its life changing vortex. Chance Neunan, a nineteen year old farmer's son, is caught up in the chaos of the times and joins the 41st Illinois Infantry. Following training, the young farmer's unit marches away from home and hearth side. Too late, he discovers that he and his first cousin, Becky Scott, are experimenting with a forbidden love affair. Neunan's departure creates a void in the protection of his and Becky's family in Central Illinois where southern leaning dissidents known as Copperheads are fermenting mischief. This clandestine society operating under various names perpetrate all manner of schemes endeavoring to undermine the Lincoln administration and the Union's war effort.

Young Neunan is involved in combat at the momentous battles of Fort Donelson, Shiloh, Corinth, and Vicksburg, and comes through the engagements a wiser man. Additionally, he begins to realize that the prejudices toward black people he has acquired from his southern born mother are wrong and the 'Contrabands' are just as human as he.

Chance is injured in January, 1864, and sent north to convalesce while on furlough. His train passage home is interrupted and he is cast into a full blown riot taking place in Charleston, Illinois, between soldiers and Copperheads.

LeCrone brings his vast knowledge of the Civil War in the West to bear in *Fire on the Prairie* and provides the reader with a visceral description of the perils, the heart break, and the glory that every soldier, both then and now, passes through. The letters between Neunan and Becky Scott are colorful and laced with colloquialisms and unusual jargon utilized by the military and civilians of that period.

'Fire on the Prairie' traverses the fortunate reader through both a history lesson and a poignant love story all in the same instance.

Acknowledgements

I wish to thank all the following persons and institutions for their assistance in the development of this manuscript and the offering of technical help when called upon.

My wonderful and loving wife, Darlene, and daughters, Gigi and Mimi, Eastern Illinois University for its publication, 'Coles County in the Civil War', Harriet Roll, of the Harvard Public Library, Ed Urban, local historian, Sue Durbin, George and Valee Selby of the Moultrie County Historical and Genealogical Society, the Marengo Public Library, and all the acquaintances I've made during my years of research and historical artifact collecting.

Dedication

Fire on the Prairie is dedicated to my wife whose understanding and assistance helped immensely in the production of this book.

Additionally, the story is written as a tribute to all the brave and true men of the 41st Illinois Volunteer Infantry, 1861- 18645.

Prologue

A T THE ONSET OF 1863, THE state of Illinois had sent military contingents numbering in the thousands to fight in the major western Civil War engagements of Pea Ridge, Fort Donelson, Shiloh, Corinth, Perryville, and Stones River. The state rushed to supply volunteers to support its most famous citizen, Abraham Lincoln, in his quest to restore the shattered union. Eventually, Illinois would provide the fourth highest number of troops of any of the states to the war effort, following only New York, Pennsylvania and Ohio. Marching away from hearth and loved ones, Illinois men and at least one woman, Private Albert Cashier/ Jennie Hodgers of the 95th Regiment, strove to give their all to suppress the insurrection. Patriotic fervor surging through the state in the early stages of the conflict was unbounded but twenty-two months after the first battles, factions of the citizenry grew bitter to the point of sedition and treason. Tired of the losses in life and the drain on the national treasury, these groups sought ways to create doubt and anxiety in order to create the erosion of morale within those who supported the federal administration in Washington.

The loyal opposition, in the guise of the 'Peace Democrats', was the less volatile of the organizations who expressed disagreement with the manner in which the Republican Party conducted the war effort. Democrats, and a mere vocal fraction of the party's membership, fabricated measures that gave tacit support to the soldiers in the field but raised loud objections to war expediency measures and the suspension of the writ of *Habeas Corpus* drafted by the president. While the 'Peace Democrats' claimed that their intentions were not meant to be harmful, in many cases their actions gave encouragement to a more sinister and lethal Copperhead element.

Some of the secret cadres making up the Copperhead opposition were guided and funded by Confederate agents working from Canada and operated under the sobriquets of; The Knights of the Golden Circle, The Sons of Liberty, The Paw Paws, The Corps de Belgique, and Order of the American Knights. Spies and contacts known to have served in various capacities with the secret groups in the Midwest were Thomas Hines; (alias Dr. Hunter) of Kentucky and George St.Ledger Grenfell, an English soldier of fortune. Both operatives had seen previous military service with General John Morgan of the Confederate cavalry at the time of his eventful Indiana raid in 1863.

Copperhead elements stirred the pots that brewed insurrection in Fulton and Hancock Counties and in East-Central Illinois near the Wabash River. Fermenting disobedience in the various sections of the state, and working in secrecy, the Copperheads promoted arson, thievery, and persecution. The southern sympathizing members struck out against the creation of the military draft, the emancipation of the slaves and the inroads that the German, Irish, and the Catholics were making in the culture of America. Their ultimate aim was to turn the people of the five pivotal states of the Midwest against the government in Washington and have the region sue for peace with the Confederate States of America.

In the spring of 1864, a riot occurred in Charleston, Illinois, pitting the 54th Illinois Infantry against the citizens of that city who carried allegiances to the southern cause. Following that affair, Clingman's Raid was mounted in the summer wherein a group of heavily armed men crossed the prairie near Bloomington on their way to the Democratic National Convention in Chicago. The rumor was that these men were bent on recruiting more comrades at the political gathering and releasing the rebel prisoners being held in

Camp Douglas on the lakefront. The apex to all this subterfuge and the Copperhead effort was the foiling of the plot of freeing the Confederate prisoners. All major participants involved were rounded up by the Chicago authorities and the fledgling Secret Service and jailed. Oddly, the only person who was given the death penalty in this scheme was the English soldier of fortune, George St. Ledger Grenfell.

Ultimately, those participants in the Copperhead organizations who escaped detection, capture, or death during the conflict, chose to relocate or renounce what they'd done and slip quietly back into the ranks of a post war, peaceful society.

Somewhere East of Vicksburg, Mississippi May 14, 1863.

"Close up, men, close up," the perspiring officer exhorted the ragged blue line as it thrashed through the underbrush and passed on either side of him.

"The dress is right, dammit! Align yourselves! You damned clodhoppers are breaking!" Captain Ansel Rouse, normally a man of calm demeanor, was a wild beast when he caught a whiff of gunpowder causing his nostrils to flare like those of a frightened colt. But fear was not in the man's vocabulary. He seldom flinched when bullets passed near, just became more agitated and profane. His salty adjectives urged his sweating command into new determination.

"You there, Nolan. It is Nolan isn't it? Close up! We'll have no slacking in this company, by God!"

A sergeant passing on the left shoulder of Captain Rouse wheezed out a half-hearted excuse for the manner in which the formation was advancing,

"Sir, it's all this danged brush and the deep ravines that's causin' the trouble."

"No excuses, sir. I'll accept no excuses. Our shining hour is upon us, and by the heavens we're going to take advantage of this situation!"

The Decatur, Illinois, native had drawn his foot officer's sword and was thrashing its blade through the tangle of briars as though he had closed with the rebel enemy. The vines, like the foes whom he was about to confront, were stubborn, bending down but springing back to snare his boots and tear at his trousers. Zipping, hissing sounds passed overhead as the unseen missiles clipped twigs and leaves from the towering white oaks through which the Union soldiers passed.

"See there men! See there! We're driving them and they're firing high! By God you are magnificent! Your mothers will be proud of you!"

Chance Neunan was cognizant of the captain's rants as he stepped into a leaf choked runoff filled with the dry debris of last fall. Briars of an unknown variety were less virulent in the shade of the giant trees and the young soldier's passage was eased for a few steps.

Mississippi air in early summer was hot and filled with a humidity that saturated every thread that Neunan wore. Chance felt his perspiration circle around his jacket collar and course down his spine to wet the seat of his pants.

His loaded 1853, Enfield rifle musket with its bayonet attached seemed to weigh a ton and was forever getting tangled in the brush and low branches of saplings.

"Sergeant! Sergeant Wilson! Fetch me a runner to carry a message over to Lieutenant Kellar!" Chance heard his Captain bellow. "Can't see him to know where the other end of the line is. It's this damned brush. Where are you, Wilson?"

Neunan watched as Rouse drew a sodden memorandum book from inside his tunic and commenced to scribble his order with a stubby, natural wood pencil. Sweat dripped from the tip of the man's nose and dropped on the paper's surface ahead of the little writing instrument. Speaking to himself in a low tone, Chance picked up the nearly incoherent sentence uttered by the concentrating officer, "Got to get skirmishers out on out right flank. We've got to know what's out beyond B Company. God help us if they hit us with cavalry. They'll roll us up like an old Persian rug."

Neunan stopped to untangle his rifle from a swatch of small limbs before pushing on. He tried to ignore the captain and sergeant who were conferring with each other next to the base of a massive oak tree. Chance looked straight ahead and avoided eye contact with either of the men. His desire was to pass silently and unnoticed out of their line of sight without drawing their attention. Bushwhacking through the jumble off to his right carrying an order could cause three things to happen; two of them bad. He could be shot by mistake by members of his own company or get gobbled up by Confederate cavalry probing for an opportunity to turn the advance.

"Well, Wilson, have you a man for me?"

"Yes Sir." Wilson turned sideways and grasped a passing trooper who had been malingering at the back of the movement.

Chance breathed a sigh of relief. Dodging out of responsibilities doesn't always serve your best interest, he thought as the line shifted slightly to fill the void of the departing man.

Somewhere in this voracious growth the 41st Illinois was struggling to cut off Confederate General John Pemberton's retreat after the fighting at Jackson. One lone road from the outskirts of that city led west to safety in the fortifications at Vicksburg for the rebel army. Bloodied by the forces of Grant, Sherman, and McClernand, the Confederates had failed to link up with General Joe Johnston's relief moving down the state of Mississippi from the northeast. Still, Pemberton's southerners were a viable, dangerous force and capable of putting up a fight. But at this moment the Confederates had chosen flight over valor.

Neither Chance Neunan nor Abe Stratton, the man to the young soldier's right, or the other three hundred eighty two men of the regiment and very possibly Captain Rouse had knowledge of where they were on the battlefield or the retreat route that the main body of the rebel army was following. They were mere game pieces as was the remainder of the brigade in the grand scheme that the commanding generals were formulating.

A Company trudged through the morass on the extreme left flank and B Company anchored the far right of the line. Squeezed between the two was the remainder of the regiment comprised of companies C, D, E, and F. If these sections performed as they usually did, then the entire conglomeration was bent backward in the form of a bow. This was not the expected military procedure but Chance knew from previous experiences that the men in these companies were more timid than those in the flanking companies. The truly lucky contingent was H Company who had drawn reserve duty and was guarding the stacks of knapsacks, pup tents, and haversacks in the rear.

Replacing his order booklet inside his high collared dress coat, the Decatur lawyer withdrew his sword which had been shoved into the leaf covered loam at his feet. Captain Rouse buttoned the woolen garment to his throat muttering to himself as he watched the line of soldiers pass.

"Won't have to worry about our left. The Iowa boys are over there and have an unobstructed view of our point of attack. It's the damned right that I'm worried about." Rouse, with sweat stung eyes followed the terrified young runner as he departed. A flight of bullets clipped more twigs from the limbs overhead.

The verdant obstruction remained void of bird or animal sounds. The approaching confrontation of the two forces had stripped the woods of everything except for the crackle of twigs, the wild ranting of the commanding officer, random musket shots, and the occasional curse of a man caught in the spiny vines.

"Damned orderlies! Can't ever find the timid little pukes when you need them. I've got to rely on some snotty nosed nubbin of a kid that I pull out of the ranks to carry messages," Rouse cursed.

"You there, Milloy! Get up there next to your messmate! Align yourself!"

"Peers like the graybacks is aimin' a mite high, don't ya think?" offered Pete O'Donnel thrashing about off to Neunan's left.

Turning his head to locate the speaker, Neunan noted that his tent mate carried his musket at the 'Charge Bayonets' position and seemed to be negotiating the brambles much more easily than he was.

"If they'd shoot even higher it would satisfy me."

O'Donnel gave a nervous little laugh that was devoid of humor.

"Look at Ol' Rouse over there. He's as giddy as a man in a bed full of virgins. That crazy bastard enjoys these little scrimmages." O'Donnel ducked under a low hanging branch.

Neunan shot a glance over at the officer and saw that a ring of white salt from perspiration had stained his kepi. "Some folks get their gratifications outta fighting, I suppose."

"Well, I sure as hell don't. Scarin' off Joe Johnston without gettin' into the fightin' was fine by me."

"The powers that be sure didn't figure that Pemberton would come outta Vicksburg and give us a tussle did they?" Chance used his hand to push away a swatch of leaves. The back of his hand to the tips of his fingers was wet with sweat.

"Hey, you two birds stop that jawin'. " Sergeant Wilson pushed through the briars from behind them. "Ain't no sense drawin' fire with all yer senseless racket."

The two soldiers went silent. Even Captain Rouse curtailed and stopped his incessant harping as though he sensed the advancing line was about to go into action.

A commotion to Chance's front, a mélange of excited talking and crackling branches that he was unable to access, rolled toward him. Instinctively, he brought his gun to his shoulder.

"Don't shoot! Don't shoot! Runner comin' in!"

Chance yelled back over his shoulder echoing the warning.

"Don't shoot! He's one of ours!"

The red headed young boy that Neunan had seen Sergeant Wilson select from the line for service as a messenger came hobbling toward the dark haired soldier supporting a staggering man. The afflicted soldier's face was pallid to the point of being marble and with his left hand he clutched a right arm that hung limp at his side. Neunan recognized the man as Webster Long who'd been selected as a skirmisher at the beginning of the day. How the red headed runner had gotten out in front of the skirmishers and back into the line without being shot was a mystery to the young volunteer.

"Wounded man and a runner comin' through! Hold yer fire!" O'Donnel yelled.

Passing between the men of the advancing line, the two were soon swallowed by the green hell of the Mississippi forest.

Chance felt the weakness in his knees, the surge of nausea sweep up his esophagus and pool back into his stomach. The quivering that accompanied this response in the tense moments after he'd seen wounded or dead comrades coursed down his wet fingers and terminated on the wrist of his musket where he gripped the weapon. He had seen how men handled trauma. Some clenched their jaw and went forward with even more resolve than they'd formerly had. Others became more careful, watchful, as if witnessing the carnage of wounds and death wrought by the implements of war eroded their feelings of invincibility. Yet, still others lost all control, throwing away any threads of duty, honor and responsibility and broke or deserted at the first opportunity. Only the oilskin wrapped letter tucked into the inside pocket of his jacket gave Neunan the strength to continue and not run from the field. The arrivals of the missives had sustained him through his trials from the time of his enlistment to the present, but the most recent one in his inner pocket meant the most to him. Mundane as it was, the information touched him with news of his neighbors, their daily tasks and the affection that tinted the words of Becky Scott.

My dear Chance;

We receive so little news about Gen. Grant and our cherished 41ˢᵗ Regiment outside Vicksburg. The newspapers provide excuses for their tardiness in covering the fighting in Mississippi by saying that all lines of communication to the North are subject to rebel cavalry raids. Earl van Dorn was crafty when he caught us off guard at Holly Springs in December, but I should think that our General Grant has learned his lesson and won't allow this to happen again. All the news appears to be speculation on the part of the papers' editors. The County Democrat newspaper has rebel General Joe Johnston bringing a relief army to Vicksburg to join with Pemberton in that city and whip our boys. The Mattoon Plain Dealer has our armies lost in the swamps and thrashing about in the woods and ravines. I don't know what to believe. All the believable news that I have are in the nice letters from you. It's really remarkable that we can get word from you in eight to ten days considering that we're so far apart. I received your letter dated April 17, and passed your greeting on to those you indicated.

Your Aunt Emma is no better. She struggles with the humidity. It makes it hard for her to breathe and the consumption worse. The weather has been unusually warm for early spring and that's why your aunt suffers so. The corn is about four inches high and the rains have really greened it up.

Can you imagine that mother decided to pluck the geese for feathers this late? We'd come out of that wet, soggy spot in early April as I'd written you about and the geese went right on their nests. I'd thought that when the goslings had hatched and the temperature rose we'd be shut of this dreadful chore. But I was wrong. Last Saturday, it was Ruthie, Alfie, mother and I who took on the gaggle. You never heard such a racket and saw such wing flapping as we had. You'd think those blue- eyed, feather dusters would learn that we intend them no harm. Mother chose an overcast, humid day and we sat out under the big oak in the yard. Little Alfie had the task of holding their necks and preventing the birds from flogging us.

Alfie had the big, blue Toulouse we call Sarah and I was making the fine feathers fly. Ol' Sarah took offense at how brother was holding her and bit him on the cheek. Well, that was the end of her. Alfie broke her neck as pretty as you please. Her poor old wings liked to beat me to death before

I could get away from her. We've had goose at three different meals and Alfie has had nothing more than corn mush and milk. Mother was quite upset with him. She rendered down the goose's fat and packed it up in a crock for the cellar. It will be used for spread on bread or as chest salve this winter. I would hope that mother won't want to stuff pillows until sometime in November. I've just now gotten all the fine fluff blown out of my nose. I shall close for now and not take up anymore of your time.

> *As ever,*
> *Becky Scott*

p.s. Are you getting your rations regularly?
Do you need anything from home?

Chance had studied the signature each time he'd read the letter. He calculated by the elongated gap between the first and last name in the signature that there had been a period of hesitation on the part of the signer. It was his impassioned hope that Becky had vacillated between formally signing her full name over her more personal first name.

Pausing next to a massive moss covered log that lay extended on the forest floor, the young private tried to collate the written words with the softness and inflections of Becky's voice. His quaking subsided as he permitted his mind to wander, allowing the hominess of her message to compete with the zip and hiss of bullets passing around him.

"You all right Chance?"

"Yeah, I'm all right. Just day dreamin' I guess."

"This is a hell'ava place to be doin' that. Jesus, this ain't no dream we're in and you'd better look sharp. There could be a passel of them gray backs come a pourin' outta the woods at any minute." Pete O'Donnel stooped forward and set his gaze in the foliage at their front attempting to glean the approach of danger.

"Thanks, Pete. I'll mind myself."

Kaskaskia River Bottom, Moultrie County, Illinois April 30, 1863.

Becky Scott stood at the swinging gate which protected the home's yard from meandering livestock that roamed the pasture adjacent to the farm house. The worm, split rail fence was effective against the foraging of cattle and horses, but winged fowl were constantly a nuisance with their droppings underfoot. It seemed as though the birds had a special affinity for the low front porch and an hourly duty was for Alfie or Becky to shoo them away. But the aimless wandering of the fowls and their imprisonment was not a priority for a teenage girl. Her thoughts were focused on the dreadful time in which she existed and the epical occurrences that weighed heavily on the mind of the nation.

It was unfair, she thought, to be sucked into events that she was powerless to control. Why should young people like herself be involved in this horrid war that maimed and killed thousands of Americans both combatants and civilians? She should have been experiencing the thrill of her budding, young body, the development of her sexuality, the immergence of her romantic emotions. Instead, she spent her days in a pall of despondency and the moments before retiring at night on her knees, praying. Beside her bed she asked God to spare Chance Neunan. Only after she had satisfied herself that her words for the soldier's physical salvation had been sufficiently fervent did she turn her attentions to her immediate family and relatives.

Dear God, guide the soul of our dearly departed neighbor, Andy Crowder, as he moves to your side in paradise. In your holy benevolence, forgive the transgressions of my cousin, Ruthie Scott, who has taken up with a soldier from Neoga. She's so silly and could use your guiding hand.

Watch over the Neunans, their farm and the crops they seek to raise. Protect them from the night riders who would do them harm in this lawless time. Lay your fingertips upon the breasts of those who would do evil things to them. Mediate the hearts of the wicked ones who choose to make war in the gloom of night. And, oh yes, don't forget my family and Aunt Emma. Help me and my family to retain our health and find peace in our lives. In your name I pray.   Becky

Champions Hill, Mississippi
General McClernand's Brigade

Neunan could tell that this was not to be another minor skirmish. The manner in which the men were aligned and the numbers deployed gave away the game. Stretching on either side of the Illinoisans were the other three regiments of the brigade and one could only guess what other brigades from the division were advancing in concert with them through the mile of woodland. The commanding generals were throwing all the forces they had at their disposal to halt the Confederate retreat and cut off their escape toward Vicksburg. *It was just as well*, thought Chance. "*Skirmishing seldom provided any clean cut victories; just nasty little engagements that got good and brave men killed. At least with this course of action if the Union forces were successful and could stop Pemberton's flight, his rebel force might be compelled to surrender outside the fortified city.*

Musket firing grew hotter and more deadly. Men were cursing and bellowing in the green tanglement at Neunan's front. More walking wounded were appearing, tottering toward the rear, passing through the blue line. Some shouted words of encouragement while others staggered ashen faced, claw like hands gripping the point of the bullet's entry as though the pressure from their fingers would miraculously close the wound. White, hazy smoke permeated the low branches and curled around the legs of the walking soldiers.

"Captain Rouse, Captain Rouse, Lieutenant Cramer sends his compliments from the right of the advance ." A bedraggled soldier with salt stains in his jacket's underarms lowered his musket and saluted.

"Yes, Son, report."

"Sir, the lieutenant says to tell you that his skirmishers have discovered a rebel battery of four guns straight ahead of you. They are masked on the slope of yonder hill. They're positioned just up from the deserted cotton field that you're about to enter."

Rouse still held the light officer's sword in his left hand and permitted the fingers of his right to encircle the French, imported binoculars which hung suspended at his neck.

"That will do, private. Let's not stampede the men by broadcasting this news." Rouse released the field glasses and reached inside his coat for the order memoranda. In a few moments he'd scribbled a message on a single sheet, ripped it from the binding, folded it and handed it to the soldier.

"Take this back to Cramer and tell him that we are obliged to have this information. He can follow my orders and flank the position if there are signs that the Rebs have provided no infantry support for the guns but I find that highly unlikely."

Company B continued on until it reached the edge of a fallow cotton field. The rails from the fence enclosing the acreage had been tossed aside by the retreating Confederates facing the Union skirmishers. In the brown stalks of last fall's crop, bags of gray clothing lay strewn. Chance's first summation was that some refugees had passed this way and tossed aside unwanted garments. But as he studied the forms further, he realized that the bundles were the bodies of men. The dead, lying in contorted positions, were opposing skirmishers killed by the Federals as they were driven out of the cover of the woods and into the open field. Their line of escape had been halted in front of their hidden Confederate guns.

Rouse had his glasses pressed to his eyes watching the fleeing survivors of the defensive line clear the fencing on the field's far side.

"Sergeants, halt the men in position." The order was given firmly and forcefully. The line stopped and awaited orders, men nervous, muskets at the ready. Two musket shots taken at long distance whirred overhead. Rouse's lens had discerned heaps of red clay shoveled before piles of freshly cut brush. Dust clouds billowed up from an unseen road just beyond the tall trees on the crest of the hill. The officer's observations told him the location of the artillery pieces and that their carriage trails had been dug in to allow the muzzles to fire at an elevation midway across the field. Swirling dust signaled the passage of several hundred men and animals which the guns were protecting on the rebel line of retreat. Rouse continued to study the topography and weigh his odds of launching a successful attack. He calculated the field was not more than thirty acres across at its widest point. A well trained cadre of gunners could get off one shot per minute from a battery position. Rouse surmised the pieces were loaded and ready for action but if he could get the regiment to the guns' point of aim and have enough men standing after enduring the charges of canister, he could take the artillery position before the crews reloaded. The appearance of only four field pieces in battery instead of the usual six, told him the battery had been bloodied, lost guns and probably had replacements from the infantry added to the crews. Rouse's calculations that the ineffectiveness of the unfamiliar foot soldiers involved in the performance of a duty that they were not trained to do, were factors that would spell success for his regiment. Aided by the magnification of his field glasses, the officer swept the hillside but found no evidence of the battery horses. Apparently the main source of movement for the artillery pieces were being picketed over the hill's crest and out of sight. Rouse's mind imagined the angst of the gun crew. Sweating, nervous, unsure of their abilities to withstand the surge of the blue formation camouflaged in the trees before them. Men stinking of sweat hunkered down along side the crocodile like tubes of the guns, mouths dry and eyes burning.

Captain Ansel Rouse lowered his binoculars, cleared his throat and spit into the briars at his feet. "We have a hidden rebel battery in position on the hill across the field." A groan rippled through the line. "On my command we will step out and in alignment, we will advance. Sergeants, you will listen to my directives and expedite them at the upmost speed. It is absolutely essential that this be done." Rouse trained his gaze on those men to his left and then to those on his right. "Sergeant Wilson, bring the drummer boys forward and place them five paces behind me. Uncase the colors and move the guard to the front."

The Decatur officer pushed his light sword into the earth at his feet, freeing his hands to straighten the buttons on his coat front and flick away a small green leaf that had attached itself to his left shoulder.

"Men, we can take those guns and when we do, we will sever General Pemberton's line of retreat." Rouse stood erect with shoulders squared, savoring what he was about to say. "Men, I'm calling on you, Illinois is calling on you, and your nation expects you to give your utmost today. We are bound for glory at this hour and I know in my heart that you are up to this task." Captain Rouse's blue eyes coursed the line of men from left to right.

"I'll meet you on yonder hillside and may God preserve you all. Now forward!"

Blue clad soldiers stepped from the shadow of the trees and into the brightness of the field.

"Sergeant Wilson, have the drummers beat the cadence."

Kaskaskia River, Moultrie County, Illinois May 14, 1863

Standing at the front gate of the fence enclosing the farm house's yard Becky Scott had placed her hands on the top palings and leaned against the hinged affair. She had pinned back her hair permitting the late morning breeze that rustled through the oak leaves overhead to cool her throat and brow. Rays of sunshine had filtered through the drawn curtains at her bedroom window and roused her from the last moments of a beautiful dream. Images of Chance Neunan, so life- like that they appeared real, floated before her. He was on a sandbar in the river, stripped of his shirt, wearing only a pair of linsey-woolsey trousers, rolled to his calves. His black hair glistened in the sun and his muscled body reflected youth and virility. Chance was smiling and waving to her to come and join him in the clear water that flowed around his feet. But the dream was disrupted by a crow of the rooster perched majestically atop the gate where she now stood. The impatient bird announced the new day had begun and it was time for him and his harem to be fed.

Becky permitted her dream to return as she stared at the lane leading down to the bottom land, focusing her eyes on nothing.

A crow, sitting in a tree outside the yard, was disturbed by the nearness of the teenage girl; it bent low to determine if she was a threat. Its piercing black irises surrounded by yellow enlarged as its eyes focused on the slender figure before the bird let go with two alarm calls.

"Hush up you dumb ol' crow and fly away. You have such an easy life compared to me."

She waved her arms and then the bottom of her apron in order to rid herself of the distraction. Her action succeeded and the bird uttered two more croaks as it flew off. Becky exhaled and returned to her romantic daydream and her vision of Chance. The images revived thoughts of the time before the horrible conflict which had come to be known as the War of Rebellion and all the turmoil and sadness it had wrought.

Becky allowed her thoughts to drift to a meeting she'd had with Chance at the spring that gurgled up at the base of the hill below the two farmsteads. It had been early June and the twilight of day had surrendered to a full, round moon which bathed everything in shades of soft blue.

Is that you Chance? Becky Scott stepped into a patch of moonlight and studied the figure in the shadows of the giant trees surrounding the spring. She was unsure of the form's identity. She hoped that it was her cousin; besides who else could it be?

Yes, Becky it's me. What on earth are you doing down here in the dark?

I came to fetch Pa some cool water. He's plumb tuckered from hoeing corn all day. Mom sent Alfie to help him but he's so small, I'm afraid that he wasn't much good.

We all work too hard at this time of the year, Becky. I spent the better part of the afternoon mowin' hay. I think that my arms will surely fall off my shoulders if I try to raise them. Ma wanted me to wash up at the horse trough but since supper wasn't quite ready, I skipped off and came down here. I was gonna get below the spill pool to do my washing.

Becky stifled a giggle.

You mean that if I'd come a minute or two later I'd have caught you half naked?

More than likely.

I thought that the least that I could do was to draw Pa a cool drink. The water in the bucket was yesterday's. He and Alfie finished your pa's field and commenced on ours over beyond the second slough.

We are forever in debt to Uncle Job and your mother, Becky. I guess that this is the second time that Uncle has bailed us out when my Dad went off to war. The last letter Mom received from him a week ago told us the company would be sent home from Cairo any day now.

In the interlude that Becky stood looking at her cousin she didn't recall replying to the thanks he was offering.

You shouldn't come here after dark, Becky.

Why's that?

Aren't you afraid of panthers?

Shaw no. Pa says they killed the last one in the county five years ago. Or was it ten years?

She squinted to make out the muscular form of her cousin but was unable to distinguish his features. Becky was certain he was studying her as the evening breezes moved one of her long tresses over her face. The deepening approach of the night was most agreeable after the heat of the spring day. She placed her left hand on a moist, moss covered bolder that protruded out of the hillside and sheltered the bubbling water. She was aware of the wetness of the stone as it dampened through the side of the cotton house dress she wore. The soil was cool to the soles of her bare feet as her cousin continued his conversation. Becky had a special affinity for Chance and the softness of his voice interposed with the beauty of the night caused her face and throat to flush. As Chance's voice droned on, Becky was not cognizant of the heavy bucket filled to its top that she was holding. She was pleased the weak light hid her slender body beneath her thin dress; else Chance's eyes would have seen the erectness of her small breasts. She fidgeted with the errant tresses that danced about her forehead.

You're pretty brave, aren't you?

Yes, I suppose. I don't fear much.

Well then' you wouldn't be afraid to go with me over ta Whitley Creek to the basket supper at the schoolhouse this coming Saturday night. It's a charity event for the school. Andy Crowder means to ask your cousin, Ruthie, to go. We could all ride together in our wagon and have a gay ol' time.

Sounds interesting and I'd like to go but it all would depend on the health of Aunt Emma. If she's better and I can get permission from the folks I think I could put together some nice vittles to help raise money.

Andy is real sweet on your cousin from Ohio, you know.

Yes, I've picked up on that. Every time they're around each other they get near to being cow eyed.

There was a pause in the conservation. Neither knew what to say. The peepers, with the secession of the voices, were encouraged to begin their singing once more. From the lower depression below the spring the tiny amphibians chimed into a discorded chorus.

You know, Becky, I've really taken a likin' to you. You've got to be about the purtiest girl in our neck of the woods and I'd wager in Whitley Township too.

Becky dropped her chin on her chest, her ears burning, her mouth dry. She knew that Chance Neunan was awaiting her answer. She was unsure how to react to his compliment or just exactly what his intent was. Chance had never spoken to her in this manner before. Becky was startled by her cousin's overture. She and he had grown up together, been playmates and gone to the one room school as the best of friends whenever a traveling school master could be hired to provide tutelage. Becky thought she knew Chance and all his peccadilloes but now, here in the romantic blue light of a June moon, everything had changed.

Chance Neunan, you certainly know how to make a girl feel good. Becky found her voice.

She was both happy and sad at the same time that her farm boy cousin could not see her blushing.

Let me see about going with you to that basket social. I'll ask the folks as soon as I get back to the house.

Neunan moved to take a step toward Becky but the darkness cloaked his intent. She turned away and started up the trail to her parents' farmstead.

I'd be most happy if you could find a way to go.

Good night, Chance.

Good night, beautiful girl.

XX

Becky turned from the gate and glanced toward the entrance to the house upon hearing her mother drop a pan from somewhere in the kitchen.

"Is everything alright, Mother?"

"Yes," came a muffled reply. "I just tipped the flour sifter off the table but it was empty and didn't make much of a mess. You go on about your business; I'm mixing up a mess of dough for some biscuits for dinner."

The young girl returned to her fond memories.

A horse snorted at the corner of the barn and Becky's heart leaped as Chance rode around the building on one of the Neunan's draft horses. The animal ambled up to the gate, its massive hooves plodding dust with each step.

Mornin', sweet cousin. My you do look pretty and worth all the trouble of riding over here.

Becky smiled to herself as she remembered the compliment.

You're even prettier than you were last night.

What brings you here? Becky brushed a stray lock of hair away from her face. I figured you'd be slaving in the hay field.

It was the misty image of Chance that returned her smile.

Dad came home early this morning. He'd been gone sixty seven days and Mom was so happy to see him she was beside herself. Such a racket that you couldn't imagine with the wailing and laughing all in the same instant.

Is Uncle at your house now?

He sure is. Sleeping I'd guess and Mom isn't up either. He showed up at the door at sometime after two and liked to scared the daylights out of Mom and me. He was dirty and still wearing his militia uniform. We got a candle lit and he slumped down in the living room. Mom made coffee and he stayed up filling us in on all his goings on. Pop said the regiment and his company got word they were relieved on account of the federally sworn troops taking over at the fort. His outfit came up river from Cairo on a steam transport the next morning and landed at Alton. There the soldiers turned in their muskets and equipment at the arsenal and then boarded the train for Camp Goode in Mattoon where they were to be mustered out of the service. Well, Pop was kinda anxious to get home to see Mother so he jumped off the train when it went through Windsor. He and Lem Welty walked a couple of miles, and being so tuckered, they slept for a time in a hay stack before going their separate ways.

Won't he get into trouble with the military? After all, he disobeyed orders and he has government property in his possession, his uniform.

I didn't ask him about the consequences of what he'd done. Mom was taking up most of his attention.

Chance swung his right leg over the broad back of the horse and nimbly dropped to the ground. He walked over to Becky and placed his tanned hands atop hers on the gate.

Mom and Dad want all you Scotts to come over to the house at six this evening for some 'welcome back' supper and I'd like to especially talk to you about the basket social.

As though it was only yesterday Becky imagined that she could feel the firmness of Chance's hand on hers. But she knew better. What she most longed for, her cousin's warm touch, seemed as though it had never happened. Her soldier love and first cousin had been gone from her for days, weeks and months. He was somewhere with the army outside of Vicksburg.

Baker's Creek Road
Champion's Hill, Mississippi

THE ADVANCE STEPPED OFF, CLEARING the tree line and entered the edge of the vacated cotton field. Marching at right shoulder shift the blue line dressed to the right while on the move. Ahead, in the midst of rust brown stalks, lay bodies in gray, festering in the hot Mississippi sun. The drummers had commenced their rhythmic beat which partially deadened the sound of the tramping feet in the dry field stalks. Away to the east, the crump of artillery guns and thunderous roll of musketry elicited nervous twitches on the men's faces.

Neunan studied the approaching hillside searching for the dreaded guns. He was forced to look down occasionally to avoid the wild sweet potato vines that sought to encircle his shoes and trip him. But he always brought his eyes back to the tree covered rise that lay ahead. He riveted his sight on the piles of brush stacked so uncharacteristically under the towering oaks.

"Close up men, close up. Listen for my commands." Captain Rouse, too, was appraising the hillock, stopping to lift his field glasses to his eyes. "Sergeant, bring up Company C, they're lagging behind."

The staff sergeant, a Clinton man named Olson, turned to look to his left when he disappeared in a cloud of dust and cotton chaff. The canister blast obliterated the man and three others at his side in a kaleidoscope of clothing, guns and body parts.

The line of men bent backward, wavering at the point of the explosive penetration. Like a snake in the jaws of a dog, the attacking line withered.

Chance had not witnessed the puff of smoke signaling the gun's ignition, nor had he heard the report. He was stunned by the destruction the charge rent in the attacking formation and the immense fear that swept through the soldiers. Wounded men on the periphery of the canister load were down, some on their knees, others lying face down shocked by the severity of their wounds.

"Sergeant Wilson, get every man down! Get down on your bellies, men!"

Chance did not have to be told more. He pitched forward, allowing his musket to fall in front of him but within his reach. Quickly, he retrieved it and pulled it against his shoulder. Shiloh had taught the men how to survive canister and grape shot. The earth and your proximity to it was your salvation. A cannon barrel can be depressed just so far even when the carriage wheels were dug in. Beneath this point and inside this zone, the soldiers were safe.

"Look for their support! You men look sharp, now! If those gun's got infantry support they'll be comin' at you like wild Indians!" Wilson's voice was muffled by the earth.

A second and then a third blast ripped over head. These shots mercifully dispatched the whimpering wounded who sat upright examining their horrific injuries.

The fourth and last report indicated that all the guns had been fired and the curious raised their heads to witness the artillery crews on the hillside working feverously at the mouths of the cannons. Battery horses made an appearance on the crest of the elevation and were being lashed downward toward the gun position by their riders. Responding to the short whips and yells of their riders, the massive animals seemed beyond control and incapable of being halted.

"Would you look at them brazin' son-a- bitches!" Cory Adams lying two men over from Chance shouted.

The Confederates were struggling to push the guns up and out of their pits while their cohorts were attempting to back the teams up to the gun trails to hitch them to the harnesses. Figures in gray strained at the spokes of the artillery pieces' wheels trying to force the guns out of their depressed positions.

Captain Rouse stood up and waved his sword toward the gun locations. "Men, they have no infantry supporting them! They're over there as naked as a newborn's ass!

Now, they mean to re-direct those guns at us!" Spittle flew from his mouth as he reached full agitation. "Rise up my hardies! Rise as if on eagle's wings and smite those bastards!" The officer from Decatur swung his sword overhead as if he was clutching a Turkish scimitar, and held its quivering point toward the battery position. "Now charge, damn you! Charge!"

Spurred by the captain's exhortations, the line rose with an angry growl and surged forward.

"Charge bayonets!" Rouse was running at the forefront of the mass of men for a mass it had evolved into. What had once been a line had morphed into the point of a spear which was closing quickly on the frantic rebel gun crews.

"Shoot the horses!" came a cry from somewhere in the hurtling midst. "Kill the damned horses!"

Company B needed no command to fire. Those in front stopped for a split second and unloaded their weapons into the large draft animals being backed to the rear of the guns.

The bay animals flinched, then neighed in pain. Those not dropped in their traces, stampeded attempting to pull their fallen teammates with them but only managing to hopelessly entangle themselves in the harnesses. Still others rolled and kicked in every direction, whinnying pitifully.

Men from B Company wearing drawn masks for faces passed around those who had fired and sent a second ragged volley into the gunners and their cannons. Splinters and fragments of wood went spinning off wheel spokes and carriages. Stricken crew members dropped beside their pieces or crumpled over their gun's axles. One intrepid officer stepped forward and attempted to yank the firing lanyard of his cannon but was riddled by bullets before his arm could flex. A lone gun was fired but the Union boys had surged around and away from its muzzle and only the barren field suffered the brunt of its load.

Chance rammed a cartridge into his Enfield and with trembling fingers attempted to place a percussion cap from his pouch on the gun's nipple.

"Don't give 'em a chance to kill anymore of us! Put 'em down!"

Neunan frantically scoped the swirling mass seeking a stationary target but the red kepied gun crews were going down so fast that he could not find a viable enemy on which to sight. Muskets and gun rammers were being swung like baseball bats and hand spikes were parrying off bayonets. But the boys in blue had scores to settle and outnumbering their adversaries as they did, they were winning the melee. Yet, the Confederates fought with the tenacity of a wounded she wolf protecting her young. They knew the importance of their mission and fought for time so their comrades on the road above them could escape.

In a few more moments the uneven contest ended. Exhausted soldiers in blue gathered around the guns and stood cheering, some with their kepis skewered on bloody bayonets.

Panting, powder stained men stood shaking hands and smiling. Captain Rouse had the colors brought to each piece and ordered three cheers given for their success and survival. Around the feet of the Illinoisans lay the debris of war. They stepped over their fallen enemies and their own dead and wounded. Canteens, broken muskets, caps, scraps of clothing, and dead and dying horses covered the hillside. Adrenalin receded back to a level stage of normality and the unhurt began to provide aid to those less fortunate. Chance walked around each gun position searching for his friends.

He found Corwin Adams, late of Adams Corners, Illinois, lying broken on the matted grass beneath the muzzle of one of the captured guns. Neunan allowed his weapon to topple to the ground before dropping to his knees beside the crumpled figure. He began to cry as the men walked among the badly wounded battery horses and shot them.

Vicksburg Fortifications, May 22, 1863.

Dear Becky,

We got into a big fight eight days ago and came very near to cutting off Pemberton and preventing the rebels from getting back to Vicksburg and safety. But we failed because of some boneheaded decision by our commanding general and the Secesh got away. The 41st was pretty badly shot up and I regret the news I am about to impart to you. The battle is being called Champions Hill by the officers and we were charged with cutting the Baker's Creek Road. We did seize the route if you could call it that but General McClernand acting as he usually does, failed to support our brigade. General Grant was absolutely furious with McClernand and all the men in the brigade have pretty much lost faith in the rooster strutting a––. I've come through with nary a scratch although I was in the thickest of the fight when we took the Reb battery. I don't know if the casualty lists have been posted at the county courthouse for this fiasco but the following men are on it. Webster Long got shot in the arm and the surgeons are waiting to see if they'll have to amputate it. John Dugan got his thumb shot off and he'll be as handicapped with that injury as Web Long is. Harvey Leiter got grazed on the right jaw but it doesn't look to be a dangerous wound. Six other soldiers from Macon and Shelby Counties are wounded or killed. I won't give their names since you don't know them. The death that grieves me most is that of Cory Adams from Adams' Corners. He fell before the guns in the last moments of fighting and a more cheerful and dedicated soldier you could not find in all the army.

Unfortunately, when the gray backs brought up re-enforcements, we were driven back and most all our dead and seriously wounded fell into their hands. The loss of these true patriots can be placed on the shoulders of the fool that commands out XIII Corps, John A. McClernand. He is nothing but a politician and not fit to command a mule team let alone an army corps. Lincoln caved in to the likes of this misfit and we in the ranks have had to suffer the consequences. Our president did do right by seeing the worth of such men as Prentiss, Hurlbut, and 'Black Jack' Logan. They know how to fight.

Don't worry about me. All our mess remains the same with Pete O'Donnel, Tom Warner, Walt Bone, Elmer Gent all fine and dandy. We chased the Rebs all the way back from Jackson to here outside the city on the banks of the mighty Mississippi. We have re-equipped and re-fitted and moved into place in the trenches dug by our pioneers outside the enemy works.

I miss home dreadfully but there's nothing to be done in that direction until we convince our errant brothers that they belong back in the Union. I'm writing a similar letter to the folks and I would like to suggest you pay a visit to the Adams' if you can find time and the means of getting to their home. This is all for now. The drummers are beating assembly for evening parade.

As ever,
Chance

p.s. What of these night riders or regulators that Ma writes of? Are they Copper- heads?

Picket Duty between the Trenches Vicksburg, May 28, 1863.

SUMMER HEAT WAS BUILDING AS the sappers in the Federal pioneer units inched closer and closer to the rebel works. Using gabions for protection, the men involved with endless digging slaved in shifts under a merciless sun. Sharpshooters on both sides made life miserable for the men of all ranks and the expert riflemen played no favors be the target a cobbler or a skilled surgeon in civilian life. Each morning at first light, the selected men found their hiding positions and awaited an opportunity to kill their enemy. Some operated within the lines and others crept beyond the protective trenches to 'no man's land 'that separated the two forces. Measures were taken by both sides to suppress this menace and although the Yankees eventually gained the upper hand in this area of warring, they never completely ended the threat.

"Dammit!" Chance Neunan winked the dust and bark fragments out of his eyes without moving his upper body. He mustered tears until they flowed hot and salty down over his stubbled cheeks. Slowly his vision cleared.

"Did you see him?"

"Hell no! How could anybody see anything with his eyes packed with dirt up to his eye brows." Neunan shoved his face deeper into the dusty mast at the tree's base. His excited breathing rebounded off the composted vegetation and up into his nostrils. The old nemesis that accompanied the onset of fear; quivering, commenced to shake his body.

"I thought that damned son-of-a-bitch had got you like he got poor Wes."

Chance turned his head slightly to peer at Wesley Lansden. The body lay ten yards away, eyes wide and brains matted into the bark of a tree growing in the split rail fence. A flock of blue bottle flies had already landed on the warm corpse.

"You're alright then, Sarg?" Chance was surprised at the calmness of his question.

"Yes sir. That Reb had his sights on you and not on me." Sergeant Bone's voice was low as if he thought that the sharpshooter could hear him from the distance from which he'd fired.

Neunan left his right cheek buried in the matted grass at the base of the tree. "Think that I can scoot backward and get behind your tree with you before he can get another shot off?"

"Don't know, but I allow that they's only one of 'em. The older man added more volume to his voice. " Shore is some kinda rifle that feller is pottin' at us with. Shore as hell ain't one of them punkin' slingers that most of the Rebs has."

Chance swallowed trying to return the moisture to his throat that his fear had dissolved.

"Well, I'm gonna move so you watch to see where he shoots from. Try to pick up where the smoke comes from over there outta the tree tops."

Neunan steadied himself, attempting to reduce the quivering. Carefully he raised his head, mindful to avoid exposing his upper body and gazed in the direction that he assumed the hidden antagonist occupied. *Might as well look around because this scene may be the last thing I see,* he thought. *Killed at 19, in Mississippi, in a non-descript field in the great siege of Vicksburg. A nothing little skirmish that contributed dittle to the Union cause except to add two more men to the casualty list. This same game was continuously being played all along the lines. A shattered arm here, a dead man there, that was the awful activity's outcome. The snakes always went to trees. They entwined themselves in the branches, hiding in the leafy canopies and striking out. They robbed their targets of a hand, a leg or a life with no compunction.*

Neunan continued to study Lansden's body. They always looked this way. Minutes before the man, lying crumpled as its life had left it, was a living, breathing being, filled with exuberance, feelings and hope for survival in all this madness. Now Wes Lansden was nothing more than a chunk of cooling meat, an object that people gaped at, stepped around or over and buried quickly to cleanse the air.

Walt Bone was a good man in a pinch. He'd been promoted to sergeant after he'd shown his mettle at Shiloh, the year before. Sergeant Bone hailed from Strasburg and had a wife and four children at home in Shelby County. Chance thought highly of the middle aged man and the sacrifices that he was making in the service of his country.

"You comin' back here, Chance?"

"Yes, give me a minute. My eyes are still full of dirt and my pants nearly so."

The sergeant chuckled.

Neunan looked at his broad brimmed hat that he'd lost in the scramble for cover.

To hell with the hat, he could recover it later.

Chance gripped his musket tightly, tensed his body and pushed backward with his left foot and right elbow. No shot greeted his acrobatics as he rolled into a wild gooseberry bush and slid into the depression where the sergeant lay.

"Damned coward," Sergeant Bone uttered as he looked across the open field.

"We'll stay here 'til dark, won't we, Walt? Then we'll skedaddle back to the lines." Chance plucked a torn leaf out of his musket's rear sight.

Bone ignored the rhetorical question. " 'Ell, there may be two that's workin' as pards up there in them tree tops yonder, but I'd rather doubt it. When them sharpshooter's work as a team, one is always loaded up and he'd have killed you sure when you craw fished back here. No, I'm near certain they's only one."

"Then we'll stay here til' dark anyway? After the sun goes down that Reb'll come shinnyin' down outta that tree and go home."

"Nope, I aim to get that sucker for him shootin' Lansden." Sergeant Bone spit a stream of tobacco juice into the leaves. "I'm goin' man huntin' and I'm gonna make that feller sorry that he ever climbed that tree or kilt a man from this regiment." A strange light appeared in Walt Bone's cold blue eyes. "You're with me ain't ya?"

Neunan did not reply, simply reached over and took the sergeant's black hat off his head. "Course I am. Time for a little revenge." The young soldier searched around in the leaves until he located a crooked limb that had fallen from the tree above them.

Walt Bone studied the topography again. In the middle of the fallow field, a lone white oak stood and stacked beneath its spreading branches stood a brace of split rails. The rails, left by the field's owner were long and thin and arranged vertically, tepee style to cure before they were put to use.

"That son-of-a-bitch is using a slug gun with a scope on it, I'd wager. We ain't got a chance in hell of shootin' across that field with the guns we got. He's not in the tree in the center of that field, that I'm sure of."

"You're thinkin' of runnin' to the tree and using the rails for cover aren't you?"

"Yes. I figured that was the plan when you borrowed my hat. We had to have somethin' to draw his fire." The sergeant looked at his hat suspended on the crooked limb and then back at the tree that appeared to be one hundred yards or more in the distance across last season's corn stubble. The bare headed sergeant rolled his chew from one side of his mouth to the other.

Walt Bone spit an amber stream over the lip of their hiding place and brought his eyes back to Chance's face. "You got yer cap on yer gun?"

"Yes."

"Check it. It could've fallen off when you took yer little tumble. I'm expectin' you to give me cover when I gallop out to them rails."

"But, you said that you didn't think that our guns would reach that far."

"They won't but I want ya to worry the bastard a little bit. When I get inta my cover, you take off down the fence line and flank him. That's the plan anyway."

Neunan wiggled to the edge of the depression and readied himself.

"Ease her up, then."

The hat rose up over the rim of the circular defile.

"Son of a bitch!" Chance yelled as the branch was torn from his grasp and the hat flew backward. He never heard the report but Bone had spied the gun flash.

"Tallest oak in that grove of trees to the left of the gate openin'," muttered the sergeant.

"Slide that sight up to the second shoulder and shoot about a foot above the tree. That'll give him some concern!"

"Be careful, Sarge!"

"I'm goin'!"

Bone was up and running, his musket slung over his shoulder, accoutrements flopping and hair streaming back. He threw his body over the top rail of the fence in front of their hole and rolled off landing in a spread legged sprint. The safety of the stacked rails was an estimated one hundred yards away and somewhere in a more distant tree a sharpshooter was hurrying to reload.

Chance watched the sergeant as he narrowed the distance between himself and the only cover in the corn field. If the sergeant hooked his toe in a corn stalk and fell it was likely that he wouldn't reach the fence rails at all. Sharpshooters didn't have the ability to reload as quickly as a soldier using the regulation musket so Bone stood a chance of carrying out the initial stage of his plan. The hidden sniper, using specialized loading material, had to seat the bullet properly in the rifle's bore for it to fly accurately. If Bone managed to stay upright, he could find a safe haven behind the rails. But what if the shooter swung his scoped rifle back to the fence row and the tree where Chance lay, put a bullet through his forehead, then methodically picked Bone's barricade apart until he flushed him?

Sweat trickled down Neunan's face as he realized that the moment of truth had arrived and that he must act. Using his thumb and index finger, he lifted the musket's sight ladder and slid the open optic up higher until it rested on the second hump machined on the base. Quickly, he cocked the Enfield and brought the arm to his shoulder. He hesitated. Something distracted his attention back to the smallish figure nearing the lone tree. A white puff of smoke issued from the far treetops and Bone was wrenched sideways but retained his balance and flung himself into an opening in the stacked pile. The ruse had worked!

Neunan took a breath, released a small portion of it and squeezed the musket's trigger. He barely noticed the recoil before he was up and running down the rail fence and toward the field's corner.

The Mississippi air was fetid and still. Not a ripple of tree leaves or the call of a bird broke the silence. The young soldier stopped running when he entered the tree line and paused to catch his breath. His quivering had ceased due to the exertion he'd placed on his muscles. He inhaled deeply and let the breath ease from his mouth. No sound came to his ears except for that of his breathing. Placing his army brogans as carefully as he could to avoid making noise, Chance maneuvered through the trees working his way behind the shooter's position. Walter Bone had fired back at the sharpshooter from the little fort he'd secured himself in. The treetop rifleman had exchanged shot for shot with Bone and both were apparently awaiting the mistake that would end the game. Neunan entered the ominous darkness of the thick woods and worked his way to a point where he'd calculated that the sharpshooter's lair was. Moving from tree to tree Indian style, Neunan approached the highest tree that looked out over the unplanted acreage. Chance had drawn a paper cartridge from his box, bitten open the charge and loaded on the run. Those that survived the shoulder to shoulder battles that took place in the war's early engagements mastered this technique and tossed aside the idiocy of their officers' massed forces commands. Crouching, he silently covered the last fifty yards without incident and eased in behind a hackberry, watching for movement above him. Neunan checked his gun's nipple to be certain that the percussion cap was in place. It was. He squinted harder into the conflicting values of deep afternoon shadows and bright shafts of sunlight.

Yes, there was a man there; a man dressed in stained gray peering out toward the lone oak. The predator had erected a scaffold of rails high in the leafy treetop much like those used by deer hunters. But this fiend was hunting men not animals. This beast was the lowest of the low and the vilest of the vile. Chance had no qualms about sending this thing to the nether world without the slightest pretense of fair play. Neunan stepped out from behind the tree, sighted on the rebel's back, and squeezed the trigger. He heard the charge's report and felt the recoil against his shoulder but the target did not tumble down in a cascade of foliage as he'd expected. Instead green leaves flew away a foot above the sharpshooter's head.

My God, how could I have missed? Dread flashed through Chance's mind. The concealed sniper, in his elevated lair, swiveled around bringing his scoped Whitworth rifle to his shoulder. At first a mixture of fear and surprise flitted across his features, then his mouth curled in a sneer as his finger slid inside the trigger guard of his magnificent weapon.

"A little spooked there, Yank? Say goodbye!"

When the report of the rifle sounded, Chance wrenched but no missile rent his coat or shattered his breast. He witnessed the sharpshooter's soiled kepi fly upward, his rifle pitch off the platform and blood spatter on the canopy of branches and twigs nearby.

The Confederate collapsed to his knees on the platform, rolled on his side, twitched a few times, then lay still.

Sergeant Walter Bone was leaning on the fence, his face the color of plaster, a swatch of red soaking the cloth of his trousers on his upper left thigh. He smiled wanly and stood his musket against the gnarled, vertical post of the field fence.

"Betcha you forgot to lower you rear sight back down." The sergeant mumbled as he placed both his hands on the wooden enclosure and steadied himself.

Moultrie County, Illinois
May 27, 1863

Dear Chance,

Father and Mother have received further word from our family near Lancaster that Uncle John has been taken prisoner and put to death by the rebels. Father was not certain if Uncle was in the service when he was taken and if he was not then he was captured and executed for being a spy. The Ohio cousins claimed that when they'd last heard from Uncle John he was a member of the 21st Ohio Infantry and stationed in Kentucky. Mother is desperate to learn more but there is little to be gleaned from the newspapers. Father has told me secretly he believes that Uncle John was a part of the party that sought to destroy the rail line running north from Atlanta to Chattanooga. Father said the plot was put together by General Mitchell in his attempt to capture that city. General Mitchell has command of sizeable Union forces in northern Alabama and an operation preventing rebel re-enforcements from coming on the rail line to Chattanooga from Atlanta would have enabled him to take the southern rail center.

If this plan was truly a military one then uncle would have been acting as a soldier and should not have been considered as a spy by the rebels. The leader of the group, a man named Andrews, claimed in statements to the Confederate authorities that he was under Mitchell's orders. While his motives were patriotic, he was taken in civilian clothing and was executed along with poor Uncle John and five others. All this information *and the many details addles my brain. All I know is I grieve along with my parents, your parents, and Aunt Emma. A black cloud seems to hang like a pall over us all.*

The crops are growing nicely. Your father has been taken with the growing season and has cleared two more acres of the slough just south of the river's bend. I suspect he's done this to get out of the house and away from Aunt Clair. He says that he will sow the new land in buckwheat and get a crop off it. Of course, he is in despair with the sad fate of his brother-in-law but he tries not to show it.

The old Kaskaskia is behaving itself and hasn't offered to flood this summer. Father says he likes her this way; asleep in her bed. As for me, I help mother a lot and she's taught me how to beat dried flax to get the fibers to make linen. I wish she hadn't bothered because it's a lot of work and now that she knows that I understand the process she'll expect me to do this chore. I do a lot of daydreaming when there is a quiet time, which isn't often, but I suppose all young people do this. After I say my prayers at night, I allow my mind to wander and I come up with some of the craziest questions like: Do you think that cousins could fall in love and marry? I don't mean distant cousins, I mean first cousins. If they have children from this marriage, will they be idiots? Aren't these silly things to think about?

Write me when you can. We get Chicago papers a week late when we can get any. Harper's Weekly has had some interesting and shocking wood engravings of the works around Vicksburg. They also ran a full page of images of the ship yards at Mound City and Cairo. One disturbing picture showed our wounded in the hospitals at that location standing at attention while they leaned on crutches. Several of the boys were missing legs or had empty sleeves.

Chance, I would just die if anything happened to you. The missives we exchange draws me closer and closer to you. I am forever looking for father's return from the post office bearing your words.

I will close this letter so I can help mother prepare supper. She's calling me, now.

Thinking of you every day and praying for your safe return.

Becky

Ed LeCrone

p.s .Ruthie has gone completely daft over her Neoga cavalryman.
She can hardy be counted on to do her share of the housework and mother
and father are getting disgusted with her. Next time, I'll write you
details of the night riders and all the mischief they're making.

p.s.s. When you think of me, think of our basket supper at Whitley Point.

Vicksburg, Mississippi
June 4, 1863

CHANCE TURNED THE LETTER OVER and over in his hands, looking first at the salutation and then at Becky's signature. There were less than subtle hints in her message that she was missing him terribly. The sun was bearing down onto the shebang that he and Pete O'Donnel had erected above their canvas pup tent. Here, in the midst of the clay revetments, the Mississippi sun seemed less than ten feet above the shelter. Soldiers in the trenches were horribly burned by the relentless rays. The shebang was a necessity to protect the two messmates and consisted of boards ripped from a plantation house sited, unfortunately, outside the Confederate lines. Several leafy boughs completed the shady roof and provided Neunan and O'Donnel with a small measure of relief.

Water, and its scarcity, was a consideration that the soldiers on both sides had to face. Preserving the daily ration of fresh beef drawn in the morning was a concern the Confederates did not have to contend with but the Union forces did. If the meat was not put to the skillet immediately, it turned quickly in the brutal climate into a seething, oozing, inedible mess. Thousands of tons of earth had been excavated and repositioned by the engineers of both armies and now that the Union forces had succeeded in putting John Pemberton's 'cat in the bag', their pioneer corps had been given new directives. The engineer arm of the Federal forces turned their attention to sinking new wells or improving those water sources which had fallen into their hands. General Grant was settling in for a long siege operation and he wanted to meet the needs of his forces.

Neunan's wool jacket hung limply on the front stake of his shared tent. Nothing in the way of a breeze disturbed the bower overhanging the canvas shelter. A crust of bread in his mess plate drew a parade of black ants that went tumbling over each other in their quest to carry off the morsel. The federal troops were well aware of the tenaciousness of Grant's plan and how it had clamped the rebels into an inescapable situation. There would be no relief for the Confederates. Union naval forces controlled the river and General Joe Johnston's rebel army had failed to unite with Pemberton at Jackson, two weeks earlier.

The command staff of the Confederate relieving army, with inferior strength to that of Grant's besieging forces, realized the futility of attempting a forced link up and had drawn off to the north. The effort that rebel President Jefferson Davis had so wanted had failed and Joe Johnston's army had become a non –entity for the time being.

Fresh baked, white bread delivered daily was a welcomed diversion from the hardtack crackers which had been the staple in the field for the Yankee soldiers. Nothing short of the news of Pemberton's unconditional surrender could have raised the morale of Federal forces more. The appearance of commissary wagons stacked high with the delectable loaves as they were driven in and out of the camps initiated cheers from the men.

Sporadic musket fire from further down the line disturbed Chance's interlude as he resumed his study of Becky's letter. A *carte de visite* of an unsmiling Becky Scott lay on the blanket between Neunan's out stretched legs.

Of course cousins could fall in love. Those of the opposite sex, closely related, often found romantic traits in their cousins. This was certainly more acceptable than having amorous thoughts about your sister or, God forbid, your mother. I know of no one in my community who has married their cousin. I think, too, that the truth of impaired children resulting from such a coupling is an old wives' tale.

"Sounds like the boys in the XVII Corps are poppin' off at the gray backs again." O'Donnel had sauntered up to the tent and caught Chance locked in reverie.

Chance looked up from his letter and replied, " Let somebody else have the glory. This brigade has had enough of that lately."

"Do I detect some bitterness there, Master Chance?"

"What a wild assed scheme that was. Launching an assault with our brigade as worn out as it was. I don't think that I'll ever get over that spectacle. We lost a ton of good men."

The younger man looked past his messmate avoiding eye contact. "Then that bearded peacock called for more re-enforcements when the rebels had thrown us back. I'm told that Grant didn't want to commit more troops but that idiot Democrat general of ours insisted."

"I'd suspect that the Illinois wonder has about run his course with the regular army officers in Grant's command."

"He's lost the respect and confidence of the men in ranks, that's for sure. McClernand is nothing more than a big political windbag."

"Got any water in the canteens, Pard?" O'Donnel wiped his mouth with the back of his hand.

"Not much in either yours or mine, Pete. This sun and heat takes its toll on you. Always got a powerful thirst."

O'Donnel knelt at the edge of the blanket, drew out the water containers from inside the tent, held them to his ear and shook them.

"Why don't you look up Walt Bone and get permission to go get them filled." Neunan folded the letter and slipped it into the oil skin packet in which he carried all his letters.

Pete O'Donnel remained on his haunches, pushed back his kepi from his perspiring forehead and shook his head back and forth in a gesture of negativity. "Won't be gettin' no permission from poor ol'

Walt. He checked inta the field hospital this mornin'. That wound in his thigh is infected and probably they'll send him up ta Memphis. Ol' Walt is done fer now."

Neunan clinched the muscles of his jaws several times, then looked down and picked at a loose thread on his blanket. He remained reticent for a full minute. "Well Pete, take the canteens anyway and go back and see if you can find the man who's been promoted to sergeant replacing Walt. If you can't find that man, look up Sergeant Wilson. He'll let you go."

O'Donnel stood up and slung the canteens over the shoulder of his muslin shirt.

"You go on and do that and I'll sit here a mite longer and write a letter to my girl." Chance opened his tarred haversack and fumbled inside for writing material. "You mind the sharpshooters, Pete. They've been awful bothersome of late."

Outside Vicksburg, Miss., May 28, 1863

Dear Becky,

We've got the rat in his hole now here on the mighty Mississippi. The Rebs are on the brow of the heights overlooking the city. Because of this we always seem to be attacking uphill on these devils. It's dreadfully hot and the brush that hasn't been cut is filled with the likes of insects that you couldn't imagine. We're infested with chiggers, fleas and any number of bee types. The Rebs have it worse though with their rations growing short and all their wounded shoved into holes in the clay cliffs with the townspeople. It's said that there is quite a lot of civilians suffering inside the Secesh lines. Our brigade is in reserve and not manning the trenches. We've used the spade and have crept up to within shouting distance of the gray backs. One of the regiments to our front learned from a Reb picket that they are being forced to eat about anything that they can get including cats. Ever since this fact was revealed that position has been bombarded with calls of: "Here Kitty, Kitty!" They, in turn retort with the vilest slurs about our ancestral lineage and our poor, inept generals. It's just one of the many ways that the two armies hope to lower the morale of the other. There's still plenty of fight in these southern boys. We learned our lesson on the 22nd when the 41st was involved with the brigade in an attack on what was called the railroad redoubt. We came away licking our wounds from the thrashing they gave us. The previous week, I drew picket duty and got engaged with a rebel sharpshooter between the lines. A man from

Company F was killed in the fracas and a sergeant named Walt Bone was wounded. We eventually got the Reb and I came out unscathed. I thank the man who watches out for me day in and day out for his attention.

I regret to learn of Uncle John's death. I should expect if our uncle was performing his duties in uniform that he would have been treated as a prisoner of war. He made a perilous choice and he has had to pay the penalty. My mother, your parents, Ruthie, and Aunt Emma must be lost in the blackest grief.

I do not wish to end this correspondence on a grim note so please allow me to address a subject that we have talked of earlier. Since you've mentioned cousins, I believe that I should try to answer the questions which you posed in your last letter. I know that you have observed qualities in me that you find admirable as I have in you. Of course, we have known each other for all our years but now as we reach maturity our thinking about these traits are different. Our foray to the Whitley School social has cast a new light on how deeply we feel about each other. I don't think that there's a shred of truth to the 'wives' tale' about malformed children being born to cousins who marry each other. It seems that I recall at least two of our founding fathers who chose cousins as brides with no children born to them that were idgets. Don't hold me to this fact since I can't recall the names of these prominent men. So, if you have ideas of going further with your feeling regarding me, then I'm all for it.

Bless you, Becky and all my relatives there on the Kaskaskia. May God look after you all.

Yours,
Chance

p.s. Keep me informed on what you know of Uncle John. Any news of Central Illinois will be appreciated.

Moultrie County, Illinois
April, 1863

CYRUS 'BUCK' JOHNSON GUIDED HIS sorrel into the timber on the south side of the road, dismounted and tied the animal to a convenient maple sapling. Tall and lean from working outdoors on his father's farm the strapping figure was a perfect specimen of a man. His clear blue eyes, chiseled nose and thin lips made him the personification of handsomeness. Buck Johnson was so striking in appearance that he would stand out in a crowd of men. This morning, however, it was not the young man's intent to be noticed but it was his desire instead to be swallowed up in the vivid green foliage of the forest. Johnson was on a mission to find and question a man whose identity he did not know who clandestinely had contacted him with a puzzling message.

Nervously he thrust a calloused hand into the front pocket of his canvas trousers in order to find the coin he carried. Buck withdrew a large copper penny with a hole pierced through its top edge and a cotton string tied through the opening. He took the token and slid it over his head and down beneath his shirt front. Then he reached around and patted the Allen and Wheelock side- hammered pistol that nestled in his waist band in the small of his back.

Can't be too careful in these times. I can't afford to be caught in some hum bug Union League scheme and taken to the hoosegow. I've got much, much more to do to derail the ugly ape president's war.

Johnson walked thirty feet into the trees and looked back to determine if his horse was well hidden. The sorrel was perfectly camouflaged. The road he'd ridden in on was not a true thoroughfare but merely a sandy path that coursed around the base of several steep hills to the south and branched off to the north into farm lanes that lead to the Kaskaskia River bottom. It was barely wide enough to permit the passage of two wagons when they came abreast of each other, or a log raft drag that was being drawn to the mill for lumber. Perched on a clear-cut hilltop a quarter mile from where Johnson was adjusting himself stood Clem Woodruff's saw mill. The irascible old man owned one of the few such businesses in the county and profited nicely from his efforts.

Four miles to the north lay Sullivan, the governmental center of Moultrie County. One of the smallest counties in the state, it had been formed not quite twenty years previously by a scission from adjoining Shelby County.

Sullivan had remained a small, muddy streeted town, its growth stunted by its isolation from any rail service. In order to reach the existing rail arteries, citizens of the county had to trek east and cross the Kaskaskia at Old Nelson and traverse eight more miles to Mattoon. Another route that could be chosen led due south and crossed the river at a shallow spot known as the Monroe Ford. From there it was not an arduous trip across the flat prairie to Windsor.

Buck Johnson peered into the dense woods, trying to visually identify the passage of a group of men through the grass and bushes. Seeing nothing that would spell an ambush, the young farmer struck out on a game trail that paralleled a small creek and flowed north into the bottomlands. Following the instructions he'd received, he was to proceed up the gurgling brook to the junction of a smaller tributary trickling downhill from the west. Johnson had no idea of just who the contact was he was to meet; only that the folded paper message had appeared in a crack in the weathered gate post on his father's farm. The missive had not been in that position the previous evening when he'd led the fatigued team to the barn. Whomever it was had been keeping him and the farm site under observation.

Short hair growing on the back of Buck's neck rose as he thought of an unseen spy watching him as he went about his business. Was this person a friend or enemy?

He had read the words twice before tearing it into minute pieces and throwing the fluttering bits into the chicken yard. 'Meet me up Wheeler Creek at the forks, Sunday, April 21, at seven o'clock. Come alone. We have work to do for the cause.

Whose cause and what cause was the writer referring to?

How could this stranger have knowledge of the sympathies he ascribed to? Was the man a mind reader or had he discovered the identities of the night riders who'd burned the haystacks of the Unionist, Benjamin Rider. No, this inquirer could not have discovered that Johnson and his two friends, John Sipes and Willard Bell had been responsible for the deed. The trio had taken an oath of secrecy, swearing never to tell anyone of their goals. Working in concert and under the direction of Buck, the group had sallied out during a violent thunderstorm at the end of March and torched Omar Olson's barn They had executed the perfect act of arson with the community blaming Olson's loss on the violence of nature's pyrotechnics.

So how could this mysterious person have any clues to the cause that he'd chosen to follow? True, at the outbreak of the war he had been a vocal opponent to the strife which was unfolding. He had displayed a lack of discretion when he'd openly proposed that a group of young men who supported the Southern effort should travel to Kentucky and join the forces forming to repel the Union invasion. Nearly all his acquaintances had failed to follow Buck's urgings. Nearly all except for his older brother, Frank. Frank Johnson had slipped away one early morning in late September of the previous year and disappeared. It was weeks later that the parents learned that their eldest had been sworn into the army of the Confederacy in a unit known as the Illinois Battalion. Reluctant Moultrie County men who'd not been as bold as Frank Johnson in matching their action with their words regarding the Unionist's conduct of the war were trapped in an environment which was hostile to them. Their failure to act, their vacillation was their downfall. Now it was impossible to cross the lines. Buck's brother was one of the few score men from the central and southern parts of Illinois who had committed themselves as he'd proposed.

Still, there was much that could be done within the ranks of the dissatisfied citizens to upset the work of the Unionist and their unjust war. Weren't pockets of resistance springing up all along the state line on its eastern side, commencing with Paris and spreading southward to Cairo? Papers were filled with suspious activities of these groups. Secret societies supporting both the Union and Confederacy were acting as para-military groups and instilling fear within those who opposed their designs. Operating in the shadows outside legal authority, the clandestine organizations presented problems for local sheriffs who were sucked into mediating differences between the two factions. It was a known fact that the constables of Clark, Coles, and Edgar counties held southern sympathies while Sam Earp of Moultrie County and his cohort, Marcus Richardson, in Shelby County maintained a neutral stance.

Buck stopped at the base of a white oak tree and looked at the size of the leaf buds. He'd been thinking too much and not paying attention to what he was getting himself into. But he was agitated and his mind wandered back to the topics that fed his anxiety.

Sullivan and the county had been settled by the hardy immigrants who had coursed their way up the Wabash, Kaskaskia and other rivers that flowed south. The states of Kentucky and Tennessee had provided many outstanding and hard working citizens to the area and yet when the conflagration that swept over the country began, a vast number of these people took up the standard to preserve the Union. Yet, there were those who were respectable and influential who opposed the war in a peaceable manner and who insisted their voices be heard. This group did not go to extremes of providing aid and comfort to the enemy or involving themselves in acts of sabotage as did the regulators or the night riders. The Sullivan city fathers, in order to appease the dissidents, passed an ordinance and had a sign erected on the courthouse lawn which forbade the carrying of side arms by any soldier in public or the harassment of any citizen due to his beliefs.

Buck snapped back to attention and became more alert, sharpening his observations of what lay in the green grass and last fall's leaves that he passed over. It was snake season and with the coming warmth of spring, intertwining reptiles would be rousing themselves and moving to the openings of their lairs. Johnson did not want to blunder onto a copperhead or a timber rattler. He crossed the creek and proceeded in a round- about route that would permit him to make his approach to the meeting place from a different, unexpected direction. A male cardinal began three notes of his song, and then being disturbed by Buck's movement, he flitted away. Woodruff's mill remained silent because of the Sabbath. Clem Woodruff was a deeply religious man, who in spite of his greed for the all powerful greenback, never fired up the mill's steam engine on Sunday.

As he neared the point of rendezvous, the young man stopped and listened. He took several more cautious steps and paused once more.

A twig snapped, freezing Johnson in mid-stride. Carefully, so as not to make a quick motion, Buck withdrew the small revolver and slipped behind an elm. He cocked the hammer and fastened his eyes on a path that came down over the hill to his left.

"Hold it right thar, Mister." A gruff voice directed, startling Buck. "Don't be turnin' around. Just you uncock that little pop gun and hang it on that stob on the tree so's I can see it."

"Who are you?"

"I'll be askin' the questions here, Bub."

"All right, you got me cold."

"Damned right I do. Now do as I say and clip that little pea shooter on the side of that tree."

Johnson did as he was told.

"Can I turn around now?"

"Yes but no funny business."

The farmer turned and faced a bearded man wearing a plug hat and a shabby corduroy jacket covered with sticktights. Buck noticed that the fellow pointing the large Army revolver at his mid-section sported trousers that were wet from the cuffs to his knees.

"You the man who sent me a message to meet you here?"

"I didn't send no message to anybody."

"Are you a Yankee regulator, then?"

"No. Are you?"

Johnson kept his eyes on the barrel of the revolver whose bore appeared to be the size of a cannon's. "No, I'm not. But I can prove to you which side I'm on."

"Yeah, how's that?'

"Will you let me reach inside of my shirt?'

"Do it slow and keep your hand away from yer piece hangin' thar."

Buck drew the copper penny up from his shirt front and held it up for his antagonist to see.

"I got the sign too." The bearded man lowered his weapon and opened his coat front exposing a similar coin suspended in a similar manner. "Looks like they's more than one of us showin' up to find out what the messenger is up to."

XXXXXXXXXXXXXXXXXXXXXXXXXXXXXXXXXXXXXXXX

Buck Johnson didn't know what to expect as he and the bearded man who said his name was Leonard walked into the clearing where five other men waited. Buck was certain that the man who had waylayed him on the path was using a false name. It would make no sense to do otherwise. Johnson had pointed out, as the two walked together, that he believed the meeting had to be some type of Copperhead society organizational gathering. The bearded man seemed to be satisfied with Buck's loyalty as Johnson shook hands with him and introduced himself as Wilfred. No last names were exchanged and both men were smugly satisfied with the subterfuge that was taking place.

Johnson did not think the leader would be dressed as the embodiment of a Southern cavalier replete with plumed hat and calf-skin boots. A short, slight man standing away from the group was just the opposite in his dress and demeanor. His clothing, while not expensive, was quite ordinary as was the manner in which he carried himself. Buck and his new acquaintance sidled into the group avoiding eye contact and any pretense of conversation. After a time, the slight man removed a pocket watch from his vest, cleared his throat and walked to a point in front of the men. He replaced the timepiece and welcomed the gathering stating he was pleased to see such a fine lot of men on this bright spring morning.

"Is there any man or group of men in our midst who does not wish to see an end to this horrible war?"

All answered with a reply that affirmed their desire to halt the hostilities.

"Good." The small man wearing the gray, wool jacket smiled indicating his satisfaction with the group's response. "Our common cause is to end this conflict and welcome our southern brothers back into the fold of unification. Our motto is; the constitution as it is and the union as it was."

"My name is Lewis. That's the only name that you need to know. I've come to you to show you how to terminate this abomination that we find ourselves in." Lewis was warming to the challenge of inspiring the gathering. "You must not shirk from your duty to end this war and support all that is dear to us; even though death or imprisonment might await you."

Johnson didn't like the last part of the sentence as it rolled from Lewis' lips. He glanced quickly at the men who had come together at the forks of the two creeks He saw no one that he recognized.

One man wearing a brimmed hat stepped from the group and raised his hand.

"Yes?"

"Will you ask us to be disloyal in the pursuit of what you've described?"

"Yes."

"Are you asking us to commit murder if it comes to that in order to stop the war?"

"Yes, I suppose if it comes to that. Our intent is not to fight pitched battles but to undermine the war effort and dishearten the citizens. We will seek not to injure women or children or the elderly. We will disrupt lines of communications by burning railroad trestles, cutting telegraph wires, pulling rail spikes and torching commissary warehouses. In short, we will do what ever is necessary to put a stop to this Lincoln madness."

A voice from the back of the group inquired, "What you'al's proposin' will take a bunch of money. Where's that comin' from?"

Lewis smiled a wan little smile as though he felt the question was frivolous.

"The Knights of the Golden Circle has contacts with Confederate operatives in Toronto, Canada. The officials there have ample funds to see to our needs as we may make our requests. While the battles rage in middle Tennessee and Mississippi we shall forge our resistance here behind the abolitionist armies."

Another member of the gathering, a red faced, bare headed fellow with his hands in his pockets, stepped out to the side of the group and stated firmly, "You know, Mr. Lewis, you're askin' us to commit treason and undermine our government like the most of us have never done before."

"True, so true, my friend. But our nation has never been involved in a war with itself. All our foes in the past have been foreign. This war is here in our backyard. We all grow weary with the financial loss in our national treasury and senseless deaths this conflict has wrought." Lewis brought his thumb and first finger to his chin and assumed a posture indicating deep thought. His gesture was a theatrical ploy meant to emphasize a point. He paced back and forth as though he was weighing the gravity of the information he intended to reveal to the men. Finally, he exhaled deeply and turned to face the gathering.

"Our agents in Washington are positive that our esteemed misfit of a president will commence a draft on the first of July to replenish the man power lost in the fighting these past three years. Are you," the slightly built speaker pointed to the red faced man in the front row, "prepared to be forced from your family to fight in this unjust war? Are you prepared to die while the financial tycoons and the wealthy merchants hire substitutes in their place? By God, I think not!"

Several of the men looked down and spat into the grass.

"Very well, this meeting is at an end. Kindly line up and provide me with a fictitious name so that I may keep you apprized of the tasks we want executed." The speaker was withdrawing a leather bound memorandum booklet from the inside pocket of his coat.

Then he abruptly held up his hand as though he had recalled an addition he'd intended to mention.

"Before you make this decision and it will be a final one, consider the gravity of your pledge. If you are false to the oath of The Knights of the Golden Circle and you betray the cause, then expect swift retribution from the men assembled here."

Lewis took a stub of a pencil from his outer coat pocket. "Now come closer so that I can explain the coding system we use in our contact messages. The encoded symbols will appear in the upper left corner of the paper above the written words. An X indicates that a railroad must be attacked and put out of use. A crucifix T tells you that a telegraph must be disabled. An inverted or upside down V are orders to burn a warehouse, and finally, the upside down V with an upside down U would indicate that damage must be done to a Unionist farmer or businessman. Are there questions?"

Leonard shook his head no.

"Good. And oh yes, your assignment once it's received is expected to be carried out within twenty four hours. Look for the messages to arrive in the same manner and location as the one you've received asking you to assemble here. If you should be caught by the authorities hold no hope for help from the society. You will be on your own regarding your defense."

The mysterious leader wet the point of his small pencil in his lips and motioned to the conspirators to form a line.

Buck was fairly certain that he'd heard the bearded man who'd nearly shot him in the woods, give the name, Leonard, once again.

XXXXXXXXXXXXXXXXXXXXXXXXXXXXXXXXXXXXXXXXX

"So what did this feller look like, Buck? Had you ever seen him afore?"

Willard Bell knelt by a flickering little fire he'd kindled out of last season's corn stalks.

"Nope, never saw the man before. He wasn't much to look at; at least he had an appearance that wouldn't attract much attention." Johnson had snapped off a few green branches from a hackberry which he tossed on Bell's fire. "Get 'er smokin'. Lord the skeeters is bad early this year."

The three were out on what Johnson always referred to as 'a raid' and had ridden their horses into a slough that edged a field of new corn. The night was dark with no moon and spring peepers began their serenade for the dismounted riders standing next to the pitiful excuse for a fire. Moisture in the earth emitted a mist which filtered around the legs of both men and horses.

John Sipes said nothing. He stood hunched with his jacket collar turned up to ward off the buzzing insects. Across the river an owl hooted in the darkened tree line.

Johnson fished three, stubby cheroots from his upper jacket pocket and passed one each to his fellow conspirators. He didn't resume speaking until he'd opened his match safe, detached a Lucifer from its stick and lighted everyone's cigar. Blue smoke encircled their faces mingling with the black smudge of the mosquito fire and the damp fog.

Buck drew on his smoke, then spit into the fire. "I did go into Sullivan and check on this feller. He stayed at Laury's Boarding House for three days and kept a horse at McCary's; anyway that's what Dorothy Pike told me. You boys know how that girl likes to waggle her tongue. She said he didn't talk much and when he left he was acarryin' a big leather valise. Said that he asked about the ford at Old Nelson. She reasoned he was headed for Mattoon with a question like that."

"What else did she say about this mysterious feller?"

"I asked her what name he registered at the desk with and she said he claimed to be Rufus Brown of Freeport. He told her he was in the farm implement business."

"Smells like somethin' fishy, don't it?" Bell rolled the cigar to the opposite side of his mouth and stared into the smoldering fire. "Anythin' else?"

"Yeah, Dorothy said Brown or Lewis or whatever the hell his name is rode out of town on one fine horse. She said she didn't know much about horses but that one was way above any like we have in these parts."

"She's lyin'." Bell grinned a wicked grin through his yellow front teeth. "We all know the little gal knows lots about studs."

"Shut up, Willie, Dammit. We're tryin' to be serious here," admonished Sipes.

Johnson glared at the shorter Bell. "Don't go puttin' down our informants. They could come in real handy in the future."

John Sipes' interest appeared to have been kindled.

"Did this man have any kind of an accent? Did he give you a clue as to where he was from?"

"I'd say the feller was a Kentuckian. He had a definite twang to his lingo different from us."

"And you ain't heared a word from him since you last seen him on Sunday?"

"Nope." I just figured this bein' a dark night we'd go out and raise a little hell on our own."

Willard Bell, smarting from the censure he'd received from his friends, dropped his cigar stub in the dirt and ground it out with his boot heel. "Peers to me like if we go off on a tear we'll be actin' without orders."

"Shut up, Willie. Orders, smorders, we'll be carryin' out our own operations just like before this Lewis or Brown showed his face around here. We ain't regular army or regular anythin' except the time we go to the crapper in the mornin'."

"Well Buck," Bell huffed, "I think that we could get inta trouble with this Lewis."

"He'll not say a word agin us. He'll probably congratulate us." Johnson flicked his smoke over the rail fence that served as a hitching rail for their horses and continued, "Haven't we done enough on our own to gain this man's attention?"

Both Bell and Sipes shook their heads in agreement with their leader's statement. The owl in the tree along side the Kaskaskia hooted again.

"What did you have in mind, Buck?"

"Who owns this cornfield we're astandin' in?"

"Why Mathias Neunan."

"I say lets tear part of the fence down and let Neunan's cows feed offa this new corn."

Bell half raised his hand signaling he had apprehensions about the suggestion.

"Yeah, Willie, what don't you like about the plan?"

"I can see gettin' after Mathias. He fit in the Mexican War and served ninety days down ta Cairo when this shootin' match first got started. He was one of the leaders in the community who supported raisin' a company for the Forty First. He's got it comin', but his wife is awful strong agin' freein' the niggras."

"She sent her boy off with the regiment didn't she? I'd say the maw had a change of heart." Buck was breathing hard. "Besides this is a round about way of lettin' me take a whack at that whelp of theirs. What's his name again?"

"Chance." Sipes was watching the agitation growing on Johnson's face.

Willard Bell's teeth flashed in the weak firelight. "Yeah, that Neunan kid really put a bunch of lumps on you over to Whitley Point didn't he, Buck?"

"Shut your mouth, Willie."

XXXXXXXXXXXXXXXXXXXXXXXXXXXXXXXXXXXXXXXXXX

Becky Scott was drying her hands on the dish cloth after finishing the breakfast dishes when the Neunan's pulled up in their wagon. Neither Mathias or his wife, Clair, made any movement to climb down from the spring seat. Becky stepped off the porch and walked down the sandstone steps which she and her father had laid the previous fall. They had taken their horse and wagon to a bend on the river where an outcropping of the stone existed. Job and his daughter drove the horse and wagon out into the shallows and then removed their shoes and waded into the warm, clear water selecting those rocks that suited them.

"Does the oak wagon spokes good to soak 'em. They'll not squeak so much when corn shuckin' time gets here," Her father had said.

"Is brother here?" Clair Neunan asked in a quavering voice.

"Pa is in the back yard repairing harness. Would you'd like for me to call him?"

"Yes."

Becky sensed something dreadful in the curtness of her aunt's reply.

"There's something wrong, isn't there?" Becky's voice cracked.

"Get Job, will you, Becky." Mathias spoke softly just a bit above a whisper.

"Oh God, has something happened to Chance. Tell me, tell me!"

"Chance is fine, it's something else." Clair reached down and patted the top of Becky's head.

Job Scott hearing the conversation in the front yard emerged from around the corner of the dwelling and hailed in a loud voice. "Well, well, what joyous event brings my relatives here for a visit?" Becky's father smiled broadly. "Becky, go fetch lil' Alfie so's he can tie up the horse and your aunt and uncle can come in for coffee and vittles."

Mathias, who was sitting hunched over holding the reins loosely in his hands straightened himself and responded to his brother-in-law's invitation.

"Nothin' good brings us here, Job. Nothin' good."

"What's the matter, is there some sickness?"

"No, we got hit by Copperhead night riders last night. They knocked down the fence on that new, two acre plot of corn and let the cattle into it."

"It's ruined." Clair added as a tear broke from the corner of her left eye. She dabbed at it with the cuff of her dress sleeve.

"We're on our way inta town to see Sheriff Earp."

"Now don't be hasty here, Mathias. Are you sure that the cows didn't push the fence over on their own?"

"We're certain. T'wasn't cows that did the dirty work, it was regulators. We found horse apples and cigar butts." Clair Neunan pursed her lips. "These men definitely mean to ruin us."

Mathias leaned back on the seat and exhaled. "We'd intended to get a late crop off that little piece I'd cleared this spring. Now we're so late into the season all I can do is put it back in buckwheat and even that may not mature before the first killin' frost."

"Let's see if that no account Sheriff Earp will get off his butt end and try to catch these ruffians." Clair continued to wipe her swollen eyes.

"I'm truly sorry folks. Alfie and me'll come over when you get back and help you tear up the ground. Maybe we can get some of the wheat seed in the dirt before the next rain."

Mathias reached down and took the hand which Job offered him. "You're a true friend and a wonderful brother, Job. We're much indebted to you." Chance's father continued to hold Job's big paw of a hand. "You get your guard up, you hear."

XXXXXXXXXXXXXXXXXXXXXXXXXXXXXXXXXXXXXXXXX

Ruthie Scott, hearing the wagon stop at the front of the house and the muffled conversation that followed was coming down the staircase to the parlor when Becky came in from the yard.

"What was that all about, Beck?"

"Oh it's dreadful." Ruth's dark haired cousin was pale and wringing her hands.

"Something concerning Chance?" Ruth stepped off the last step and going to Becky, took her by the arm.

"No thank goodness, but it's something nearly as bad. The Copperheads have ruined one of Uncle Mathias' corn fields. I'm afraid that it's beginning in earnest now."

"Do you mean to say that there will be more evil things done?"

"Yes, Ruth, this is only the start. A terrible avalanche of such acts will engulf us if we don't take steps to stop this craziness. One side will start the chain of events and the other will retaliate."

"Dear me, dear me," The visitor from Ohio stood shaking her head in bewilderment. "Whatever can we do?"

"Come with me into the dining room and sit down." Becky led Ruth to the table and pulled a chair from under the furnishing and motioned for her to take a seat. Then she seated herself across from Ruth.

"We'll go about our business in a peaceful manner and not speak out or make a public display of our feelings. We must be cautious and try to escape the rancor of the rebels supporting Copperheads and the Peace Democrats. Both groups are of the same ilk in my estimation."

Ruthie placed her index fingers from each hand on her temples and rubbed in a circular pattern attempting to console herself. "Oh, if only Chance and my Addison were here. They'd know what to do. Those despicable ruffians would get chased out of the county. Chance and Addie wouldn't allow them to terrorize the good Unionists in this community."

"But they aren't here. We've got to bond together tighter than ever to protect our family and property."

"Do we have any idea who these rascals are?" Ruth's green eyes flashed as she spoke.

"They could be anybody in the community. The culprits could be our banker, a businessman, even the fellow who owns the general store where we purchase things. The opposing organization is very secretive. It's said those who are hard core Copperheads identify each other by flashing a copper penny and using a symbolic handshake."

Ruth folded her hands and rubbed them together before asking, "The ring leaders, the ones who wish to remain unidentified probably incite the younger, more impulsive ones don't they?"

"Yes, I should think so. It's said through the local gossip such men have recruited some young ruffians from the Whitley Point area including that bully, Buck Johnson."

"The blowhard that Chance beat the tar out of at the school basket supper?"

"Yes, that's the man."

Ruthie looked out the window as though in a trance. "How long ago was that?"

"Just over a year ago, I guess."

"Was it? It seems like a lifetime ago."

"I went with Chance and you went with Andy Crowder."

The red headed girl sniffed and unfolded her hands. "I wish that you wouldn't talk about Andy."

"You can't ignore his existence, Ruth. He was a special part of your life."

Becky Scott's voice rose.

"I just don't want to be reminded of him, that's all."

Becky angrily stood up and slammed her chair under the table with such force that the plates on the mantle rattled.

"Shame on you, Ruthie! Poor Andy couldn't help it if he got himself killed at Shiloh! Shame, shame, shame! You could have grieved his death longer than you did! You're insensitive and uncaring!"

The dark haired girl spun on her heels and tramped out of the room. She never looked back to see how badly she'd hurt her cousin with her admonishments. The heart wrenching scream that erupted told her that Ruth was shattered.

Vicksburg, Mississippi
June 8, 1863.

THE MEN MAKING UP THE squad were selected at random from the company at roll call by Lieutenant Cramer. Two changes were made in the entrenching party when a pair from the first group begged off sick and shuffled off to see the regimental surgeon. Jason Cramer instructed the men to leave their muskets in camp and fall in with shovels drawn from the sergeant. The dozen men were mystified by the order but only mildly protested among themselves as they passed through their regimental trench system and struck off on path out of sight of the Confederate lines.

"Is it true Sergeant, that ol'McClernand has been relieved of command?"

"Can't say. Not supposed to say. You boys'll find out at evening review." Bernard Wilson bit a chew from a twist of tobacco as he walked at the front of the group.

"Come on Sarge, you know and we probably won't get back for review," a voice chided the NCO.

"Nope, I got strict orders."

"The word is Grant was so confound mad with 'Prince John' he'd have cashiered him outta the army if he could've found just cause. The word has it that the brigade will go to the old regular, E.O.Ord. Now, there's a fightin' cuss for ya." Tom Warner trudging beside Chance Neunan chimed in.

"Well, I'm for stayin' as far outta the fightin' as I can." Pete O'Donnel adjusted the shovel handle onto his opposite shoulder. "Uncle Johnny was my kind of general. He never saw a retreat that he couldn't turn into a glorious charge in the newspaper."

O'Donnel winked at Neunan and Chance smiled back.

"You men cut out the jabberin'. You sound like a bunch of old ladies at a quiltin' party," Wilson ordered.

Chance looked over at Pete O'Donnel as the contingent tottered along on the uneven ground. The husky young man was two years older than Neunan and had become his most trusted friend since Andy Crowder's death at Shiloh fourteen months earlier. O'Donnel hailed from a forty acre farm located on the prairie that lay on the heights over looking the Kaskaskia. He, like Chance, was unmarried but unlike his friend, Pete involved himself in experimentations with the opposite sex whenever the opportunity presented itself. Unfortunately, the war and the constant movement of the army prevented the youthful farmer from much success in his endeavor. The five man mess had taken in O'Donnel as regimental attrition and conditions dictated. Pete had made his appearance at roll call with a group of recovered patients who had been left at the military hospital in Cairo, Illinois in the latter part of March. A bout with bad water had knocked the soldier low but his absence from the Company had saved him from participating in the battle of Shiloh. With the loss of Walt Bone from his thigh wound, the mess was reduced to four but this was a more workable number for the intimate group with Elmer Gent continuing to share a tent with Tom Warner and Chance with O'Donnel bunking as a pair. Neunan found Pete affable, resilient, and a man who conveyed a quick sense of humor. On top of these qualities, O'Donnel knew Chance's moods like a book. Walt Bone, being an NCO, had the luxury of having his own pup tent but his duties were so demanding that Chance was puzzled at when the individual found time to eat or sleep. Now the dependable and stalwart man was gone.

"Hold the talkin' way down now, boys. We're gettin' near the end of the salient." Wilson motioned with his hands extended, palms down.

Then he held up his right arm halting the column. Sergeant Wilson paused, surveying the terrain for some landmark he'd been ordered to locate, seemed satisfied, then began walking backwards drawing a wavering line in the red clay on the hilltop with his shoe heel. "This is where we dig, boys. We'll get a start, then get spelled by another squad in four hours. The colonel wants an extension onta the line. Now bend to it and mind yer loud gabbin'."

Some engineer with shoulder straps had seen a need for the new breastworks and had queried headquarters as to what regiments were in reserve at that particular time. Then someone on the command staff had taken out a map of the brigade placement, unrolled it from its case, and discovered that the XIII Corp was being rested in the rear after it had been bloodied in the assault of May 22. The Corp was in limbo with a command shakeup and why not put these soldiers to good use. Chance mulled the sequence over and over in his head as he shoveled the clay into a lumpy pile in front of him. He had a demonic desire to heap the earth as high and as quickly as he could before the detail's effort was discovered. The squad had none of the protective earth filled woven cylinders known as gabions to hide behind and at that moment, all the diggers were feeling very exposed. Neunan knew that on the morrow the gash in the earth would be observed by some Reb officer's binoculars and their sharpshooters would move into their secreted dens as if they were vultures circling fresh meat.

"You there, yes you four. Prop yer shovels agin a tree and take a blow down the hill in the shade. You boys been thowin' up a powerful pile of clods and it's time for a rest." The sergeant in charge took a time piece from his watch pocket and looked at the time. "You fellers get back up here in fifteen minutes. Any of you got a watch?"

"Yes, I do, Sarge." Tom Warner patted the waist band of his trousers.

"Well get on." Wilson waved his right hand toward the base of the hill as though he was shooing chickens from his front yard back in Illinois.

Neunan, O'Donnel, Warner and Gent descended the steep slope as ordered and found refuge from the skin searing sun. Beneath the overhanging boughs of the trees that had been spared in the fighting, they took long pulls on their wool covered canteens and allowed the tepid water to soak down their parched throats. Chance had removed his blouse and left it hanging on a bush on the upper reaches of the hillside. Growing drowsy as the sun dissected the leaf cover overhead, Neunan scooted back against the rough bark of a live oak and closed his eyes.

"Well, would you look at that? How in the Sam hill did those women get up here through our lines?" Elmer Gent had walked up the incline away from his three friends and stood at an angle on the hillside and watched a fine, delicately constructed carriage drawn by a spirited horse make its approach. Chance rose from his reclining position, and like the others, marveled at how such a vehicle and the magnificent animal that towed it had escaped the clutches of the occupying Union army.

Hardly had the white horse been reined to a halt before a dark haired young woman hailed them.

As the four stared in astonishment, the attractive young lady leaned forward from her cushioned red seat and offered up a gourd ladle dripping water.

"Come boys. Mother and I have brought you some nice cool water."

An older but equally beautiful woman sitting alongside the speaker smiled and added, "You soldier boys should cool off. Y'all have certainly worked yourselves into a sweat."

Chance took the ladle and looked into the hazel eyes of the younger lady. *Where had these two come from and how had they prevented either of the armies from confiscating their conveyance and their animal. Both pieces of property would be very valuable to the opposing forces.* Chance handed the dipper back and smiled his gratitude.

"My name's Lila Leigh Samples. What's yours?"

"Name's Chance Neunan of the Illinois Volunteers."

"Oh, what regiment?"

"I can't tell you my outfit."

"That's alright, Mr. Chance. I can see the numbers on your big ol' hat and I can make my own deductions."

"'Spect you can, Miss. This feller here beside me is Pete O'Donnel."

"Most pleased to make your acquaintance, Mr. O'Donnel. This is my mother, Nora Leigh Samples. She owns Stanford Glen. That's our plantation. That's where we live."

The mother smiled sweetly. "Why you soldier boys are workin' yourself to death in this heat. Y'all should get some niggers to do the kind of work that y'all's doin'."

Gent and Warner hadn't taken part in the introductions and the married men could see no reason to join the conversation. Both tipped their cap visors and started up the path to the growing line of entrenchments.

"Hey, Tom, tell Sergeant Wilson I've got a touch of sunstroke and Pete is stayin' with me here to help me cool off." Chance had removed a red bandanna from his pocket and was wiping his face.

Tom Warner nodded, took out his watch, looked at it and put the piece away before joining Gent on the incline. Both O'Donnel and Neunan were left to continue their flirtations.

The young men liked what they saw. Lila was wearing a low cut filmy dress, white gloves and a broad straw hat with a veil which she'd turned back. Sitting as she was, her dress was pulled tightly against her thighs revealing a well-proportioned womanly figure. Nora, Lila's mother, was probably not more than sixteen years older than her daughter. Chance had learned during his short stay in Dixie that the girls in the South very often married early in life and procreating was an expected duty.

A lull in the conservation followed the departure of Warner and Gent. The older woman who had said little at the outset motioned to O'Donnel to come to her side of the carriage. Upon his arrival, she dipped a striped cloth in the water bucket and began to bathe his perspiring face. Chance watched the two as they whispered to one another. It was easy to forget these ladies were rebel women who were supporting their brothers and husbands residing inside the Vicksburg breastworks. Their relatives were being deprived every hour of food and comfort by the ever tightening entrenchments that Chance and Pete were helping dig.

Neunan was infatuated with the lithesome Lila. She had a way of tossing her head and laughing lightly as she carried on her coquettish conversation. Becky Scott was tucked away on the carte-de-visita in his haversack back in camp. She was a thousand miles away but Lila Samples, in the flesh, was within touching distance. It had been so very long since Chance had talked with a physically attractive woman and the enjoyment he was deriving from the experience was exhilarating. It was not until the plantation mistress removed her gloves and stroked the back of Chance's hand did he learn what the intent of the two females was.

"Now be still so's the other two men climbing up the path won't hear and come back and I'll show you something. Come look under this piece of carpeting here at my feet. It's a real surprise."

Neunan stepped to the surrey's side and looked.

"Did you ever see finer blackberries? Mother and I had our driver pick them just this morning. Mother and I would dearly love to have you and ...what's your friend's name?"

"Pete. Pete O'Donnel."

"Yes, you and Pete come by the house tonight for some fresh pie." Lila had not only drawn the carpet section from the top of the wooden bucket but she had made certain that the edge of the tapestry hiked up her crinolines to reveal the smooth, white calf of her left leg. Only after she was certain Chance had feasted his eyes on her charms did the young lady permit the carpet piece to fall back to the floor of the carriage. She smoothed her flowered garment and smiled coyly at the young soldier at her side.

"Would you believe the Yankees haven't found our cow?" Nora was holding Pete's face in her cupped hands as she spoke. The striped cloth was in a wad on top of O'Donnel's head. Lila leaned even closer to Chance, her lips a fraction of an inch from his cheek. "If you and Pete come tonight to Stanford Glen, Mother and I will serve you fresh pie with real cream and sing a few songs. Mother is a very talented pianist. She took lessons as a little girl at the academy in Atlanta. We've been lonely and refined women such as us don't generally go about offering such invitations to just anyone. You soldiers appear to have the proper upbringing and well, our own boys have been awfully busy with this contrary war."

Chance looked into her eyes. The dreamy, spell binding web she had woven was pulling him emotionally and physically to her. "But your home must be almost inside the lines isn't it?" His question came as a soft whisper.

Lila gave his hand a little squeeze. "No, it's in a bulge between them by a mile or more. Here, I have a map drawn on this ol' envelop that will help you find us."

Chance looked over at Pete and saw he was having a similar close contact discussion with Lila's mother. A woman was a woman to O'Donnel and the difference in age meant nothing to him. The lad from the upland farm was possibly more desperate than was Chance in his desires.

"I don't know. It's mighty risky, Lila."

She fluttered her lashes ever so slightly. "We'd make it worth your while." Lila shifted her body on the seat so that she was even closer. Her movement exposed her cleavage and she tightened her fingers on Neunan's hand.

Chance was in the young woman's power and he knew it but couldn't decline the mystic invitation.

"We'll be there. Will it be safe for us?"

"Surely. Why all the boys who would do you harm are bottled up in the city. We'll have a delicious time." Lila loosened the pressure of her fingers and resumed her stroking of the back of Chance's hand.

"What time shall we come callin'?"

"About nine o'clock would be fine."

"Why so late?"

"You silly soldier boy. How are the two of you going to dodge the picket line any earlier?" Lila faked disgust and tossed her head. " You Yankees never bother to think things out."

Lila withdrew her hand and smiled for the last time before leaning against Nora and exclaiming, "Chance and his friend Pete will come over to see us tonight and we'll show them a fine time won't we, Mother?"

"Certainly, my dear." Mrs. Samples gathered the cloth from O'Donnel's damp hair and dropped it on the floor of the carriage. "You gentlemen are not to say a word to anyone. We don't want the whole Yankee army traipsing over to the plantation and eating us out of house and home."

XXXXXXXXXXXXXXXXXXXXXXXXXXXXXXXXXXXXXXX

The sirens' song was entwined throughout the classics and well known to both Neunan and Pete O'Donnel; but here they were groping their way in total blackness attempting to locate a darkened house between the lines of two embattled armies. The lure of the unknown excited them as they neared their destination.

Finally, after what seemed like hours, the two turned and followed a graveled roadway that branched from the main road into virgin forest. Chance stopped and lighted a sulphur tipped match on two different occasions in order to examine the wrinkled map which Lila had slipped to him. As they trudged on, a noise of an unknown origin caused Chance to stop and look back behind them.

"Did you hear that, Pete?"

"No, I didn't hear nothin'. You're just jumpy."

"No, there was somethin' back down the road. For a split second I saw a tiny speck of light."

"I turned when you did and I didn't see a thing."

"You keep your eyes peeled, anyway."

The two went one hundred yards further and stopped as the tree lined road way opened.

"There, that must be it." Neunan spoke in a low voice.

The house loomed before them, its black bulk contrasting with the sky that had grown lighter with the rising of a half-moon. The manor resembled so many of the upper class dwellings of the southerners living in the Vicksburg area. Few of this type of habitation remained whole within Yankee lines for they had been scavenged to the foundations by the invaders. Chance squinted at the main building and made out the columned veranda that spread across the entire front of the structure and one window showing a sliver of light through drawn curtains. Spaced in a row beyond the plantation were outbuilding and small cabins that apparently were slave quarters. All of these tiny abodes remained without light. Pete tugged at Chance's sleeve and whispered, "Looks to me like their darkies has run off."

Both soldiers knelt at the edge of the graveled walkway leading to the manor's front door. Neunan's heartbeat was quickening and its tom-tom like thumping seemed to be shaking his tense body.

"Come on, Chance, let's go."

"Now wait a minute, Pete. Let's not rush into this. Let's look around a bit."

"Yeah, but they're waitin' in there with open arms."

"Hush. Maybe Forrest's men are waitin' in there for us 'stead of the ladies."

"Chance Neunan, you do beat all. I ain't tusseled with a real woman for over a year and here you are spoilin' all my fun. You want to go off playin' scouts and Indians. What's come over you?"

"It's all about caution, ol' man. Didn't you notice anything suspicious about those two this morning when we first met them?"

"Nope. The only thing that I noticed was that they didn't have a mattress in the carriage and it was broad daylight."

"Didn't you see that both Lila and her mother were wearing white gloves and even though they claimed their driver had picked the fruit for them, neither of the women had a speck of berry juice on those fancy duds. When Lila removed her gloves, I noticed she had stains under her nails."

"So she lied about having her livery man pick the berries. She probably figured that doin' such a chore was beneath her and her ma."

"Lila lied to us about having a nigger driver. I'd say that those huts over there have been vacated from the day Grant's army moved into this area."

"By God, Chance you've made me begin to suspect these gals, now."

"You got anything to defend yourself with?"

Pete O'Donnel patted his pockets as though he hoped to find some type of weapon he knew was not there. "Nope. All I was figurin' on doin' was bedding Mother Nora."

"Then you stay here and I'll go up to the house and take a look-see."

"Be careful, Chance. You've got me worried."

Neunan made his way up the graveled roadway until a cobble stone walk joined it and passed through a wooden fence gate. As he stopped to listen in the cover of a giant magnolia bush at the corner of the dwelling, the soldier swore he heard a faint whistle from a direction that O'Donnel did not occupy.

Then only the familiar night sounds enveloped his ears. Chirping insects, the call of a whippoorwill and a bull frog's deep bellow resonated from the darkened surroundings. Carefully, Chance stepped up onto the veranda, edged to the lighted window and peered in.

Lila Samples sat sewing some type of garment next to a burning candle whose flame barely pushed away the shadows of the room. Nora Samples stood primping before a free standing gilt framed mirror, turning first to the left and then to the right admiring her slender figure. Two pies sat on white napkins on a carved table positioned in the center of the room. The grandeur of the now sparse furnishings did not match the haute décor of the walls and ceiling and it was obvious several pieces had been removed. Chance noted the lack of heavy chairs, sideboards and cupboards. But nothing else seemed amiss and as determined as he was that he and Pete were about to be entrapped, he could detect not the slightest thing to indicate a potential ambush.

"What'd you find, Chance?" O'Donnel had moved up to the base of the magnolia tree and was crouched down.

"Shhhh. Keep your voice down. Nothin'. Maw is fixin' herself up for you and Lila is sitting sewin' ". It all seems blamed strange but I can't find a thing that'd give away a plot against us that they might be hatchin'."

"Well, let's go. Looks like we've fell inta a good thing fer once."

"Alright , but if anything goes bad, make for the window."

Chance took a position to the side of Pete and watched as his friend tapped lightly on the massive front door. The situation was still bothering Chance but the Colt Root revolver he was touching in his front trouser pocket gave him a degree of confidence.

A pin point of light pricked the darkness down the lane from whence they'd come. Neunan saw it before it winked out. The phenomenon occurred so quickly that Chance was unsure if he'd really seen anything. His attention was diverted away from the tiny spot of light as the massive portal swung open and Lila stood in its opening.

"Mother, the soldier boys are here." Lila, holding a flickering candle, stepped aside and allowed the young men to sidle past her.

"Oh good, you're here!" Nora came forward and took their hats. "We surely thought you'al had been lost in the woods. Why it's near to being ten o'clock."

Pete wrapped his arm around the older woman's waist, nuzzled the side of her neck and whispered, "Me and Chance would've walked a dozen more miles just fer a piece of that pie and yer company."

Nora Samples laughed lightly but did not twist away from O'Donnel's embrace.

"You Yankee boys sure know how to flatter a woman. Come here to the table and I'll cut you a piece of pie just like Lila and I said we would. Then after you eat, we can all do what ever you'al would like."

Lila moved forward and took Chance by both his hands, her face beaming. Chance nudged the door closed with his hip and followed his enchanter. Lila was bewitching with her sparkling hazel eyes and long black hair. She led him to the table and sat him at one of the two chairs which were placed there. Pete continued to stand with his one arm around the mother as she bent forward and scooped slices of the juicy dessert into milk white china bowls. The older soldier placed a kiss on her cheek and Nora jabbed him in the ribs and half-heartily pushed him away.

"Lila, dear I believe we've forgotten the cream. Would you be so kind as to go and fetch it for the men? Perhaps Chance, here, will accompany you. It is awfully dark down there in the cellar."

Mrs. Samples glanced at Lila, and as she did, Neunan believed that he detected the passage of a message between the two. He stole short looks at the women in an attempt to determine what was in the offing for him and Pete.

"Oh Mother, must I? It's scary down there."

"I'd be glad to help you get that cream, Lila." Chance stood, took a candle and lighted it from one sitting on the table and walked to the attractive girl's side.

Neunan followed Lila as she carried the candle from the parlor, through the sitting room, and into the kitchen where she stopped and took a crockery pitcher from a shelf. She walked a few more steps, bent over, threw back a small rug and opened a trap door in the floor. She hoisted the bees wax candle to reveal wooden steps leading downward to a subterranean chamber. A musty coolness wafted up and brushed past them into the kitchen. Lila led the way down the decline of the staircase which creaked in protest as the pair passed over it. As their shoes touched the graveled floor, she stopped and passed the candle to Chance.

"Please go ahead of me. I'm deathly afraid of spiders." Announcing her fear, Lila turned to face Neunan as he squeezed past her. When their bodies touched, Chance paused and placed the candle on a stone outcropping from the wall and drew Lila to him. The pitcher hung precariously from the girl's hand as her arms encircled the soldier's neck and their lips met. Her kiss was hot and demanding as Chance's hands groped her backside. She offered no resistance or complaint as they forced their impassioned bodies against each other. Then, as abruptly as she had given up her body, she stopped and pushed Chance away.

"Take the candle. I'll direct you. It's only a little further. Besides we'll have time for more of this once you've eaten." Her finger tips flipped the hair above Neunan's collar.

The flickering candle did a poor job of illumination as they entered the enlarged portion of the cellar. Hogsheads and casks stacked one on top of the other lined one wall of the damp intersanctum. Nearing the back of the room, Chance had moved ahead and torched several cobwebs that impeded his progress when suddenly, his eyes picked up a faint glimmer of white that seemed to float before him in the humid darkness. Leaning forward, he brought the candle closer; its glow broadening and brightening the cellar's corners and crevices.

Chance stiffened. Then he drew back in horror! Protruding from a stack of wooden crates was a shoeless, waxen white, human foot!

Stricken with fear, Neunan cried out and turned to run but before he could take a step a huge, black mass knocked him sprawling in the gravel of the floor. The figure rushed past the soldier's twisting body and threw itself onto Lila Samples. The unexpected assault sent the puny candle flying before its flame extinguished against the cellar wall. In the darkness, Chance rolled under a stout table and fought to untangle the small revolver from the fabric of his pant's pocket. Sounds of a struggle, grunts, scraping shoes in the flooring and open handed slaps reverberated in the storage chamber.

Finally the fight ended with two hard blows landing on flesh and a desperate little scream. Then only silence. Chance exhaled and eased the hammer of his gun back, the cylinder rotating in his hand as he fought to see what had happened.

"You all right, Yank?" a masculine voice whispered in the murk. "Hey? She didn't get you did she?"

Chance remained quiet, testing the direction from which the muffled inquiries were coming.

A match rasped against the stone wall and a crouching man emerged from the gloom. He located the extinguished candle, lit it and held it aloft to extend its illumination.

"Come on out from under that table. It's about over. That little hellion isn't goin' to hurt you none."

Neunan leveled the pistol at the speaker and using his free hand, grasped the moldy table top and pushed himself upright .

"You can put that away, too. I saved yer bacon, Boy. She meant to stick you in the gizzard and feed you to the hogs."

Lila Samples lay in a disheveled mess, her skirts hiked above her thighs and a trickle of blood running to her chin from a cut in her lip.

"Who are you?" The young soldier kept his firearm directed toward the man's midsection.

"Carl Enoch, Second Iowa Cavalry."

"How come you're not in uniform if you're in the army?"

"I took a little French leave to find a friend of mine who was listed on the company rolls as a deserter. You can move a damned sight easier at night without all that brass on yer clothes." The cavalryman spit into the gravel at his feet. "Looks like I found my friend." He nodded toward the protruding foot. "I knew he wouldn't desert. He comes from good stock and he wouldn't do that. He'd have come back to camp if these she-devils would've let him." Enoch held his right hand up to the light as he examined a barked section on his knuckles. "He won't be goin' anywhere now except back home in a pine box." Enoch's lip curled in a snarl as he kicked gravel on the reclining girl. "She's seen to that."

"There's no need for that." Chance protested.

"No need! Hell! Take a look at what she had in the pitcher."

The cavalryman kicked the shards of crockery apart revealing a worn butcher knife that glistened in the candlelight.

"She came damned close to placin' that blade between your ribs. You'd be just like my poor Billie there. You'd be coolin' out over night, get stripped of your clothes and buried in the orchard along with your pard tomorrow mornin'. They'd stick you in the ground alongside who knows how many more that came here for pie and 'deserted'." Disgust caused the Iowa soldier to spit out the last part of his sentence.

Chance lowered his gun. *So that had been their scheme. Lure in either single soldiers or pairs of them, dispatch the unsuspecting guests and take their belongings, clothing and shoes. The soldiers would never inform their friends of their intent and their disappearance could only be considered as desertion by their officers. The Samples used their ill gotten loot to barter as chattel and to feed information to Confederate spies working outside the city. In this way mother and daughter supported their deteriorating lifestyle.*

"Get up you little bitch!" Enoch had Lila by the arm and was pulling her to her feet. He viciously jammed an ugly Colt army revolver into her bruised cheek and growled; " You give us away afore we get upstairs and you'll be deader than last fall's hogs."

Lila rolled her eyes toward the hulking soldier as she tried to twist herself out of his crushing grip. The blood from her cut lip had coursed down her throat and was reddening her dress bodice.

"You Yankee sons a bitches!"

Enoch grabbed the young girl by the nape of her neck and squeezed so hard that her features contorted in pain.

"We'd better see to your friend upstairs." He thrust the pistol barrel even deeper into Lila Sample's cheek and put his face close to hers; "And you keep your pretty mouth shut!"

Neunan pushed the little Root down in his waistband and led the pair up the staircase. Enoch had the younger Samples in a full nelson and his pistol at full cock an inch away from her temple.

They eased their way through the darkened rooms, the glow from the candle only barely penetrating the gloom.

Pete O'Donnel sat bolt upright from where he'd been lying on a horsehair couch and pulled his long-john underwear over his shoulders. His eyes widened when he saw that there were three figures in the doorway.

"I didn't expect you back so soon from the cellar, Darlin," came the elder woman's voice from behind a dressing screen that sat in the shadows.

Before he could stop her, Lila freed herself from Enoch's grasp and was running toward Nora.

"Momma, watch out! They're on to us!" Lila bolted between the Iowan and Chance and made for the screen. Mother Samples, with the litheness of a cat sprang from behind the panel and snapped off a pistol shot that struck flesh and bone. The discharge flashed in the room like a lightning bolt, partially blinding Chance as he dived for the floor. The candle spun skyward as a responding shot deafened him. Another shot followed the first and then the room was plunged into blackness. The suffocating stillness mingled with the stench of burnt power as Neunan groped for the evasive little pistol once more. A strange dripping sound commenced and continued until Enoch broke the suffocating quiet with a whispered question.

"You Sucker boys hit?"

This fellow from Iowa certainly has an air of assurance about him, thought Neunan.

"No, I don't think so."

"Speak up! Are you alright?"

"Yes."

"How about your pard?"

"Yeah, I'm not hurt."

"I think I hit the ol' lady before the candle got blowed out. You got your piece out?"

Chance thumbed the side hammer back. "Yes."

"I'm goin' to strike a match and anything that moves, you shoot. Your partner ought to get off that couch and on the floor."

"I'm there." Pete wheezed.

"Yer naked friend better stay put. Ain't no sense in shootin' him by mistake."

"Yes sir, I'm not movin' a muscle."

A Lucifer sputtered into life and was placed on the wick of a candle Enoch had righted on the table.

Lila Samples lay in a pool of blood, her hazel eyes glassing over as she stared upward at the ceiling.

"Peers like the ol' lady shot her daughter."

The Iowan stepped over her body, then turned and looked down. "Too bad, I was going to take out a little revenge on her for what she'd done to Billie but that's all off now."

Enoch reached down to an ankle protruding from beneath the collapsed dressing screen and pulled Mrs. Samples forward into the ring of candlelight. She was in her corset, her left breast bared, hanging limply like an over- ripe fruit. The first shot from the cavalryman's weapon had entered the woman's mouth and passed out the back of her neck. Carl Enoch knelt beside the partially robed woman, touched her throat seeking a pulse, then picked up her pistol. He shoved the small firearm in his belt .

"Is she dead?" O'Donnel asked.

"Just like her bitch of a daughter." Enoch groaned as he stood up. "Hate to spoil your fun, Sucker boy, but these two have done away with better men than you."

Pete stood shaking. "What do you mean?"

"What he means, Pete, is that while you were crawlin' all over Mrs. Samples, her daughter was supposed to be guttin' me in the cellar. Then when she got finished with me, she was going to come upstairs and stick you." Chance let the hammer down on his revolver and put it back in his pocket.

"Damn 'em!" Pete's breath hissed over his bared lower teeth and snarled his denunciation of the two harlots who had deceived them.

Chance looked down at the bodies and in spite of the feeling of anger that he had toward them, a wave of compassion mixed with nausea flooded over him. He had seen scores of dead men throughout his short tenure in the federal army but here was a new experience he'd rather not have been exposed to. The enormity of what he and the other two men in the room had passed through weakened Neunan's knees. It seemed wrong, beyond comprehension, that women should die in a man's conflict.

Chance picked up a bedspread that had been hanging on the dressing screen and covered both bodies. His stomach went queasy as he watched pooled blood soak up into the fabric.

"I'd expect we'd better make our exits, boys. Those shots will carry for miles on a still night like this." Logan spat on the carpeting as if he was clearing his pallet of a bad taste. "If either side catches us here we'll hang for sure. We could never explain this away."

"We owe you our lives." O'Donnel was adjusting his suspenders over his shoulders.

"You don't owe me nothin'. I had this place under surveillance from the woods for the past three days. As I told your pard there, I've been lookin' for my neighbor boy, Billie Pearson and you fellers just happened to show up for bait in this scheme."

Chance thrust out his hand and the Iowan took it. "We're sorry that you found your friend like you did."

"Hell, I had to find him. I'll be takin' him back, too. He won't be recorded as a deserter in this company."

Pete finished dressing and stepped forward to shake Enoch's hand.

"I tried to warn you boys that somethin' was up and I thought one of you had seen the glow from my cigar but I guess you didn't. When you knocked on the door and went inside I shinnied in through a cellar window and poked around tryin' to figure out what these two witches were up to."

The cavalryman tipped his revolver muzzle upward, cocked the hammer, and turned the cylinder permitting the spent percussion caps to fall to the floor. Enoch reminded Chance of so many men who had been caught up in the swirling conflict and who seemed to thrive on the life and death circumstances of war. Enoch showed no outward remorse from his involvement in the deaths of the mother and daughter. Neunan doubted that the Iowan would give the occurrence another thought.

O'Donnel had his hand on the brass door handle as he spoke: "We'd best get outta here before the provost shows up."

Chance went back to Enoch and gripped his hand one more time.

"You and your pard get goin'. I'm stayin' here for a few more minutes to tidy the place up. You boys stay off the road as much as possible. Like I say there'll be patrols everywhere tryin' to find out where all the shootin' took place."

Chance and Pete had barely covered a mile on their return when they were alerted to the approach of the first cavalry detachment. The jingling equipment and the thudding hoof beats sent the pair into the bushes before they were spotted. As they knelt in the thicket permitting the riders to pass, Pete nudged Chance's shoulder and motioned to an orange glow topping the tree line from the direction they'd just come.

"Is that the moon, Chance?"

"No, it's too late for the moon to be rising. The moon won't raise twice in the same night."

"Fire, then?"

"Yep. The Iowa fellow wasn't kiddin' about tidyin' up the place."

"He was a cool one warn't he."

"Yes, he was. I'm glad that kind of man is on our side."

Scott Farm, Moultrie County, Illinois
June 9, 1863

Dear Chance,

 I have not received a letter from you for what seems an eternity. Perhaps your letter has been intercepted by the rebels as was the soldiers' mail this past December. I miss your sweet words and long for your safe return. Even though you try to mask your feelings toward me with your descriptions of army life, I can read between the lines and know that you truly care for me. I'm missing you terribly and am jealous of the number of missives which Ruthie receives from her Addison. The 5th Illinois Cavalry is operating somewhere in Arkansas but they must not be too involved since her man seems to have all kinds of time to write.

 As for us here in the second bottom, we go about our daily business. Yesterday, after Ruthie and I had weeded and hoed the vegetable garden for two hours, we asked mother if we couldn't go to the river and wade and cool off. It had grown dreadfully hot and we girls found the rocky riffle where the Kaskaskia makes a gradual drop for some fifty feet. You know the spot. We removed our outer garments and after a time we decided to swim like you boys do. Ruthie told me that I had a Venetian body, whatever that is. I assumed that she was paying me a compliment. I told her that she was splendidly formed as well and Addison would be in awe if he were to lay his eyes on her at that time. We sat for the rest of the afternoon together on that big gray bolder that the water spills around and talked our heads off. I feel that I've gotten to know my cousin *in a way that I'd never known her. We told each other of our dreams and all our little secrets. I won't tell you what I talked to her about until you return and I can look into your eyes and tell you.*

Father and Alfie hoed corn all day yesterday while we girls played in the water. Well, we had worked hard in the morning. Anyway, Father says that the corn is beginning to joint and this will be the last time that it will be worked. Alfie and father killed three 'spreadin' nighters' on the sand ridge in the middle of the field. Ruthie says that we are calling these snakes by the wrong name. She says that she'd seen such snakes in a volume of biology called 'Serpents of the World' that her grandmother back in Ohio owned. According to her the variety is really named, Spreading Viper, and that they don't have a speck of poison in their body. In fact, she says that they only have one tooth in the roof of their mouth and they feed on toads. It seems that the snake uses that tooth when it tries to swallow the toad it's caught. Seems Mr. Toad puffs up to keep from going down Mr. Snake's gullet and gets the tables turned on him when his skin gets poked by that tooth. Then it's 'psst' and down he goes. Ruthie says the reason that a dog gets so sick and throws up after it shakes a 'nighter' is because the snake puts out a protective musk that causes sickness. That Ruthie is a gosh danged jewel sometimes.

Now, I shall tell you some news which I'm not sure your mother has written you about. Forgive me if the news is upsetting to you, but I feel this is something that should be brought out. The Copperheads have been pulling some shenanigans around here that's got good Union people upset. Your father had two acres of corn ruined three days ago by these cowards who took down his fencing and let his cows into the field. It happened at night. Uncle Mathias and your mother are certain Copperheads were responsible. The Decatur newspapers owned by the Republican element say that there are two secret societies operating as Copperheads. They are the Sons of Liberty based in Indiana and the Knights of the Golden Circle from Ohio. Of course the Democrat papers say that this is all so much Unionist foolishness and all that's happened has been a bunch of accidental incidents. Yet both sorts of papers report pine tar poured on sixteen sheep at pasture over in Coles County and rail spikes removed from a track crossing a trestle in Alton.

Oh, Dear Chance, if you could only come home. Your folks are so afraid and convinced this is just the beginning, and they are targets because of their strong Unionist beliefs.

When father found out Ruthie and I had gone to the river alone, he scolded us something terrible. He said that it was a dangerous time and young girls should not do such things without adults with them.

I shall close for now and pray that your letters come to me in torrents. I hope I haven't upset you.

> *Yours,*
> *Becky*

XXXXXXXXXXXXXXXXXXXXXXXXXXXXXXXXXXXXXXXXXXX

Neunan dropped Becky's letter and lay back on his knapsack. The 'traveling bureau' made a descent substitute for a pillow but in the Mississippi heat one had to make certain the black enameled covering was not exposed to the sun to ruin a man's shirt or stick to the back of one's neck. The regiment had been issued a number of inferior pieces of equipment by an unscrupulous contractor and the knapsacks were cursed ever since. Chance had traded around with the members of the company who were sent to hospital through sickness or were wound casualties and found a good one that was not tacky. The pup tent which Chance shared with O'Donnel was far from spacious but at this particular time Pete was off drawing two days ration from the commissary wagon and Neunan could stretch out. Shortly Pete would return with freshly butchered beef wrapped in an old cloth, a loaf of army white bread, dried beans, green unroasted coffee, desiccated vegetables, a half cup of vinegar, and a small portion of sugar. Then, since it was his day to cook, Pete would go to the mess fire and cook the raw food ingredients so that they would not spoil.

Neunan did not have food on his mind. Becky's letter jolted him into the realization that most or all the gossip about the Copperhead threat at home was not gossip but the truth. Dissidence in hot beds of southern sympathy such as Oakley and Mt. Zion in Macon County as well as locales in Moultrie, Coles, Edgar, and Clark counties had formed into secret groups threatening armed resistance against the government.

Chance took up the folded letter and re-read it. He had to know more and he had to go to the source of the information, Becky. He knew that his mother would try to shield him from the trepidations that she and his father were dealing with. Neunan removed pencil and paper from his haversack and began to write.

Dear Becky,   *June 12, 1863*

I'm not sure of why you haven't received my most recent letter. All our mail is going out by boat on the Mississippi, and there have been no rebel actions to disrupt it. Admiral Porter controls the river from Minnesota to the south and his half brother, David Farragut from Vicksburg to the Gulf. There is one fort below us between Vicksburg and New Orleans that the Rebs still hold called Port Hudson but they're besieged there just like the gray backs are here. The 41st is still being held in reserve and except for getting involved in some trench digging, we do very little.

Chance had discretely decided not to reveal his and Pete's close call with the rebel women at Stanford Glen.

Our camp is a good quarter mile back and down from the trenches. We are out of sight of Confederate observers and only in danger when we are called into the trench line. General Ord, being an old regular, has had us lay out a company street, dig sinks for our daily use and allowed us to construct more elaborate shebang's over our dog tents. That poppin' jay of a McClernand didn't like our brush structures and said they were unmilitary like. We'll that ol' fool is back in Springfield where he belongs. I hope he never gets another command. So you can see we've dug in for a long siege and I feel that we'll be successful with the likes of John McClernand out of the army.

Now, Becky, be truthful and tell me what's going on with these Copperheads in our area at home. Surely mother and father went to see Sheriff Earp about their loss. What action has he taken? Doesn't Decatur have a Provost Marshal post located there? Aren't people going there to voice complaints? And what of our State Representative, Franklin Sims? Isn't he doing anything? It's no longer dissenting when property is destroyed and people put in fear of losing their lives.

I will anxiously await your next letter.

As ever,
Chance.

p.s. Dearest Becky. Please forgive me for so crudely forgetting to respond to your inquiry regarding my feelings. My tender thoughts of you grow stronger with every minute we are apart.

Neunan Farm, Moultrie County Illinois, June 15,

Mathias Neunan tied Sally to a post set next to the wooden trough and allowed the Belgian to drink from the algae covered water. Becky and Ruthie Scott came bouncing around the corner of the house and relieved him of the letters addressed to them from the bundle which he carried. The two girls were giddy with delight at the two missives each had found in the packet brought by the older man from the post office in Sullivan. Mathias' gray eyes sparkled at their youthful exuberance as they bolted to a swing that he'd suspended from an apple tree in the yard. He had come to expect their visitations every time he returned from the county seat for they knew that he would fetch letters from the boys to which they gave special interest.

The war news had been both good and bad. Grant's army was choking the life out of the Confederates at Vicksburg and the newspapers were reporting it was but a matter of weeks before General Pemberton would be forced to surrender. On the down side of the news, Lee and his Army of Northern Virginia were massing to launch an invasion of Pennsylvania with an intention of capturing that state's capitol, Harrisburg. If Union General Hooker could not defeat them, then the Confederates had an opportunity to capture Baltimore or even Washington.

Clair looked up from the basket of hen eggs she was cleaning with a cloth as her husband entered the kitchen. "Did I hear the girls outside?"

"Yes, they're sittin' in the yard swing as contented as can be readin' those letters I brought. They always see me comin' home from town on the upper road and cut through the timber and down past the spring. I don't think that I could steal past them if I tried."

"So what did that good for nothin' Sheriff Earp tell you he'd found with his investigation?"

"Nothin. He said he'd come out to the field and looked in the fence corner where we told him to but I don't think that he did. That man's as worthless as teats on a boar."

"Mathias! There's young ladies outside and I'll not tolerate such man talk in their presence!" Clair gave her husband the look that only a disapproving wife can give.

"Yes, mother, but you know those girls won't be conscious of anything until they've finished those letters."

"I'll still not hear anymore of an excuse for using such a terrible comparison."

Mathias was fifty- eight years old and had just turned that age the previous February. He felt every jolt and bump in the road during the weekly trips to town. The trek of four miles was never easy in any season but it was a necessity for purchasing provisions and learning the news and happenings going on outside of the Neunan and Scott enclave overlooking the river.

He went to the dry sink and removed a coarse linen towel from the drying rod at the top of the piece of furniture. He poured water from a pitcher into the large, porcelain basin and soaked the cloth in the water. Mathias mopped his sun tanned face and whiskers before sponging the drawn tendons in his neck. The farmer stared out the window at the Scott girls occupied with something one of them had found in her correspondence. He slipped his gallowses off over his shirt, unbuttoned it, pulled it from his burly shoulders, and laid the garment on a hickory slated chair next to the stand. Then he examined the tiny red opening high on his right shoulder that oozed clear pus. The doctors called the medical phenomenon supplication which meant that the wound he carried would not heal and would never do so as long as he lived. The leaking orifice was a reminder of his impetuous youth when he and other young men had gone off to fight the Mexicans. Mathias was not as wild and impulsive as his comrades for he was a married man with a tearful wife and small baby boy back at their home in the tiny town of Watson. Clair could not understand her husband's decision to leave her and the one month old, Chance, alone and expect her family to provide them subsistence. But then women never understood war, that was the nature of the sex.

It was in a far off place in a location marked on the military maps as Buena Vista that a mere boy wearing a gaudy fusilier's uniform shot Mathias with a seventy caliber musket. Only the skill of an unknown surgeon and Providence spared the young American soldier's arm. While the appendage was saved, Mathias had been burdened with a shattered clavicle tip and a bone disease that constantly wept from the small opening in his upper arm. Partially crippled, Mathias came home mustering out of the service at Alton and was re-united with Clair and little Chance. His brother-in-law, Job Scott wrote him from Moultrie County and told him of the glowing opportunities that waited in the occupation of farming. Money for a start in the new endeavor was obtained through a dowry Clair's parents had retained for her. Fortunately for him, the in- laws had saved back the distribution until they had seen a change in his outlook on life. The returned veteran purchased acreage along side that of the Scotts in a second bottom overlooking the Kaskaskia and soon had the small family prospering.

XXXXXXXXXXXXXXXXXXXXXXXXXXXXXXXXXXXXXXXXXX

Mathias had allowed his patriotism to get the best of him once more in the spring of '61, when the United States fort in Charleston, South Carolina's harbor was fired on and forced to surrender by Confederate troops. He'd heeded the call to duty for three months emergency service to man the works at the strategically located Fort Defiance at the confluence of the Mississippi and the Ohio.

Shouldering a musket, he engaged in the rudiments of re-training with his regiment. Job Scott, recognizing the determination possessed by his brother in law, agreed to plant the spring crop and watch over Clair and the boy while Mathias served his duty. Now he and the regiment stood on the depot platform at Mattoon amid crates and barrels of supplies destined for Cairo. They watched as a steam locomotive with white flags attached to each side of its cow catcher came high-balling down the tracks rattling south on the rails of the Central Illinois line. Attached to the bell clanging engine were flat cars laden with the canvas covered guns of the crack First Illinois Light Artillery from Chicago. Shortly following this train came another with its engine displaying a pair of green flags and towing passenger cars filled with boisterous Zouaves and colorfully uniformed militia units from the northern counties of the state. Six trains and three hours later, the stationmaster appeared amid the waiting regiment and wormed his way through the anxious men. He made his way down the glistening rails to a lone switch. He bent and unlatched a safety device, then pulled a lever across his body to move the rails to his left onto a siding. The soldiers lost interest in the rail worker when someone announced; "Say, there's a speck on the horizon. Maybe that'll be our ride down to Cairo!"

An engine with a funnel spewing a column of white wood smoke came into view within a few more minutes and the regiment put up a cheer. A half mile from the depot the engineer commenced his braking procedure and the clicketty –clack of the wheels were replaced by hissing steam and the squeal of iron on iron as the troop train was eased onto the siding. Mathias Neunan's second tour of duty had begun.

XXXXXXXXXXXXXXXXXXXXXXXXXXXXXXXXXXXXXXXXX

"Did you have any letters addressed to us from Chance?" Clair had risen from the table and squeezed in alongside her husband to wash her hands from the basin.

"Yes, there's one there on the chair." Mathias wiped at the clear liquid again "That looks infected, Matty." Clair used her pet name for Mathias as she brushed away the towel that he was holding over the wound. She gently touched the spot with her fingertips.

"It's nothin', Mother. Probably got it riled up rebreaking that corn ground that the Copperheads ruined. Sally's rein passed over that shoulder and it rubs the spot a lot."

"Yes, I suppose that's the cause of it looking so angry. Let me put a cloth over it and you leave your shirt off for a little while." Her gray eyes narrowed as she examined the breach in her husband's skin. "Does it hurt?"

"No, Clair, it don't."

XXXXXXXXXXXXXXXXXXXXXXXXXXXXXXXXXXXXXXXXX

Buck Johnson was loafing by one of the eight hitching rails positioned around the public square in Sullivan. A mid-June rain storm the previous night had turned the unpaved street into a rutted quagmire. The city fathers had made an attempt at municipal improvement by having the cross walks at all four of the square's corners covered with bank wash sized stones. This effort accomplished little in the preservation of the citizens' footwear since the unintended dikes dammed the rain water in miniature lakes between them.

Johnson stood on the boardwalk which extended out from the front of Bailey's Grocery and General Store to the street. He casually took his time smoking one of his signature cheroots as two teams of draft horses passed pulling a flat bed wagon loaded with bricks. The animals strained to move their heavy burden in the slimy morass, snorting and shaking their massive heads. Sitting high on the wagon's spring seat, a bearded man cursed and applied the whip liberally. Buck shifted his gaze from the commotion in front of him to the infamous sign detailing what was expected in the way of behavior from the military personnel who entered the town. His eyes continued their sweep until they came to rest on two figures standing on the steps of the wood framed courthouse. Samuel J. Earp, the sheriff of Moultrie County, was completing his first term in office and was stretched to the breaking point in attempting to mediate the civilian differences regarding the war. The handlebar mustache he wore beneath his prominent nose and the extremely wide brimmed hat with its left side turned up identified him as one who was resolute and not to be dallied with.

His deputy, Homer Hoskins, was shorter, stockier, and clean shaven. Both wore open topped gun holsters with revolver handles protruding from them.

Johnson ignored their inquiring stares by looking away. His ears detected the approach of footsteps from behind but he did not turn around.

"You wanted to see me, Buck?" Johnson recognized John Sipes' voice.

"Shut up, smile and keep walkin'. I'll meet you in the alley behind Bailey's."

"Why?"

Johnson turned, smiled and tapped his hat brim with his finger tips. "Do as I say, damn it! I'll be along shortly."

XXXXXXXXXXXXXXXXXXXXXXXXXXXXXXXXXXXXXXX

John Sipes was tired of waiting. He was nervous and fidgety, not knowing why Buck had been so short with him. He was ready to walk off and forget the whole thing but he knew that his actions wouldn't go over well with Johnson.

Buck came striding up the shaded alley that passed behind the buildings fronting on the square. He extended his right hand with the little finger bent back into his palm. As John Sipes received his grasp, the leader of the gang's left hand took his fellow henchman's elbow.

"Good job, John. I just wanted to see if you'd recognize our signal."

Sipes ignored the compliment and dropped Buck's hand. "Why did you act that way toward me around on the square?"

"Didn't you see our lawman and his toady watchin' me from the courthouse?"

"No."

"Then you've got to be more alert. You can't go goofin' about without keepin' yer guard up."

"Do you think Earp is on to us?"

"Naw, he hears lots of shit but I don't think he believes much of it."

"Then he's straight? The society h'ain't got him on the payroll?"

"Let's just say that he's takin' his job way too serious." Johnson dropped his cigar butt in a water puddle in the wood ashes that partially covered the alleyway. All the business proprietors who had stores fronting on the main street disposed of the ashes from their wood stoves out the back door.

"Can you get hold of Willie?"

"Yep. He's over to Lindlay's bar right now. Are we goin' on a raid?"

"Yes."

"Is it a official raid, one ordered by this Lewis feller?"

"Yes. I've got his note here in my coat pocket."

John Sipes would have liked to have seen the message with all the secret markings on it but thought better of asking. Buck didn't handle questions that had to do with his authority very well.

"How soon are we goin'?"

"Tomorrow night. Union man by the name of Hostetler up on the Little Okaw has a barn lot full of horses he intends to sell to the government for cavalry mounts. Either you or Willie will ride into the farm yard and yell that the stock has all run off and leave. It'll be dark and they won't be able to identify you."

"Well, that don't amount to much. All's he'll do is turn out the family and round them horses up again."

"The plan is to touch off the barn when he's got the boys and the Mrs. out helpin' him herd. We'll make it look like one of his little kids set down a lighted lantern wrong in the barn in all the hub-bub."

"You are a smart one, Buck."

Johnson didn't acknowledge the platitude.

"Get Bell and meet me at the Sheep Ford on the little river at eight o'clock. By that time it'll be dark enough for us to operate." Buck paused as if he were turning the scheme over in his mind making sure he hadn't left anything out. "Loaf around here for five minutes or so before you go over to the tavern and talk to Willie. Fer danged sure don't use the handshake. We shouldn't use that at all in public places."

"Understood."

"We've got to avoid bein' seen together as much as possible."

"I'll watch that too."

In the Trenches, Vicksburg, June 28, 1863

Dear Becky,   June 28, 1863

We are hunkered down in the trenches supporting 'Black Jack' Logan's brigade. We had a big blow up beneath the Secesh lines three days ago when we exploded a mine under the Rebs. Our boys weren't involved in the diggin', it was the miners from Galena that belonged to the Forty- fifth regiment. They packed a chamber with gun powder and touched her off on the afternoon of the twenty-second. The blast blew men, logs, dirt and anythin' else you can imagine into smithereens. It even blew a nigger who was working for the graybacks into our lines. The surgeon who examined him said that it was truly a miracle that he landed as he did in an unhurt condition. He said he didn't allow that the poor man would ever hear again. General Logan sent three regiments into the breech but the Rebs recovered faster than he'd expected and trapped our boys in the hole. These poor fellas have been fighting for three days now without any let up and it looks like we won't be able to get them out of their tight spot. If they do get captured by the Rebs they'd better not be mistreated because in a matter of days, ol' Grant is goin' to capture the city. There'll be hell to pay if they abuse our men in any way.

The 41st is having an easy time of it although we do get sniped at once in a while by the Secesh sharpshooters. Most of the Reb's attention at this time is that big, gapin' hole they've got in their trench line. Almost every night, Admiral Porter's gunboats drop shells into the city and it's a marvel to watch the cannonade. The beauty of the affair is the burning fuses of the bombs as they rise above the hilltops and then arch downwards out of our sight followed by an ear poppin', WHAM as they blow up.

I've told you we've dug close enough to the Reb lines that we can shout insults at each other. They aren't near as scrappy as they were a month ago. Our boys have fun with them by yellin' to them, "You fellers better watch out for our new general." They shout back," Who'd that be, Yank?" " Why it's General Starvation, that's who!" The graybacks don't much like that at all. We had some concern when we learned that Joe Johnston is coming back toward Vicksburg with a sizeable army to try to rescue Pemberton and his men. We've got 'Uncle Billy' Sherman guarding our back and our General Ord tells us we've got nothing to worry about. Ord says that 'Uncle Billy' and his boys are more than able to whip the likes of Joe Johnston should he bring his army closer.

Our mess remains the same with me, Pete O'Donnel, Tom Warner, and Elmer Gent, hail and hearty. The weather is hotter than Hades durin' the day and it fogs over with mist from the river at night. We've been exposed to the sun for so long that our hides are the color of ripe acorns.

I've described way too much war news but I thought you'd like first hand reports rather than the stuff you read in the papers.

Write me and tell me the news from home. I trust something is being done about the rascals who are causing everybody so much trouble back there.

Is my soldier mail getting through to you as it should? The U.S. Post Office is doing a great service to the soldier by letting us mark our envelopes with our names, company and regiment and penning 'Soldier's Mail' at the top of the envelope.

I hope that Pa and your father don't complain too much about payin' the postage due on your end of the route but you've got to remember that we don't have much money and no place to find stamps. Your father must really hate to put postage stamps on all the prose you and Ruthie write to this Addison feller and me.

> Thinking of you,
> Chance

p.s. We are in General Lauman's Brigade of E.O. Ord's Division. The regiments in the brigade are the 3rd Iowa, and the 28th, 41st, and 53rd Ill.

Scott Farm, Moultrie County, Illinois
July 3, 1863

My Dear Chance,   *July 3, 1863*

    Ruthie and I received two letters apiece in the batch of letters your father brought back from the post office in Sullivan last week. It was so good to hear from you and that you are well. Rest assured all is well here except for Aunt Emma's health. Things have quieted down a good deal since Sheriff Earp has started to get interested in the nighttime goings on. He's been investigating these scoundrels and trying to find out their identities. I suspect, however, there are several rings of operations involved in these Copperhead societies and we would be surprised to learn the names of the upstanding citizens who are working to disrupt our government. In the estimation of just about anybody of the Union persuasion our county sheriff is dealing with the lowest of the low. In any case the law is finally showing some gumption.

    We've gotten news from the Mattoon paper that Clark County is having its Copperhead troubles too but much of it is coming from their sheriff. It seems the law official is strong for the Peace Democrats and has decided southern sympathies. He's been helping deserters from the Union Army with money and directing them to safe places where they won't be found by the Provost Marshals. It seems the Provost office in Terre Haute received word a boy who'd deserted from Clark County was residing in the county jail in an unlocked cell. The provost notified the sheriff and informed him that the soldier should be turned over to them. The sheriff, and his name escapes me, informed the marshals that they had no jurisdiction in Illinois and that he would not co-operate. Well, the provost and a detachment of soldiers left Terre Haute by train, crossed the state line and took the boy into custody at gun point. The Clark County sheriff has thrown a fit and says the sovereignty of the state has been soiled by this intrusion. 'I'm using words from the newspaper here in front of me'. The Provost Marshal's office has told the law officer to 'go blow smoke'. Of course our beloved state representative, Franklin Sims, is getting into the argument and saying that army officials have committed an outrage against the state by using such heavy handed methods . Father has been right all along about this man and his dark leanings. Now let me tell you of more homey things. Ruthie and I discovered from the letters sent her from Addison Reynolds that his unit is now serving outside of Vicksburg. In Ruthie's last letter from him, he and the 5th Illinois Cavalry were operating in Arkansas but it seems they've crossed the Mississippi and are scouting outside the works somewhere. Wouldn't it be wonderful if you boys could look each other up?

Your father's buckwheat has sprouted and is growing fast. The rains have come exactly as needed and all our crops are looking well. Aunt Clair has added to her vegetable garden and for some reason is growing more of most everything. Uncle Mathias shot two groundhogs in her patch last week. I told Auntie that she should get a dog to solve that varmint problem but I don't think she will.

Aunt Emma gets along from day to day. As I've told you, she has trouble with the heat. When I visit, she keeps the house all shut up and dark. She says that it's easier for her to breathe that way but I can't understand how.

The cherries are all ripe and Ruthie and me have been picking daily using your father's old rickety ladder he's allowed us to borrow. Do you remember how sticky your hands and forearms get when you pick cherries? I wish that I could be with you right now eating cherries from the same bowl but I know that this cannot be. Not now, but I pray soon. I think of you every day.

Love,
Becky

Vicksburg, Mississippi, July 4, 1863.

Dearest Becky,

It is a glorious day for our army and the true citizens that wish to see the Union as one once more. General Pemberton surrendered thirty thousand men and all their arms and artillery to U.S. Grant today. The Gibraltar of the West is today in Union hands. The Rebs are a sorry lot, down in the mouth and skinny as fence rails. As soon as the terms of surrender were agreed to, Grant rolled the commissary wagons into the city and commenced to feed the citizens and the raggedy soldiers. All the Secesh boys formed up, roll was taken by their officers and orders given to stack arms. We captured enough muskets to exchange theirs for all our old and foreign junk some of us have carried for the past two years. Getting their late model British Enfields and American Springfields have brought smiles to the faces of many a Yankee soldier boy.

It's said that Grant has paroled all the graybacks and sent them home instead of shippin' them north as he did after Fort Donelson last year. The rebels have to sign an oath pledging they won't fight against the U.S. government until they are exchanged with a like number of Union fellas their government holds as captives.

'Black Jack' Logan's brigade was given the honor of being the first Yankee force to march into the city. The brigade bands struck up a military air, every regiment's color guard was sent to the front and we followed behind.

The colors belonging to the Forty-fifth Illinois were selected to be hoisted on the Warren County Courthouse flag pole in the center of the city because that regiment had fought so long and with such courage in the crater. What a spectacle that was with the old flag, shot full of holes and blood stained rippling in the breeze off the river!

Grant forbid any wild cheerin' of any kind saying that the Rebs had fought hard and felt bad enough about the affair as it was.

Pete O'Donnel and Tom Warner slipped off after the ceremonies to see what they could see although they weren't supposed to go. They took a quick tour around the town to explore the caves where the townspeople existed and the damage that had been done in the shelling. They described the caves carved in the clay banks as being damp and full of stink. On the way back, Pete and Tom cut off a piece of the little oak where the two generals met and talked over the surrender. Pete says that the souvenir hunters had taken about everything off the trunk and only a stob remained. Tom said that the city was all shut down with soldiers serving as Provost Guard on every street corner. He described the big holes blowed in the streets and the roofs torn off the houses and businesses. They came sneaking back after they'd got stopped twice and asked for passes that they didn't have.

Oh, such a glorious day! Let us hope that Hooker can defeat Lee in Pennsylvania and give the Rebs a double whallop.

Yours Always,
Chance

XXXXXXXXXXXXXXXXXXXXXXXXXXXXXXXXXXXXXXXXXX

A few days after the fall of Vicksburg, General Grant began the readjustment of the positions of the Corps that had fought with such tenacity in subduing the Confederate forces in the city. News reached the Union command on July 9 that General Nathaniel Banks and his army had starved out the rebel troops garrisoning Port Hudson three hundred miles downriver.

Another round of jubilation swept through the Union soldiers' camps for the men felt that with the latest capitulation coupled with their victory and the one at Gettysburg that surely the end was in sight.

Tom Warner squatted on his haunches at the mess fire watching his mucket filled with coffee simmer.

"Well if that don't beat all." Elmer Gent wadded the newspaper he'd been reading and tossed it into the hot embers.

"What don't beat all, Elmer?" Warner looked up and then back to the newspaper blazing next to his coffee container. "Say, that ain't the newspaper printed on wall paper by the boys announcing the Vicksburg victory is it? I wanted to save one of them things for a keepsake."

"Naw, I saved you an extra and put it with mine in my haversack. What I was amazed with from readin' the paper was that George Meade got command of the Army of the Potomac whilest they were chasin' after Bobby Lee. Ol' Meade got the most fight outta those eastern boys up in Pennsylvania than any of the officers we've seen lately."

"Yeah, he did. Here, all along we figure Hooker was leadin' the army but it turns out he got relieved whilest the Potomac boys was on the march."

Pete O'Donnel came over to the fire from the pup tent he and Chance shared.

"Word has it the XIII Corps is bein' pulled off the line and sent to Sherman to chase off Joe Johnston and his rebel relief army. Since we've bagged all the Rebs here, Grant's got real tired of watchin' his backside. He's gonna beef up Sherman's forces and run Johnston and his Reb army outta the state and away from here for good."

"Sounds like a practical plan to me." Warner removed a soiled cloth from his trouser pocket and mopped at the perspiration on his face. Then he took up a stick lying next to his shoe, hooked it under the bail of his mucket and lifted it from the ashes. "Guess we won't be gettin' that white commissary bread no more if we go inta the field." Tom's voice trailed off.

"Nope. It'll be hardtack again. I'd have thought the bakers would've been givin' us flat rocks to chew on in order to get our gums and teeth inta shape fer the ordeal to come." Gent smiled at the little joke he'd created.

Pete O'Donnel started on the first stanza of the mournful soldier's song entitled; 'Hard Crackers Come Again No More' but when he came to a section where he couldn't remember the words, he started to hum.

On the Pearl River
July 16, 1863.

My Dear Becky,   *July 16, 1863*

Oh, woe are we here in the old Forty-First. We have gone from the highest plateau to the lowest pits in morale within the last eight days. After our army's stunning victory at Vicksburg on our nation's birthday and the rousing news Meade had defeated Lee in Pennsylvania, our division marched from the trenches to a new peril. Our brigade was bad mishandled in what was to be a skirmish that turned into the darkest bit of butchery that you could imagine.

Our General Jacob G. Lauman, against the objections of his junior officers, sent us in a charge against the rebels at the Pearl River. The fool must've judged us to be supermen since the graybacks outnumbered us by more than seven to one and held breastworks holding fifteen artillery pieces. These guns were sighted on a six hundred yard field we were ordered to cross that had only corn stubble for cover. We commenced our charge and suffered a terrific fire as we neared their field works not realizing the rebels had strong forces on both our flanks. The volleys were deafening and the boys fell like sheaths before the scythe but we pressed on. Finally, our own colonel, Isaac Pugh, saw the futility of our efforts and ordered a retreat. But he was too late; for some of our boys continued on and crossed into the Secesh lines and were captured. Somehow Pete O'Donnel and I made it back across that shot swept field to our lines. Our clothes were riddled with holes, I had my hat shot off my head and my cartridge box ripped off my right hip. Pete's musket stock was broke by a ball as well.

Tom Warner has a real bad bruise on his right shin from a spent bullet or a rock that ricocheted up outta the corn stalks. He can hardly walk to or bend at the cooking fire it hurts so bad. Poor Elmer Gent has not showed up at roll call during the last two days. We can only hope he played off before the Rebs flanked us and made it into the deep timber. We three are still praying for him to put in an appearance in camp.

All regimental flags were lost except for that of the Fifty- third. Our brave color bearers carried ours right into the Confederate barricades and that's why so many wound up in the hands of the rebels. I am told our regimental was carried by five different boys, all who were shot down and killed. Every national color of the brigade's four regiments was lost save the Forty-first's. Sergeant Henry Strearer, wounded two times, carried our banner over the field and back again.

I tell you, Becky, our little regiment was near to being shot to pieces. We lost over two hundred men in the 41ˢᵗ alone in this boondoggle. I had hopes of more coming crippled out of the woods but this has not happened.

The list of missing men that you may know or might have been mentioned in my letters are: Elmer Gent, father of three, Enos Hicks, Paul Foster, Ezekial Ritter, Stephen Vaughn, John Walker and others. I have only a partial listing of the wounded. They are: Samuel Powell, Jasper Craig, Tom Seymore, Willard Hicks and several others. I will not mention the dead for my head and my heart grows weary at this point. No one of us can soften the blow of their deaths and all will be missed, sadly missed not only by their friends in uniform but more so by the families that grieve for them.

It angers me to think the army has not freed itself from the incompetent, uncaring idiots like Jacob Lauman who sacrificed this brigade as he did. He sent us to the slaughter in order to gain political fame. There is talk around the camp fires that this beast will be arrested and court martialed. I hope he is given the sentence of death for I would gladly step forward and put a ball into his black heart. But this will not happen. Blunderers like him are always preserved by the army and he probably won't be demoted in rank either.

I close with a heavy heart and wish for better times to come.

Yours,
Chance

In Camp, Pearl River, Mississippi
July 18, 1863

CHANCE NEUNAN SAT COATLESS ON a blanket spread on the ground before his tent involved with the task of grinding green coffee beans which was a necessity of the soldier's daily ration. His tin mess plate served as the mortar and a flat rock he'd found along the river bank was his pestle. Chance was in a melancholy mood due to the disappearance of the mess's friend, Elmer Gent, and the heavy casualties the brigade had absorbed. The young man knew that he was an enlisted soldier in a dying regiment. The 41st had been so disseminated in the action on the Pearl River that he sensed the unit would never recover. Nor even with the recruits and draftees would the old regiment renew its e*sprit de corps* .

Harvey Ballis from Whitley Point, looking like a lost dog, came wandering up the company street passing by stacked muskets and smoldering cook fires. He edged over to where Neunan and Tom Warner sat and started talking to the older soldier. He was concerned with finding a new bunky and aquiring a place at a mess fire. Ballis had lost his messmate, Orval Simpson, in the fighting and he was lonely and desperate.

Following General Lauman's arrest, Colonel Pugh had succeeded the errant officer and saw that the shattered brigade was pulled from the firing line. After the stunning loss of so many good men, the Union army had initiated a more sensible flanking movement that eventually forced the Confederates to give up their strong position and retreat across the river. It was in the day following the rebel retreat that Ballis, accompanied by the detailed grave diggers, went onto the field and commenced their grisly work. He found his messmate, stripped of his shoes and accoutrements, swollen and dead at the base of the Confederate breastworks.

Warner rose painfully and continued his conversation with Ballis.

"I'd allow we could be pards if you need one. I know it's a lot easier to get through this craziness if you got a friend to look out for you. But I'm tellin' you right out if Elmer Gent comes back, you'll have to move on."

"I'll agree to that, Tom. I ain't got no bad habits and I take a bath whenever I can."

"You don't smoke ner chew?"

"Nope."

"There's nothin' worse than rollin' outta yer tent in the morning' and puttin' yer knee in a cud of tobaccy that some galoot has spit out."

"That'll not happen with me."

"An another thing, you go ahead and draw Simpson's rations until the sergeant catches on. I'm doin' the same with Gent's portion and we'll be eatin' high 'til they catch us."

"It'll be fine then, fer me to go fetch my gear and bunk with you?"

"Shore."

"I'll have to turn in Simpson's shelter half."

"I'll talk to Sergeant Wilson about that. It might be we could keep it and use it to button an end into our tent. Do you know these fellers here? They're the ones who we'll be sharin' the fire with." Warner nodded toward Neunan and O'Donnel.

Ballis stepped forward and shook O'Donnel's hand, then grasped Chance's. Ballis hesitated and squinted at the face beneath the newly purchased black hat as though he was trying to recall the features from a previous meeting.

"Hey, ain't you that feller that beat the hell outta Buck Johnson two years ago over ta the Whitely Point School social?"

"I suppose that was me." Chance grinned a crooked grin and shook the offered appendage. "You must've been in attendance there or you wouldn't have recognized me."

"I was there and if ever there was a blow hard bully who needed a beatin' it was him."

"I get word from home that Johnson seems to have taken up with the Copperhead crowd."

"I hear the same thing. He's got a circle of toughs that are of that stripe. Cowards that's what they are. And that ain't all. The folks write and tell me every place outside of Decatur is all infested with Copperheads. You can call them everything from Peace Democrats to whatever but these people seem to take joy in trying to derail the war effort."

Pete O'Donnel folded his arms over his chest and asserted that if he was lucky enough to survive the war, he intended to look up a few of these people when he got home.

"You need help with haulin' your things over to here?" Chance offered.

"I'll give him a hand." Tom said as he smiled at Ballis. "You're sure that you ain't got no bad habits?"

"No sir."

Johnson Family Farm, Moultrie County, Illinois July 18, 1863

CYRUS 'BUCK' JOHNSON HAD LOST hours of sleep during the past week as he'd lay in hiding awaiting the mysterious person who delivered the tiny notations to him. Each of the past seven nights he'd kept a watchful eye on the weather split gatepost but no one had made an appearance. His vigilances were long and the regional field leader of the Knights of the Golden Circle was growing impatient with his detective work.

Buck lived on the family farm with his aged parents who had no knowledge of their son's clandestine operations. Their oldest son, Frank, had abandoned his obligations to the farm and left at the war's outbreak for the South. There, from the smattering of letters they received from their boy, he revealed his allegiances to the Confederate cause. The Battle of Perryville, Kentucky, marked the end of the correspondence and the parents fell into a morose state, locked in heavy grief that disassociated them from tilling the fields. Buck was called on to take over the farm's management as his mother's and father's efficiency faded into lethargy. Both Zack and Elva were aware of Buck's raucous behavior and late night forays but they either did not care about his doings or were unable to put together the events that would tie him to the local Copperhead depredations. Being his own boss without having to answer to any authority allowed Johnson to work ten hours a day in the field, and night ride from six to eight hours as the need arose.

Suddenly a slender figure appeared in the gloom and scratched at the splintery split in the gatepost. Johnson's surveillances had finally been rewarded.

"Don't move Mister." Buck's command was forceful but not a shout. The hammer on his Army Colt clicked back. " I told you not to move."

Johnson struck a match on the metal tire of the wheel of the wagon he'd chosen for his hiding place. He held the flame aloft illuminating the space between his body and the small figure.

"Well, well, it's Bobby Stennet. What are you doin' out this late or is it mornin', lil' Bobby?"

"I meant no harm to anybody, Buck," stammered the teenager.

"Who sent you?"

"Whatta you mean?"

"Don't play dumb with me, kid. You gotta message for me. Now, who sent you?"

"I'm not supposed to say."

"You tell me or I'll beat the tar outta ya." Buck grabbed the youth's shirtfront and twisted.

The cowering neighbor boy threw up his hand as a symbol of surrender.

"All right, all right, Buck, it was Judge Blackwell. He gives me fifty cents to make the delivery of these folded papers, all late at night."

"Why don't you come here in the daytime?"

"Can't. The judge says that this is all secret."

"The old coot is payin' you a mighty poor wage to go gallivantin' around in the dark." Johnson uncocked the weapon and lowered it. "You read any of these notes?"

"No, I was afeared to."

"Who'd have thought that ol' geezer was involved in somethin' like this?" Buck mumbled to himself. The Copperhead leader's entwined knuckles felt the frightened boy's heart pounding through the flimsy shirt that he wore.

"Involved in what, Buck?"

"Never mind, kid. It's best you don't know anymore than you do. For your own health, you'd better leave the notes where the judge tells you to and not be tempted to read any of them."

"I won't. You're scarin' me real bad and I don't think I want to work for the judge anymore."

"No, you keep on doin' what you're doin' and you can come early in the mornin' and not anymore at night. The folks are old and they won't take any notice of you if they should happen to see you."

"All right, Buck, I will."

"Good, now get on outta here so's I can go up to bed."

XXXXXXXXXXXXXXXXXXXXXXXXXXXXXXXXXXXXXXXX

A bright July full moon bathed the forest road in pale blue light as John Sipes and Willie Bell awaited the arrival of their leader. Both sat their horses and pealed their ears for the approach of Buck Johnson. Only the swish of their horses' tails and the creak of their saddles disturbed the quiet of the night. It was nearing mid-night and all the creeping and chirping insects had ended their serenades and sought shelter from the dew that was forming on the tree leaves and grass. The two sat motionless and watched the vapor brought on by the moist air form about their mouths and noses as they exhaled.

"Jesus! What in the hell was that!" Bell exclaimed, his voice high pitched with fear as he spun sideways in his saddle.

"Shut up, Willie. It ain't nothin' but a danged screech owl. For God's sake, I don't think you'd last five minutes out here alone."

Bell was been definitely shaken by the call and the proximity of the bird.

The pair then hunkered down and turned up their collars. They feared their horses would whinny and give them away if the on coming footfalls turned out to be someone other than Buck Johnson.

"That you, boys?" The gang of two recognized their leader's inquiry.

"Yeah."

"Then foller me back into the thicket and we'll be away from the road where we can talk. I've found out who the messenger is and who's responsible for sending the directives."

"Who's the man you've got with you, there?"

"I brung along Orris Whitchurch. You fellers all know him, don't you?"

Both Sipes and Bell leaned forward and squinted to make out the bearded man's features in the pale light. Whitchurch made no reply but extended his greeting by touching his hat brim with the tips of the fingers on his right hand.

"We know him, Buck. What we want to know is if he's true to the cause?"

"He is. I'll vouch for him. My brother, Frank, and me has knowed him for years. Ain't that right Orris?"

"Right. I'd do anythin' to dump that ugly ape outta office and bring back the Union to what it was. That's why I'm askin' to ride with you fellers."

"Satisfied boys?"

"If you say he's on the level, then that's good enough fer us." John Sipes answered.

Buck led his expanded group of raiders deeper into the woods and dismounted in the thorn apple thicket he knew so well. His henchmen did likewise. After a few moments of adjusting their crotches and pulling down their coats, Johnson began.

"As I mentioned, I've found the identity of the contact who's givin' us the targets he wants taken out but I'll not tell you who he is."

"Why not?" Willard Bell asked crisply.

"For secrecy and it ain't this Lewis feller. Lewis is a lot bigger fish than this man I've uncovered. Our area contact is small potatoes compared to Lewis. Enough said."

"But you got a directive?"

"Yes and the raid won't be near as easy as the horse run off and the barn burnin' we did last week. We're to derail a train full of army supplies on the St.Louis, Alton, and Terra Haute railroad west of Windsor tonight."

"Tonight?" Sipes and Bell were incredulous at the order. "It's nigh onto mid-night and we're an hour from the ford on the river and makin' a crossin' durin' the day ain't no cup of tea and it'll be even harder in the dark. It's another hour and a half just to get to Windsor from Monroe Ford." Willard Bell voiced his concern.

"Does that mean you'll not go, Willie?" An uncomfortable silence followed. Buck found a pocket watch from somewhere on his person and a match safe. He removed a Lucifer, struck it on the serrated lid of the holder and gazed at the dial. He looked from his watch into, Bell's darkened face, expecting an answer.

"I'll go. A man can complain cain't he? It's just like yer wearin' us out tear assin' all over the country."

"Don't expect to get back home before the roosters crow." Johnson snapped the cover on his watch closed.

On the Pearl River Line, July, 30, 1863

THREE MEN IN THE MESS stood upwind of their cooking fire and took turns watching the sweet potatoes roast on the flat rocks they'd taken from the chimney of a burned out slave cabin.

For a paltry fifteen cents, O'Donnel had purchased the spindly morsels, from an old black peddler who'd passed through the camp. The potatoes were the earliest digging and not as full and robust as if they'd been harvested in late August when they would have reached maturity. Tom Warner, a master with the use of a stick at the cook fire, deftly turned the small tubers so that they would cook evenly and not burn.

"Not much in the way of mail today." Harvey Ballis announced as he wormed his way into the group. "Only a couple of letters and one appears to be bad tiding. It's addressed to you, Chance."

Ballis handed an envelope to Neunan that had a thick band of black ink penned around the edges of the paper.

The young soldier's hand shook as he took the missive, turned and walked to a spot on the backside of his tent. He knew well the significance of the black trimmed envelope and he wanted isolation so he would not appear weak to his friends if the message was truly devastating.

Dearest Chance,   *July, 22, 1863*

It is with a heavy heart I inform you of the passing of our beloved Aunt Emma eight days ago. I found her dead in her gown sitting in a chair at her kitchen table. I had brought her noon meal to her as I always do and that is the way I discovered her. Our Aunt had followed her family members from Ohio in search of a better life but I fear the hard trek weakened her. I will always think of her as a gentle, respectful woman who loved her family and her God. She possessed qualities which would have made her a perfect wife and a wonderful mother but unfortunately for us and the world, she took no interests in matrimony.

We buried her on the hillside near the farm lane leading down to the river bottom. Father found a large stone which he and Mathias managed to place on the site by using our horse and the mud sled. Both say they'll have her name chiseled on the rock when the weather cools and before corn shucking. Alfie and me found small stones and placed them around the edges of her grave plot.

Chance, your father is not well, I fear. His old Mexican War wound has acted up and is festered. He carries on but we all know he is in pain. I pray for your father, Uncle Mathias, and the departed soul of Aunt Emma every night. I know your father has a strong constitution and he will overcome this setback.

Other happenings that demand our attention and which you should know about are: a barn fire that consumed the building of a Mr. Hostetler who resides with his wife and family up on the Okaw River. It seems the farmer had a pasture full of prime horses which he wanted to sell to government purchasing agents for cavalry mounts. Someone let the fences down and while the Hostetler family was occupied in rounding up their animals, the barn burned. Our well thought of sheriff, Sam Earp, came out to the farmer's place and looked around. He concluded someone had accidently knocked over a lighted lantern and caused the loss. Of course, all the folks here in the neighborhood suspect that the Copperheads were behind the affair.

The most sensational happening occurred last week when a section boss and one of his workers found a rail on the St. Louis, Alton, and Terra Haute rail line outside of Windsor torn loose. Apparently a farmer, who lived close to the spot where the sinister event took place, was up at a late hour helping a cow deliver her calf. Instead of going up to the counterfeit crew doing their awful work, he smartly went into town and roused the section boss. The Sullivan Express newspaper report says that two rail workers and the farmer boarded a hand car and scared off the ruffians. Their action saved the place from becoming the scene of a terrible accident. All this took place on a low trestle over Skull Creek. Now I don't know exactly where that place is except that its west of Windsor. Isn't that a scary name for the incident to happen in? And the story doesn't end there. There's more to the suspicious affair.

Two freight haulers headed south out of Sullivan the next morning found the drowned body of a man named Orris Whitchurch in a drift just west of the Monroe Ford. They'd come up on his horse grazing on the river bank and went looking for the missing rider. I'm told the Kaskaskia is at its normal stage for this time of the year and it seems queer to most folks that a man could drown there. Sheriff Earp, who's investigating the death, figured Whitchurch missed the riffle in the dark and got into a deep hole. He went on to say the man must have panicked and got his foot caught fast in his stirrup. Of course, Earp couldn't make any connection with the attempted destruction of the rails and a man who lived eight miles away and crossed a ford that he didn't know much about during the nighttime..

Chance, we need you back at home as soon as possible. The Union people are growing disheartened with our young men away and all this devilment going on. Aunt Emma's death reminds me we all have but a short time on this earth as mortals. The poor thing, so kind and simple in habits was taken from us at age forty-eight. I think of that as I put on my gown in my room at night. I stand before my mirror in the lamp light and imagine my wedding night with you. I know I would make you a good wife. I am strong, well proportioned and believe I can give you as many babies as you would want. Think of me every waking moment that you are safe and alone.

Love,
Becky

On the Pearl River Line
August 1, 1863

Dear Becky,

The news you related in your letter received today was a basket full which set me back so I am feelin' pretty down. Aunt Emma's passing was a huge shock to me. Death always shakes me in spite of how much I've seen. Its happening reveals to me that we mortals are each but a mere grain of sand making up the tiniest portion of the thousands of mountains that God has created on earth. Our being and passing is nothing more than a flicker in our Father's grand order of things.

There, Becky, I've given you my thoughts on our mortal existence. I grieve for my Aunt Emma and her passing but I know she is in a better place.

Dad's failing health hits me hard as well. He was always strong when he needed to be and gentle and a good teacher when there were things to be taught. He was able to step back and study problems and find a way to the answers. Your father and Dad, although they aren't blood relatives, have much in common. My Dad has told me on more than one occasion of how indebted he is to Job for his suggestion our family settle on the Kaskaskia.

Harvey Ballis from over at Whitley Point has joined our mess with the disappearance of Elmer Gent. Harvey, when we first met, informed me that he was at the school social the night that Buck Johnson and me had it out. He says the young roosters over there still talk about that melee. Ballis looks like he'll be fine in the group and is sharing a tent with Tom Warner. Tom is doin' better after just one visit to the surgeon about his shin. He says that the 'saw bones' is such a counterfeit that he's afraid to go see him anymore. I was going to have a dollar deducted from my pay for losing my cartridge box in the retreat of the twelfth. That affair shouldn't be called a retreat but a grand skedaddle instead. If we'd have had time, me and Pete could've picked up a bushel of boxes but it seems like we were in a kinda hurry. Anyway, Sergeant Wilson stepped up and pointed out to the ordinance clerk that the piece of equipment had been lost in battle. The fellow changed his mind and struck the entry in the report. If that galoot had his way, he'd have had Pete owing a month's pay and then some for his musket that got shot up.

Becky, I think of you as my fiancée even though we have not made a formal announcement. It would be best if we waited until I get back to make known our intentions.

May the things that trouble you clear away in the warmth of a sunny, blue sky.

Yours Always,
Chance

p.s. It will be next to impossible for me to meet up with Addison Reynolds. The cavalry is forever on the move and they provide valuable service to the army. I've greatly changed my opinion of these fellows.

Scott Farm, Moultrie County, Illinois
August 12, 1863

Dearest Chance,

I received your latest 'Soldier's Mail' in a bundle that my father picked up in Sullivan today. Mathias was not able to make the trip at this time due to a crippling bout of arthritis that he claims has been brought on by the infection in his body. He spends a lot of his time now, sitting in the willow rocker on the front porch.

Mr. and Mrs. Winford Dixon came over from their place on the high road to offer help. Mrs. Dixon said she knew how trying it was to nurse anybody let alone as big a man as Mathias is. Father told me Winford took him aside and offered to come and help with the corn shucking when the crop was ready. The old fellow said that neither he nor his wife knew just how far your father's health had slipped. The corn won't be ready for at least a month to six weeks and who knows; maybe your father will be recovered. The Dixons brought a nice peach pie and a large kettle of chicken and dumplings.

Cousin Ruthie received word from Addison that he is in the military hospital in Mound City suffering from a broken leg. He writes that his horse slipped and fell on him while he was serving as a vidette near Jackson, Mississippi. Ruthie is frantic and says that he's probably worse injured and not telling her everything. She says she's going to take the train down to Cairo and volunteer to be a nurse with the Sanitary

Commission. That way she can see for herself what her beau's injuries are. We expect her to leave as soon as she can pack and get transportation to the tip of the state.

The Copperhead activities have quieted down because it's rumored Sheriff Earp has enlisted strong Union men who'll commence night raiding against the disloyal element and anybody who supports the designs of this distasteful plague. It looks as this is going to turn into tit for tat in the county.

Oh yes, more good news. Last week in Sullivan, two cavalrymen rode onto the courthouse square rigged out fully with sidearms and carbines. They dismounted in front of our offensive ordinance sign, removed hatchets from their saddle bags and chopped the thing to pieces. Then they set the kindling on fire and stood watching the pile burn up into ashes. Not one person, loafer, shopper or businessman came out of the establishments to voice a protest. Sheriff Earp and Homer Hoskins were out in the country doing their investigations and the troopers mounted up and got away 'scot' free.

It is amazing how three major victories in one month can stiffen a person's spine. All the Unionists have taken new hope at the toppling of the wretched sign and feel the governments and their own endeavors are on the up swing.

God bless you, Chance and all your friends in blue who seek to restore the Union.

Love,
Becky

North of Sullivan, Moultrie County, Illinois
August 14, 1863

THE THREE MEN COMPRISING BUCK Johnson's Copperhead band had assembled on the prairie at the intersection of two roads, one of which led due north toward the hamlet of Heritage and the other to the Lucus grist mill situated on a small creek that flowed into the Kaskaskia. It was unusual for the threesome to meet in daylight and expose themselves to any travelers coming up from the Old Nelson river ford. But Buck reasoned they had the advantage of an open vista and any interlopers could be spotted at no less than two miles away. If his gang had to disperse quickly they could do so without being identified. Johnson had loaded ten sacks of flour on the floor of the wagon behind the spring seat on which he sat. The lower legs of his dark checked pants were dusted with white powder from the mill. Sipes and Bell sat leaning over in the saddles of their mounts waiting for Johnson's team to stop throwing their heads up and down in a restless desire to keep moving.

"Dammit, Buck! We shoulda gone back after Orris or at least tried to find him to pull him out've the river." John Sipes knew Johnson's temperament and that he did not take criticism well. But the gang member had his dander up at the way the leader had deserted Whitchurch in his time of peril.

Johnson leaned back in the spring seat of the green Studebaker wagon and sighed as though he thought an infantile proposal had been offered.

Then he directed a disgusted look into the face of his protesting group member.

"Now what could we have done? It was dark, his horse floundered and more than likely he brained Whitchurch with one of his hooves in the water. There wasn't a damned thing we could've done. Besides, wasn't it you that panicked when we heard the hand car coming outta the darkness and wasn't it you that spooked, mounted up and took off like a strippedy assed ape. We ran our horses practically to death before we got to the ford. You was so damned sure that Earp and Hoskins was on our tails. Jesus!" Buck sent a stream of tobacco juice over his left thigh.

Willie Bell had sat silently taking in all the words of recrimination. He shooed a fly off his horse's neck with a flick of his hand. The sorrel shied but Bell brought its head around and tightened the reins in his hand.

"Either Orris lost that big Allen & Wheelock in the river or Sam Earp took it off his body and didn't say anything about such a revolver to the newspaper reporters. If he's got it he's probably wondering what a law abiding citizen is doin' carryin' such a piece of artillery." Bell stroked the side of his horse's neck. "I suggest we lay low for a while and not take on anymore 'raids'."

"Do you think that the sheriff is on to us?" Sipes' voice had calmed.

"I think he is getting' smarter by the minute, that's what I think." Johnson hooked and index finger around the cud in his cheek and flipped it into the dust next to the wagon's front wheel. "This whole damned affair was one big boondoggle. We didn't get done what we set out to do and we lost a man in the tryin'." Johnson adjusted his position on the seat and continued; "We're bein' asked to do what I think is more than our share and we're bein' asked to do some powerful dangerous things. If we ever get caught in this stuff we will do hard time or even worse."

"Are you expectin' this Lewis to come sniffin' around lookin' to see what was the cause of the failure of this last raid?"

"No, I'm thinkin' we'll not see the likes of Lewis again. I'm goin' to our local contact and askin' for some money. This Lewis said that there was plenty in the Society and we have run up some expenses. Right?"

Both Sipes and Bell answered in the affirmative in unison.

"Would you want some help when you go see this mystery feller?" John Sipes leaned forward resting his forearms on the bow of the saddle.

"I can handle it. The fewer people who's in the know about what this gent is involved in, the better."

Vicksburg, Mississippi
August 23, 1863

Dearest Becky,

We are back near the fortifications located at Vicksburg but we are no longer in the XIII corps. We have a new campsite and a transfer to General McPherson's XVII Corps. We are outside the city about two miles and far enough away that you must have a pass to visit the site of our army's grand victory. We are being re-fitted with new and discarding our old and worn out stuff. The area between the works and our camp is one big groundhog wallow. Red and yellow clay is all rooted up and there is little brush or trees in all this desolation. Nearly every speck of vegetation was either dug up or shot away in the fighting. Every morning each company must fill details to go further to the east and cut wood for mess fires since all the rail fences and houses were pulled down for same during the fighting. We are seeing more and more niggers coming into the lines and a sorrowful lot most of them are. The older ones have no life in their eyes, I guess, from having been worked and beat near to death. I met a young man with his wife and small baby that walked into our end of the company street and struck up a conversation with me and Pete. His way of talking was difficult to understand and he would not look us in the eye when he spoke. He told us he'd been lucky in that he'd been able to keep his wife and not be separated from her and his child. Just like in 'Uncle Tom's Cabin' it wasn't unusual for the slave owners to break up a family if a profit could be made from it. He seemed to have promise if given a chance to be outside the rusty shackles that he was used to. Pete and I got some' tack' and salt pork for him and he thanked us many times over. I asked what he intended to do, since the army was having a time feeding all of the contraband. William, that was his full name, and nothing more since the slaves don't get surnames because they are, in the eyes of the owners, nothing more than an animal. William said that if he could find a place of safety for his family, he'd join the USCT. That's the unit initials for the United States Colored Troops. So I took a piece of writing paper and wrote U.S. Sanitary Commission and Quaker Relief Program. William took the paper and although he could not read, he seemed to realize the importance of the marks on the paper. He went to his wife and in a dialogue I couldn't understand they cried and embraced each other. Then they went on up the street. I have come away from this experience with a new opinion of the darkies, especially the younger ones. I would expect the intrusions through our lines will end soon mostly because these slaves are bein' rounded up and placed in camps of their own. The government needs hands to pick the cotton that's been left in the fields just like these people once did for the plantation owners. Only this time, the former slaves, and that's what they are, they're free now, will be paid a wage for their toil. It truly is the day of Jubelo.

Rumor has it that once we're refitted and some of our recruits and draftees are taken in, we'll be sent on an expedition to Natchez, Mississippi. If this is true, I'll get a 'carte de visite' taken in my new uniform before it gets ruined.

All the mess fellows remain as they were. We are far enough from the sloughs and the river that the 'skeeters' aren't bad. Please write more often.

Love,
Chance

Sullivan, Moultrie County, Illinois
August 31, 1863

Buck Johnson made his way across the freshly dragged dirt street to the two story brick home that sat three blocks from the city square. The smell of manure emanating from the small barn at the back of the property told him the resident kept a cow and probably a carriage horse in the shelter. What was to be considered a back yard was enclosed with a six foot high board fence with the slightest opening between the palings.

The Copperhead gang leader had cut a notice from the Sullivan Express that evening which advertized an upstairs apartment in the home before which he stood. The clipping was shoved down into his left coat pocket and in his right was his small thirty-one caliber Allen and Wheelock pistol. The newspaper notice would give him an alibi for being in the neighborhood and the gun was a back up for circumstances that might arise if he was unable to convince the inquirer of his false intent.

A bell chimed from a church belfry somewhere across town indicating the hour was nine p.m. Dogs barked in the darkness as they always do whenever they hear a disturbance. Only a single light shone in any of the habitations sitting on either side of the long residential street. Above Buck, up the outside staircase, a light shone brightly through a slit in the newspaper covering the inside of the entry door. Next to his shoulder the house's lower windows remained as black of the inside of a hat.

Buck tested the lower step's wooden tread to ascertain its rigidity and when he found that it made no creak, he moved up to the landing to the lighted door. The smell of linseed oil and turpentine assailed his nostrils as he paused and peered through the sagging paper.

A thin, balding man was occupied with applying paint to an inner wall of a bare room. Two large kerosene lamps elevated on stepladders lighted his work site.

Buck grasped the door knob and tested it to determine if the portal was secured. It was unlocked and opened easily. Quickly, Johnson stepped into the room as the old man turned to investigate the source of the cool air that had touched the back of his neck.

"Who are you and what do you want?" The painter's eyes narrowed then widened as he recognized the muscular visitor. "Wait, I know you."

"I'm glad that you do, Judge. You always are able to find me when you want a dirty job done."

"You fool! You shouldn't have come here!" The advocate's eyes glared.

"Hold yer horses there, Judge. Let's not be quick to label me a fool."

"Why are you here? Step away from that window and stand next to the wall. Dammit, we should never be seen together." Judge Blackwell placed his brush on a lower step of his ladder. "You've come to see me and try to explain that mishap at the ford?"

The ringleader did as he was told, taking a position against the inner wall.

"Glad to oblige, Judge. Just you don't think yer on the bench and runnin' the show 'cause you ain't. As to Whitchurch, well, that couldn't have been prevented."

"I don't think you and your renegades are of any use to us after that disaster on the Windsor rail line a few days ago. Any ten year old could have brought that assignment off."

"That warn't my fault. Some dumb farmer was up at the wrong time of the night."

"We won't tolerate excuses!" Blackwell's face was flushed in the lamp light.

"I suppose Orrie Whitchurch drowned on purpose." Buck's voice was growing heated.

"We don't give a damn about him. The fortunes of war, you miserable puke. Now you've got Earp aroused and on your trail. How Lewis ever enlisted such incompetence I'll never know!"

"Not your trail, our trail! It's gettin' a lot closer to home now, Judge. You're up to yer eyes in this shit pile just like us."

"Leave!"

"No, I ain't goin'! I want some of the Knights' war chest and you're gonna give me some. The feller named Lewis said you had plenty and we've been doin' some awful dangerous assignments. I figure that a couple of hundred greenbacks will quiet things down."

"Quiet things down? Is that a threat that's you're going to talk to some one?"

"Maybe."

"Where's all the fervent support for the cause gone?"

"Money will restore it."

"Not a penny!" Flecks of spittle from the old man's lips sparkled in the lamp's light as he issued his adamant refusal.

"You ain't runnin' a damned courtroom now, you old bastard. Go get me a couple of hundred in cash and be quick about it."

"I most certainly will not!"

"Yes, you will. You'll not call fer help ner nothin' else. I got you by the short hairs and you know it."

"Get out you miserable tramp!"

In a movement faster than Johnson thought the old man capable of, Blackwell bent forward and picked up a claw hammer he'd been using to open paint containers. In one fluid motion, the tool came flying end over end at Buck's head. The judge's aim was errant and the old man's only accomplishment was the creation of a divot in the plaster in the wall behind the gang leader. Forgetting the pistol in his pocket, Johnson took up the tool which had fallen at his feet and in a rage, attacked Blackwell, laying the hammer flat against his skull in two sharp blows. The second strike dropped the judge to the floor where bright red blood gushed from a gash on his temple and his body commenced to convulse.

"Lester, what's going on up there? Did you fall?"

Panic seized Buck at the sound of a woman's drowsy inquiry from a room in the lower section of the house. He allowed the hammer to drop from his grasp as he surveyed the room and attempted to get a grip on his searing nerves. Then he went to the stepladder, removed the burning lamp, extinguished the flame and laid the device on its side as though it had toppled over. Using the toe of his boot, he tipped an open paint can onto the floor and just as quickly, he lifted the limp body of Blackwell and carried it to the door. The portal came open with a shove from his hip and in one motion Buck sent the slender man's form tumbling end over end down the staircase. Johnson looked back into the room, swiped a handful of blood from the floor and smeared it on the door knob and jam. Another swipe left a blotch of red on the banister.

"Lester, Darling, answer me."

Buck checked the sole of his boot and saw no tell- tale crimson coloring there. He bolted down the stairway and swerved around the crumpled form lying on the stone walkway at the bottom. His ears made out the sound of someone's footsteps climbing an interior set of steps as he shinnied over the backyard fence. A series of shrieks and screams propelled him down the darkened street.

Dogs all over town started barking. They always do whenever they're disturbed.

XXXXXXXXXXXXXXXXXXXXXXXXXXXXXXXXXXXXXXXXX

Sipes and Bell had ridden over to the Johnson place to inquire of the elderly parents just where they might find their son. Zack Johnson had seen the riders approaching and met the two at his front porch. He waved to them and bid them to dismount but they declined the invitation. He told them his son was checking on the maturity of the corn in an upland field and attempting to get an idea when the grain could be harvested. Bell and Sipes thanked the old man, clucked to their horses and rode on down the farm lane where they expected to find their leader.

Buck was discovered sitting on the top rail of a fence, a sizeable chew of tobacco in his cheek, holding a golden ear of corn in his hands. He rolled the ear over and over tossing it from one hand to the other.

"How'd your meetin' go with our contact?" Sipes loosened the reins in his fingers, allowing his sorrel to lower its head and nibble grass at the edge of the dusty lane.

Johnson ignored the question seemingly oblivious to his gang members' arrival.

"Whatta you think? Should I shuck the corn by the ear now and scoop it into the crib or would it be better to cut the stalks and put it up in shocks so's I can use 'er as I need it?"

Willie Bell looked at his partner and asked his initial question again.

Buck raised his eyes slightly and sighed.

"It went bad. Real bad."

"You didn't draw no money from him?"

"Nope."

"Did ya even meet with the feller?"

"Yep. I left him dead."

"Damn, Buck! That ain't the way you operate."

"It is now. I killed Judge Blackwell in Sullivan last night."

"Oh real Jesus H. Christ! That's bad." Willie Bell sat up in his saddle and looked back over his shoulder as if he expected to see a cloud of dust rising from the hooves of the mounts of Sheriff Earp's approaching posse.

"Ol' Blackwell was our agent? Who'd ever have thought it?" Sipes was staring intently at Buck with an incredulous look on his face.

"Buck we don't have to tell you that you're in a deep stack of shit now."

"I don't think so boys. When I asked him for some money, he got plumb irritable and tried to brain me with a claw hammer."

"Then what?" Bell allowed his horse to sidle next to Sipes' animal.

"Well, the judge missed me with his tommy hawk style hammer throw and when he did, I took it up and used it on his damned old bald head. He went down like a knocked ox and then I throwed him down the outside staircase. I made it look like an accident. Nobody saw me come or go."

"Nobody saw you at his house?"

"No, it was nine o'clock or so and there wasn't anybody out on the street. His ol' lady heard the commotion from downstairs but I was outta there before she came to check on him."

"Damn, Buck."

"It were a close call." Buck added non-chalantly as he sent a stream of tobacco at a grasshopper clinging to a dead grass stem at his feet. "I guess I'm getting' right good at makin' murders look accidental."

Both Sipes and Bell appraised their friend in a new light.

"Where does that leave us now with the Knights?"

"We're lone wolves, I guess. What I done broke the chain in the Golden Circle and I don't know if they'll try to repair it or not. It's likely that we won't get used anymore."

"What do ya think we should do, then?"

"Split up and lay low in case Sam Earp is gettin' a bead on us. If I didn't have the burden of the farm and the folks, I'd light outta here for the South but I've got responsibilities. I am goin' to be scarce for a couple of weeks 'fore corn harvest. I'll get the Stennet kid to get in the wood for the folks and do the feedin' while I'm away. I got a cousin at Mt. Zion and another one on Long Creek. I'm goin' ta pay them a visit and see what devilment they've been up to."

"We'll get together when you get back, then?"

"Shore. But don't 'spect ta see me in these parts fer at least three weeks. Things has got to cool down."

Scott Farm, Moultrie County, Illinois
September 16, 1863

Dear Chance,

The corn leaves are starting to rustle and the shucks are drying which means that in another few weeks, we could get our first frost. All the pumpkin and squash vines are dying back and all the biggest produce that's been hiding under the vines are exposed. It looks like we will have some gorgeous big pumpkins. Mother keeps mystifying us with all the squash dishes she puts on the table at meal time. Yesterday, we had acorn squash cut in half with melted butter and cinnamon and sugar on it. It was really grand. That with the last of the pole beans as well as fresh baked bread. The chickens are happy getting all the poor tomatoes that were left in the garden thrown over the pen fence to them.

Last week we had a tragedy in Sullivan which happened to one of our most outstanding citizens, Judge Blackwell. The old gentleman was painting an upstairs room which he wished to rent out when the ladder that he was standing on twisted and up ended. He struck his head on the floor, staggered out the upstairs door and fell down the staircase. The undertaker said that his death was instantaneous. The entire city is in mourning and three churches have had memorial services in his memory. Our community has suffered a great loss with his passing.

Your father is still pretty much tied to his chair but insists on sitting outside on the porch as much as possible. Aunt Clair puts a shawl around his shoulders and gives him little things to do so that he doesn't feel worthless. Yesterday, Mr. Dixon came down and met with Uncle Mathias and father to discuss when they think the buckwheat could be taken in. He says with the war on the grain should bring a good price.

Yesterday evening, I visited Aunt Clair and we had a long talk. She brought up the subject of freedom for the blacks which I thought was quite queer. She talked for a time of how badly she felt about shaping your prejudices toward the Negroes. Aunt Clair allowed that her mind had been poisoned when she was a little girl growing up in Kentucky. I didn't really know how much education she'd received as a young lady and her training in a young women's academy until we got into the conversation. I guess the guidance that she gave you in English grammar is why you can write such descriptive letters. Anyway, I didn't tell her of what you'd written about the blacks in your last letter.

Ruthie left for Cairo three days ago and we expect to hear from her any day now. I really miss her because we did so much and shared so much together. Mother misses her as well even though she didn't do much in the way of work around the house.

Have you had your likeness made yet? I can hardly wait to see what you look like in your fine, new suit.

Love,
Becky

Natchez, Mississippi
November 20, 1863

CHANCE TUGGED HIS OVERCOAT COLLAR tighter to his ears and held the *carte de visite* of *Becky* up to the weak afternoon sun. Then he unbuckled the strap on his haversack and removed the newly received likeness of himself. Carefully he unfolded the brown paper protecting it and placed both images side by side on the blanket on which he sat. It was the twentieth day of the eleventh month of the year 1863. The frost had come early and turned the usually verdant countryside to various hues of hickory nut. The seasonal change had caught the brigade off guard and each morning's assembly and roll call came complete with cold shoes, icy musket barrels, runny noses and the ever present camp coughs. The soldiers who were unlucky enough to have not had gloves sent from home felt the cold creep up from the metal of their shoulder arms and chill their bodies through.

How many times had he looked lovingly at the pale, perfectly formed face with the dark eyes and thought of her? In the likeness which Becky had sent him, she had parted her hair down the middle and pulled it back severely in what he assumed was a bun at the back of her head. He knew she would be much more comely if she had chosen a different hairstyle. She was astonishingly beautiful when she took her hair down and permitted the wind to swirl her tresses around her face.

Chance moved the two likenesses closer together until their edges touched.

A right handsome looking couple. A little young, perhaps, but then he could grow a beard, which would make him appear to be more mature. Would Becky be agreeable to his growing a beard?

An acrid whiff of smoke wafted up from a campfire in the lower elevation. It was a reminder that all army camps, Federal or Rebel stank. They were all the same, a few worse than or better than the others depending on the commanding officers. An approaching visitor could detect the camp's location from a mile away depending on the direction of the wind. His ears would first acknowledge the sounds; the beating drums, the shouted commands, the whinnying horses, the chopping of firewood. As the distance diminished, the visitor's olfactory sense sharpened and he became aware of open sanitary sinks, smoking wood fires and the throngs of unwashed bodies clothed in unwashed uniforms.

Neunan had asked for and received permission, after close order drill, to leave the confines of the company street and sit on a nearby hillside. The company street was noticeably shorter as a result of the casualties that the unit had incurred in almost two years of warfare. Tents that had been penned with the space of a foot between each other as per regulation now had five feet between them. Chance had to escape to find individual solitude if only for an hour, from the closeness of military oppressiveness. He was tired of the never wavering demands of obedience to directives and the ever present male proximity.

As he gazed at Becky in the *carte de visite,* he tried to calculate how long it had been since he'd actually touched the girl pictured on the stiff piece of cardboard or experienced the sensation of her breath on his cheek. His thoughts drifted to a time never to be revisited. It was a time wrapped in a soft film of pink, swirling about Becky, Ruthie, Andy Crowder and himself.

It was in the first blush of conflict when young men in blue uniforms promenaded through the graveled walkways of Camp Macon with beautiful, young girls holding their arms. The girls were stunning in their long dresses and brimmed hats and often paused in their walk to look adoringly into their soldier's eyes. They turned their heads so their scented curls caressed the smoothness of their throats and fluttered their eye lashes in response to every word uttered by their escorts as though they were listening to Hannibal himself. The young ladies spoke in tinkling syllables that they wove into webs encircling the men's hearts. It was a time of good manners, shiny brass, cleanliness and smooth faces.

Camp Macon at the north-west edge of Decatur was chosen for a training location because of its lofty oak shade trees and several flowing springs which would provide the men learning how to be soldiers a moderate degree of comfort. Orders had been decreed that the trees were not to be violated and the commanding officer, Isaac Pugh, had sited the sinks on lower ground in order to avoid polluting the springs. However, thousands of tramping feet created a different problem for the encampment, dust. In a matter of days the regiment appeared to be wearing buff colored leggings over the lower portion of their trouser legs as they marched about performing drills they were being taught. A small creek crossed one corner of the camp and flowed toward the Sangamon to the south and this source provided a natural bathtub for the men. In the elementary stages of soldierly instruction the green recruits got themselves tangled with each other and jostled about like apples in a dunking tub. The newly formed 41st Illinois had been issued the short, eight buttoned blouses, called by the officers, state militia issue. But the apparel was renamed by the men as organ grinder's monkey suits. French style kepis, along with an assortment of accoutrements, and obsolete, foreign muskets of an unknown origin completed the soldier's image. Those lucky enough were housed in the tepee like, cone shaped, Sibley tents capable of sheltering twelve soldiers. The companies formed later were issued wall tents meant to accommodate, four very small men. Chance was fortunate enough to be assigned, with Andy Crowder, to one of the more spacious Sibleys. He stood and laughed until his sides hurt at Crowder's antics as a war chief engaged in his version of an Indian dance inside the doorway of their lodging.

After three weeks both Neunan and Crowder allowed army life was agreeing with them. Fair food, clothing that was well made though dreadfully hot in the early August sun and sleeping in the open air was doing wonders for their health. The 41st was taking pride in its appearance and the sharp manner they snapped to attention when the colonel rode by on his daily review. Isaac Pugh was genuinely interested in the men's *welfare, even inspecting the quality and cleanliness of the bakery and the condition of the regimental sinks. The general had his junior officers issue passes to those boys who wished to leave the perimeters of the camp to pick blackberries but when he learned a thoughtless few had sneaked into saloons in Decatur, he had the offenders march the outer boundary of the parade grounds with knapsacks filled with rocks. Colonel Pugh was insistent on another aspect of military training that his compatriots commanding sister regiments neglected and this was musketry practice. Each soldier drew twenty rounds at least three times per week and blazed away at a six foot by six foot target standing two hundred yards away. At that time, Sergeant Bone and Sergeant Wilson stood along side the shooters and instructed them on methods which would improve their marksmanship. Chance and Crowder had watched in amazement as the buck and ball loads whizzed out over the prairie at the rifle range, struck the ground and ricocheted up into the targets. Those leaden missiles that flew high traveled on and clipped small twigs and leaves from trees in a far off fence line. Of course, the practice sessions would set off a chorus of yelps and howls from the dogs residing on neighboring farms. Sometimes the first blasts from the assembled musketeers would frighten a prairie chicken into a cackling flight.*

But the activity Chance and Andy Crowder most looked forward to was the Sunday afternoon dress review and the evening serenade by the regimental band. Citizens from miles around turned up in carriages or walked out from town to observe the brave young patriots who soon would be marching away to the front. Becky and Ruthie had come at every opportunity that arose and as the time neared for the regiment to debark for its posting the young girls' gazes became longer and more intent. Becky Scott was as lovely as ever. Her skin had been tanned to a tawny hue from her exposure to the outdoors and on the days of the visit she had taken extra care with her dark hair, brushing it until it glistened in the sun. Chance thought he had never seen Becky's eyes so large and liquid as they were on that Sunday. Her cousin, Ruthie, was fairer even pale, for with her red hair she had to avoid the sun else a hundred freckles would emerge on her cheeks and nose.

The boys were given no leave of any kind for the past three weeks. The army had learned a trained soldier was far too valuable to be allowed outside its authority in the last stages of training where he might decide on 'French leave' and disappear.

Chance could only hold Becky's right hand in his as they walked on the loose gravel pathway at the conclusion of review. Andy Crowder and Ruthie followed at a respectable distance talking softly and making promises to each other. As the two couples passed groups of young soldiers, the beauty of the two girls sent many a lonely boy's heart into a quiver.

They sat on a blanket under the burr oaks, sipping lemonade and eating fried chicken and pickles, the girls relating all that was happening on the Scott, Crowder and Neunan farms. Little Alfie had caught a great many bull frogs at the river using a bit of red flannel on a hook. The boy had speared the amphibians through their lower jaw bones with a 'Y' shaped sapling stick as he would pan fish, but the frogs were not about to go quietly up the hill to the house and Alfie had to do them in singularly before they pounded the snot out of his left leg. On a visit to the Neunan's one afternoon of the preceding week, Chance's mother had sat with her niece at the kitchen table and shared reheated coffee with her. During their conversations, Clair told Becky that she'd wished Mathias had never permitted their only son to enlist. Ruthie brushed crumbs from her bodice and contributed that Ellis Crowder had taken in a huge amount of hay with the assistance of Andy's two younger brothers.

As the shadows lengthened and the time for the concert grew nearer, Chance rose and helped the two young ladies put their utensils, napkins and food scraps into a wicker basket. Then he'd taken Becky by the hand and led her away from Andy and Ruthie. They crossed the creek and walked into a secluded spot beneath a naturally formed bower consisting of wild grape vines. There, Chance removed Becky's flowered hat and allowed it to fall loosely at her back where it was suspended by its yellow ribbon. She looked into the taller boy's eyes attempting to read his intent but deep inside she knew what he wanted. Was it right to be wrapped in the embrace of her first cousin, to offer her hungry lips to him?

Chance's hands went to the small of Becky's back as he hesitated, questioning what he wished with all his heart to do. Their foreheads moved closer and touched as they breathed in the warmth of each others soft breaths. Then their lips met. At first with just an exploratory inquiry, a soft touch, not more than a brush. They drew back for a moment and studied each other's face. Both their lips formed the word, yes, without uttering their surrender aloud.

XXXXXXXXXXXXXXXXXXXXXXXXXXXXXXXXXXXXXXXXXX

Another spiral of smoke rose from the smoldering fire pit and ascended to where Chance sat. The suffocating sensation brought Neunan back to reality and he picked up both images wrapping them in brown paper before he secured them in his tarred haversack.

"Hey Chance, come on down here, Pete's back from sick call."Warner hailed from the plain below.

O'Donnel stood next to the stained pup tent which he and Chance shared, a heavy muslin cloth wrapped around his throat with its ends protruding from his overcoat collar. His face was rosy from the affects of the heavy cold that he carried in his lungs.

"Well, what did the Doc tell ya, Pete?"

"Not much more than I already knew. He gave me a concoction of black strap molasses and sulfur to take by mouth and some foul smellin' volcanic oil chest rub. The stuff tastes awful but I've noticed it's slowed my coughin' down already."

Tom Warner joined the pair. He'd unrolled the cuffs of his overcoat in order to protect his gloveless hands from the cold.

"I'd hope that if the rumors is true that we're goin' inta winter camp on the Big Black River above Jackson we get it done damned quick. We all will have to get something substantial built afore the snow flies. At least somethin' that we can heat."

Ballis hunched up his shoulders as though he was entertaining the thought of the icy blasts that were to come. "I talked to an ol' nigger yesterday that'd been born and raised down here. He told me they didn't get much snow at least not the amount we get back up north. The feller went on to say that they do get fierce ice storms and frost."

Harvey Ballis kicked the butt ends of the logs deeper into the center of the fire then stomped his right foot to shake off the glowing embers that had landed on the instep of his shoe.

"You fellers all done with cookin' or boilin' for the time bein'?" Ballis didn't wait for a reply before fumbling in his overcoat pocket to withdraw a fine, white silk handkerchief with initials embroidered in one corner. He wadded the cloth and threw it into the smoldering edge of the fire.

"What did you do that for?" Pete O'Donnel questioned. "That was a mighty fine hanky."

"Aw, I've learned my lesson with that thing. I traded a plug of tobaccy fer it with a soldier outta C Company. He told me he'd took it off the body of a dead rebel cavalryman out on the picket line. It was awful nice material and I thought it'd be the berries to send home to my Mom, but that Shelby County feller pulled a fast one on me. The Secesh must've been dead fer a month 'fore he was relieved of his accessory. I washed it and washed it but I never could get the stink out of it."

Tom Warner shook his head and pursed his lips at how his mess mate had been taken in with the shoddy exchange. Waving the smoke away from his face, he stepped back from the swirl of sparks Ballis had ignited and smirked at Pete O'Donnel.

"We'll know yer gettin' better, Pete, when Chance thar, starts complainin' that yer eatin' more then yer share of the grub."

O'Donnel came back with a wheezy laugh that erupted into a volley of hacking.

"Don't mean to worry ya none, Pete, but my ol' Granny had a cough sounded jest like that a couple of days before she turned up her toes." Warner was grinning.

"Shut up, Tom." Pete hocked and spit in the dead grass between the tents.

XXXXXXXXXXXXXXXXXXXXXXXXXXXXXXXXXXXXXXXXX

The black banded envelope had arrived three days later and once again Neunan had received permission to climb the hillside and sit alone beneath the skeletal, dead oak in the sun. Every man in the army felt empathy for the unlucky soldier who received such a missive and gave them silence or dropped their heads in a display of understanding.

Becky's latest letter and the dreadful news it contained struck Chance in the chest like the kick of a mule. He sniffed up cold air through his nostrils and swallowed allowing his eyes to fill with tears. His vision blurred as he dropped the letter from both hands and clutched it only between his thumb and index finger. His shoulders shook as his body convulsed with a sadness he had never known. Mathias was dead. His father was no more. He would never see his father in his mortal form again. The twenty years of memories of Mathias Neunan were all he had. There would never be more. His father would never see the children that Chance would father, or hold them in his arms or kiss their rosy, smooth cheeks. Fate had been cruel to a good man. The second devastating revelation in Becky's letter was her description of the autumn flood which had swept away the crops in the bottomland. Just as harvesting was commencing, an unnatural deluge swept down the river from the east and forced the stream out of its bed. The erosion of the banks tumbled trees and buildings into the maelstrom and sent muddy water into the sloughs drowning the ripened crop. Job Scott said the river was at least two and a half miles across and at the highest stage that he had ever seen. Beneath the flotsam being swirled southward was several thousand dollars worth of unharvested grain.

The last heartbreaking information was the most stunning of all as if his young mind could have handled anything more. Job, Becky's mother, Clair Neunan, and Becky were moving back to Ohio. Becky wrote that she'd cried for hours over the decision but her father had pointed out surviving the winter with no more food or forage than they had would be impossible. The houses would be shut up; the farm animals would be sold, except for the draft teams. The implements would be left in order to be on site when they returned in the following spring. As much of the furnishings and food that could be transported via wagon, would accompany the family to Zanesville in eastern Ohio. There Job and Clair had two brothers who were involved in agriculture and who would provide housing and assistance during their time of need. Becky went on to describe how the family had interred Mathias on the hill along side Aunt Emma. She closed with the fervent hope that Chance would be patient and not do anything rash such as deserting. She pledged to write him as soon as the family arrived in Zanesville and provide him with an appropriate address.

The young soldier raised his head and wiped his eyes with the cuff of his rough woolen overcoat. Absolutely nothing in his young life had prepared him for the ordeal that he was now facing.

XXXXXXXXXXXXXXXXXXXXXXXXXXXXXXXXXXXXXXX

Chance blew on his fingers to warm them as he and Pete O"Donnel huddled at the back of their tent completing the packing of their knapsacks. They rolled their gum blankets around their wool ones and tied the two ends together. This arrangement would allow them to sling the blankets over their left shoulder to create a 'horse collar' for marching. Thankfully, there were three regimental wagons on hand to transport their over-laden knapsacks to the winter camp on the Big Black. At this site the XVII Corps and it's newest brigade would dig in for the approaching cold weather. The troops would excavate several feet into the earth, tramp down the dirt of what would become the floor and lay down boards which had been scavenged from area slave cabins. The next step was to erect low walls of notched logs and design roof supports over which their shelter halves would be stretched. At the end of the dwelling opposite the door, a chimney made of sticks and mud or stacked hogs' heads would be placed. At this point, the simple hut heating devices came about through the ingenuity of the soldiers. Having heat, removed the major angst that plagued the troops and from this point the men turned their attention to creating bed frames and tables for their accommodations. The major task was to eliminate the seepage of water through the board flooring and chink the log walls. This camp location would be the home for the 41st through Christmas and into the spring of 1864.

Chance had written to the Dixons, the old couple who lived on the high road, and who had offered to assist the Scotts with the fall harvest. This correspondence he'd ferreted away in his haversack until the new camp site was reached. Neunan was desperate to contact Becky and his mother and he hoped the neighbors would have received word from them even though he hadn't. Not one morsel of news had arrived from his love interest and as he placed his knapsack on the gray painted army wagon, his spirits had dipped to their lowest ebb. He waited beside the baggage conveyance for the regimental postman to guide his horse through a minor traffic jam and receive his missive. In less than an hour, the army would be on the march, all the tents would be struck, the repugnant sinks would be filled, and only the depressions in the ground where the fire pits were once located would be left as evidence that a large group of men had spent a portion of the lives on the site.

The Forks of the Kaskaskia, Moultrie County, Illinois December 22, 1863

CONFEDERATE AGENT LEWIS SAT ASTRIDE his dapple gray horse in the midst of the softly falling snow. Buck Johnson had no idea how the man would find his way to the rendezvous point in a forest where he had no previous knowledge and was unfamiliar to him, but there he was. The mysterious man watched intently as Johnson maneuvered his horse through the black trees to where he waited.

"Hello, Mr. Johnson. I thought perhaps that you'd bring some of your associates with you."

"Nope, just me. I like to work alone. A feller don't attract much attention that way. How in tarnation did you find yer way out to this spot?"

"I have sources to assist me as you well know."

Buck didn't respond to the man's assertion. Lewis was wearing a tobacco colored plug hat and a capeless gray overcoat.

"Did your visit to Macon County prove fruitful for you?"

Buck Johnson looked at Lewis, his countenance revealing his astonishment that the agent knew of his recent travels.

"Er, well, yeah."

"Tut, tut, Mr. Johnson, your expression displays your perplexity. Just remember, I have contacts that are always watchful."

Johnson didn't respond, only sat quietly as if he were a little boy who'd been caught with his hand in the cookie jar. The snow was picking up in intensity, hissing against the trees as it slanted down.

"As you're well aware, we've had a death and a breach in our chain of operation due to the incident in Sullivan." Lewis' horse shook the snow from its mane. Waiting until the animal quieted itself, the agent continued. "My superiors believe and I have concurred that you would be the best man to take over the deceased's position."

Buck smiled a mischievous grin akin to a cheater who had, against the odds, been declared the winner in a spelling contest.

"I can see that you feel confident of being able to perform that task. I have observed your audaciousness and ability to lead." The snow was building on both men's garments.

"Shore I do. I know I can handle the job. What's the pay?"

"Why Buck, may I call you Buck? Compensation had not been an issue with our former director."

"Well, pay makes me work a hell'va lot better."

Lewis raised his chin and looked up into the slate colored sky as though he hadn't expected such a request.

"Very well, then. We can supply you with payment commensurate with the risk involved."

"Commensurate, what's that?"

"Equal to, that the word's meaning."

"Let's start with a thousand then. Me and my boys ain't asked for a cent or been offered anythin' for the work we've did."

"That's a pretty stiff fee, Buck."

"You told us at the first meetin' that the Knight's had a bunch of money."

Lewis' gloved hands remained on the bow of his army saddle. "All right then. You shall receive such a sum."

"In greenbacks. I don't want any Secesh paper."

"You couldn't spend that species up here, you fool." The agent's demeanor was growing sour. "Agreed, then Mr. Johnson. I apologize for my harshness."

"You watch who yer callin' a fool, mister." Buck's dark eyes flashed in anger. "You got it on ya?"

"Yes."

"What do you want done?"

"Nothing. Absolutely nothing. Sit tight for the time being. Momentous events are in the offing in the next three months and we don't want to tip our hands any more than we already have. The society wants no little harassments, no raids. We want an absolute stand down by all our operatives. Understood?"

"Yes, sir. Now about that money...."

Big Black River, Mississippi
December 28, 1863

THE WEATHER FAILED TO MAKE any dramatic change as the camp situated northeast of Jackson took on a lived in appearance. Some Christmas packages from home had been delivered but Chance received nothing so Pete O'Donnel shared his with his messmate. From the brown paper wrapped box, jars of peaches, pears, and cherries appeared. A can of oysters came out next as well as a pair of mittens, a woven scarf, and a pocket knife. Packed flat on the bottom of the box were hard bound copies of 'Tennyson's Selected Poetry' and 'Loreson's Guide to the Southern States'. Pete's mother had put all the items in a loose filling of dry oatmeal which the soldiers emptied into moisture proof tins for later consumption as breakfast food. But individual letters came few and far between to the soldiers' enduring their dreary respite in the smoky camp.

In the late morning on the third of January of the new year, a man from a Michigan regiment came down the street inquiring if any of the mid-westerners had received correspondence from home within the past week. He stopped and asked the question of Warner who was cleaning his musket in front of his hut. The soldier said the rumor was that rebel bushwhackers had intercepted the mail two different times during the previous seven days.

Neunan, hearing the conversation, unlatched the short door on his shelter and stepped out over the threshold.

"Then, this would account for all the messages we've sent out not getting a reply." Chance struggled to get his bulky overcoat over his shoulders.

"Peers that way. I spoke to a yellow leg cavalryman who patrols on the road to Jackson and he says that they's mail scattered all over hell up that way."

Neunan's shoulders drooped as he realized his missives to the Dixons trying to locate Becky were probably mired in the icy muck of the roadway.

That night between tattoo and taps, Chance rewrote his letter to the Dixon's in Moultrie County. Pete left his messmate to allow him to compose his inquiry in solitude and talked quietly with Ballis and Warner outside the hut. Neunan could only hope that this letter of desperation would reach the old couple and they would respond with an address where he could contact Becky once more.

Neunan was wrapped in his blanket but was not asleep when O'Donnel opened the small door to their hut and came in. He clutched a handful of broken branches and went to the tiny sheet metal stove which they'd purchased from a sutler, slid the lid aside and put in the fuel.

"You asleep, Pard?" Pete asked.

"No, just lying here thinking."

"You seem to be doin' a lot of that, as of late."

O'Donnel shed his clothes and pulled his heavy wool blanket over himself, then added his overcoat to the covering. He floundered in the darkness, adjusting the placement of the coverings until he got them to his satisfaction.

It was not long before the small stove was glowing red and both men became restless pulling back their bed clothes and lying in their long underwear on the straw that was their mattresses.

The two lay in silence and listened to the crackle of the fire in their tiny stove.

"Chance?"

"Yes."

"I can't sleep."

"Neither can I."

The heating device continued to sizzle and spit. Pete sighed in weary disgust.

"I've never heard you say a word about the fight at Pittsburg Landin'. You war in it, right?"

Neunan lay in repose, reticent to the question for a few minutes.

"Yes. Why do you bring that up?"

"Well, most of the fellers have talked about it quite a lot, but not you. I had an early case of the *summer complaint* and it knocked me low. I missed that battle, thank God."

"You were damned fortunate."

"I suppose I was. You lost your best pard there, didn't you?"

"Yes, Andy Crowder."

"I don't recollect ever meetin' him. He was in the company acourse, but we wasn't ever introduced."

"He was a good boy." Chance barely whispered in the darkness. O'Donnel couldn't see the tears in his friend's eyes.

"Do you want to talk about him and the fight? It'd probably be good for you to get it off yer chest."

Neunan exhaled softly, as though he had been waiting for someone to ask him about his participation in the battle.

"I helped my father and Uncle Job kill lots of hogs when butchering season came in early December of every year. I'd seen gallons of blood before but nothing like what gushed out of Andy. One moment we were peering into the gray smoke and in the next I heard him grunt and pitch forward. It was all I could stand; Andy's blood all over me and 'minies' zipping around my head like a jillion bees."

Pete O'Donnel rolled over and faced Chance.

Then the grieving soldier felt the warmth of Pete's hand on his arm.

"I ran, Pete. I ran like a dirty coward."

"That's all right, Pard. Lots of the fellers did." Pete could hear the pain in Neunan's voice. "You don't have to continue if you wanna stop."

"No, you asked to hear my story and I'm going to finish." Neunan wiped away his tears with the heels of his hands. "I didn't quit running until I reached the end of the 41st's line which was extended to the river. I got me a musket and got back into the fight picking up cartridges from the boxes of the wounded and dead. Then, our position started to cave just like we did at Donelson. Right when things were looking their worst, the 9th Illinois bullied in along side of us and we held. They saved the army and weren't a minute too soon either. Later when the news swept through our ranks that the rebel commander, General Albert Johnston, had been killed, that regiment claimed it was one of their marksmen that got him."

"Gosh, all hemlock, Chance, that's a heck'va story."

"Let me finish, Pete. That's just a part of my adventure. I was delirious, out of my mind and shaking like a leaf. My head was on fire and I was having trouble with my eyes. I pitched my gun and made for the landing. I figured we'd got our asses beat so I was looking for a way to save my skin. The bluffs overlooking the river were jammed with our troops who'd run off. It was an insane asylum. Then it started to rain, and rain, and the thunder and lightning came. Lightning crackled so close above the trees it made a person dodge. Lord, I've never seen such flashes in all my life."

O'Donnel readjusted himself before saying, "I'm listenin', Chance."

"Got any water, there? I've got to have a drink before I go on."

"Sure, here's a little in my canteen."

Neunan took a swig of cool water and returned the receptacle to Pete. He leaned back against his knapsack which was his substitute for a pillow.

"Then, Blooie! The dangest racket you've ever heard shook the woods and water. General Don Carlos Buell had two timberclad gunboats and a load of transports full of fresh troops on the opposite side of the Tennessee River. They'd come to reinforce us and the Tyler, one of the Navy boats, had let go with one of its big cannons. Just hearing that ear splitting sound put some mustard in men's britches on both sides that night. Directly, in the damnest pour down I've ever seen, Buell started unloading his men at the wharf. They pushed and shoved sulkers and wretches like me aside so's they could disembark. Oh, those boys coming down the gangplanks did give us Billy hell for the way we'd fought before they'd got there.

"Is that all?" O'Donnel mumbled.

"Just about. I stayed up nearly all night watching transports off load men, ammunition, light artillery and God knows what else. They had big bonfires going in spite of the rain and that scene with all the thousands of troops milling around had to have been a preview of what hell would look like. It wasn't any use to try to sleep because both the navy's gunboats, the Tyler and Lexington, were shooting shot as big as scalding kettles into the rebel lines at fifteen minute intervals." The young soldier paused to swallow and lick his dry lips.

"Next morning, the storm had cleared out and a more miserable throng of men couldn't be found anywhere. Sometime before daylight several squads of armed men and mounted officers began forcing us broken bunch of sorry specimens into make shift companies. I was given a handful of cartridges and a musket and sent forward as a member of the rear support for the fresh divisions that'd landed in the night. I staggered along, mind in a muddle and every bone and muscle of my being hurting like the devil. I'm glad the mob I was in wasn't called on to do anything on that Sunday. We were all tuckered and dispirited. We'd have broke for sure if we'd been fired on."

Chance stopped talking and waited for his messmate to make further inquiries.

O'Donnel was snoring.

XXXXXXXXXXXXXXXXXXXXXXXXXXXXXXXXXXXXXXXXXX

"Dress right, Dress!" Sergeant Wilson's command came crisp and sharp in the chill air of early morning.

"Count off by twos! Count!"

"Ready, Front!"

Captain Rouse's blue eyes swept the assembled line of the shrunken company. The formation was much shorter than when the unit had marched out of Camp Macon eighteen months earlier.

"At ease, men!" the officer stood ramrod straight, a red worsted sash and light infantry sword belt encircling his trim waist. "This morning this company has been given the honor of manning the blockhouse located on the west end of the rail trestle on the Big Black at Cocker's Gap. Our detachment will consist of twelve men, eight to be stationed inside the fortification and four outside walking a sentry beat. Sergeant Sawyer will be in charge and he will see that the rotations will be adhered to in an equitable manner. Each soldier will be on guard duty for not more than two hours at a time due to winter conditions. We will be on post day and night until we are relieved by another detachment from Company H at the end of the week. Is this understood?"

"Yes sir." came an unenthusiastic answer.

"Good. Now every number two man step forward and count from the left to the right commencing with the number one. You will count consecutively until twelve is reached." When the count was finished, Rouse turned to Sergeant Sawyer and stated, "These twelve will comprise your guard detachment. Have them fall out and collect what cold weather garments they can and gather any rations they have in their quarters. We'll send up additional commissary needs later this afternoon." Rouse swiveled to his left to face the NCO standing at attention and gave the order, "Sergeant Wilson, dismiss the rest of the company except for this detachment."

Neunan was filled with dread and foreboding at his unlucky selection. The guard platoon would be in an exposed position far away from the safety of the camp. Anything could and probably would happen to them.

"Men, upon your return from collecting your necessities, Sergeant Sawyer will march you to the rail siding where a flat car and engine will convey you to your post. Be vigilant at all times! Irregulars and a small squadron of rebel cavalry are operating in the area you are being called upon to guard. It is essential that the rail line be kept open for our communications and supply. Sergeant, take over your troops."

Sergeant Sawyer, who had a small farm in Todd's Point, saluted his commander smartly and spun about on the heels of his shoes.

"Squad, assemble here in ten minutes. Dismissed!"

The men rushed to their huts and began to rummage through their meager stock of clothing and food.

Pete ducked under the low door jam and laid a hand on the younger man's shoulder.

"Tough luck, ol' friend. What a shitty detail to be on."

"Yeah, it's pretty nasty, isn't it?"

"I got an extra vest and I'm givin' you my mittens and scarf outta the Christmas box 'til you get back. You'll need 'em worse than me."

"I'm beholdin' to you, Pete. Would you have an extra pair of socks?"

"Shore and you can have 'em." Pete bent over the ammunition box that he used as a bureau and took out the items. "I talked to a feller from Company I last week that had pulled similar duty and he said that they've got lots of ponchos in the block house so you won't have to lug one up there."

"Could you spare a little tack, too?"

"Yeah, I've got five you can take but Captain said you'll get supplies after you get up to the bridge."

"You know the army. Nothin' ever goes the way they tell you."

Sergeant Sawyer's voice bellowed from the company street calling for the squad to assemble.

Pete O'Donnell stepped out of the hut ahead of Chance, then turned and grasped his hand. "I'll be thinkin' of ya, Pard," as he averted his eyes away.

Neunan looked down to avoid looking at Pete and having him see the tears running down his cheeks.

XXXXXXXXXXXXXXXXXXXXXXXXXXXXXXXXXXXXXXXX

The rain fell in whipping sheets in the blackness of the night. It splashed on the ties and formed rivulets that coursed off the gravel and into the grass at trackside. Chance had found a poncho in the warmth of the blockhouse and had pulled it over his head before assuming his guard duty and this outer garment was saving him from being drenched to the skin. The tops of the rails gleamed silver in the weak light thrown out from a distant campfire smoldering on the side of the Memphis and Charleston Railroad. Even with the *impermeable*, the shoulders of Neunan's uniform jacket were growing more sodden by the minute and the water in his shoes caused his feet to slip inside the slick leather.

Damned weather and my damned luck to draw duty in the outdoors, he thought. *Here I walk as miserable as hell while the majority of the boys lavish in the warmth and coziness of the blockhouse. Ah well,* Chance paused to adjust his hat so that the water was directed more efficiently off its brim, *my relief is laying in a threadbare pup tent trying his best to keep his ass dry and probably shivering like a hound shitin' peach seeds.*

Neunan marveled at the two relief sentries' ability to keep the green pine bough fire going in the downpour that he was enduring. The flickering fire, as dismal as it was, gave Chance hope that his beat would eventually be over on this appalling night. In the ebony pitch that surrounded him, Neunan was as lonely as he'd ever been. The depression seemed to come more frequently now that things had turned into misery on the home front. The melancholy which crept over him as he and Pete O'Donnel spooned in their woolen blankets inside their little hut was a threat to his acceptance of where he was and what his government expected him to do. He had, for a time, tried to avoid becoming close to Pete. He'd lost too many good friends in his career as a soldier. Gone were Andy Crowder, Wes Lansden, Cory Adams, and Walt Bone. While not killed in the madness of war, the sergeant was crippled and would not resume his place in the ranks or physically be the same again. But in O'Donnel's case, he was just too caring and sensitive to be held at arms length as a friend. The Moultrie County soldier paused and turned the tompion in his musket's muzzle to determine if the wooden stopper hadn't swollen in the dampness. The wooden device had to be removed if the weapon was to be fired and wise was the soldier who checked the tompion periodically. Neunan cringed at the thought of the job he'd have to perform on the morrow when the soaked firearm would have to be dealt with. He'd have to pull the load with a ball screw and rinse and dry the bore before the musket could be reloaded. Chance stopped at the end of his beat and tucked the musket's muzzle under his glistening poncho. As he gazed off into the wet, he allowed his thoughts to roam once more. His mind settled on Becky Scott and gradually he pushed back the chill which was attacking his body and brought her lovely face into focus. Where was she and what would she be doing on such a night?

Would she be wearing her night gown and have pillows at her back as she sat composing a letter to him? She had written him so many over the past year and a half and while his missives had been fewer, he had indicated his love for her during the last months. If he, through some miracle, could fly through the night over the hundreds of miles that separated them and land outside her bedroom door in Ohio, would she welcome him? Would she submit to his enfolding embrace and surrender herself to him in the warmth of her bed as the wind rattled the windows outside? As the rain lashed the roof over their heads, he would hear her soft whispers and twinkling laughter. Her skin would be silky and fragrant and her lips soft and warm. Beneath his finger tips, her quivering body would be his to take. Chance tripped over a rail spike but righted himself without falling. His impassioned vision fled from his mind as he returned to the reality of where he was and what he had been ordered to do. With the deluge pouring down, it was next to impossible to hear anything other than the falling water. He turned on his heels and began the march toward the 'corn stalk' bridge span some hundred yards in the distance. Ahead, Chance made out the dark blockhouse and the hewed timbers of the trestle put up by the engineers to cross the Big Black River swirling in the crevasse below. In the daylight the intricate lattice work of the timbers making up the bridge was a sight to behold. One's first impression was that such a framework could never bear up under the weight of a steam engine and its cars laden with military goods but the marvel did.

The cloudburst prevented the young soldier from hearing the footsteps rapidly approaching from behind him or see the three figures as they closed the distance which separated them. One of the dark forms slipped on a rail and screamed a muffled epitaph that spun Chance around to confront his antagonists. From the hip position he jerked the trigger of his musket and was blinded by the flash of the explosion. The weapon's stock stung Neunan's hands as the first man emerged out of the gloom and swung a gleaming bowie knife at his throat. The sentry parried the movement and followed that with a bayonet thrust that impaled the rebel through the face. Chance felt the blade punch through soft tissue until it struck bone before making a sickening, grinding sound. Struggling to withdraw the angular spike, the third man bowled Neunan over and grasped him by the neck opening of his poncho.

"You Yankee son-of-a –bitch, I'm gonna cut yer guts out!" The bearded man cursed as the two rolled back and forth between the rails. Neunan tried to pin the man's arms down but his opponent was much larger and stronger. He fought with his fists and fingers, tearing at the rebel's face as they grunted and grappled in the hammering downpour. Then a numbing pain surged through Chance's right side and his arm lost its strength. He felt the air leave his lung and he fought to inhale. The second knife thrust gigged through his rubber material of his rain coat and skittered off his cartridge box which had fortuitously been twisted over the vital organs of his stomach.

Blackness swirled around him and immersed him as he waited for a third penetration from cold steel but the killing gig never came.

"Jesus, God! I think that bastard blinded me!" Came an unbelieving oath.

"Is he dead?"

"Yeah, I think so." The rain gave no let up and lashed the men even harder.

"You damned son-of-a-bitch, come down here and try to take over our country."

With that Chance felt a boot go into the small of his back followed by a tremendous shove that sent him rolling down the railroad embankment. With no impediments to stop him, his agony- racked body tumbled end over end finally landing with a thud against a mulberry bush. As he passed in and out of consciousness, Neunan was aware of strange popping sounds and orange flashes coming from the direction of the trestle. Then an ear splitting explosion followed by a teeth rattling concussion pounded his face into the moist earth. The bridge had disappeared in a blinding flash sending pieces of timber skyward to disappear in the gloom. Chance covered his face with his good arm as flaming debris fell from overhead and thudded all around him.

XXXXXXXXXXXXXXXXXXXXXXXXXXXXXXXXXXXXXXXX

A drop of water fell from the leaf of a hackberry bush onto the gray flesh of a hand and another plopped on an eye lid. A chick-a-dee picked at the splintered end of a six by six bridge timber which hung in the branches of an oak tree that loomed over the twisted figure of Chance Neunan.

Chance stirred and licked his cracked lips slowly with his tongue. Then he opened one swollen eye and surveyed his surroundings.

I ain't dead yet but I'm damned near to being so, he thought. The muscles of his body were stiff and his clothing clung in a sticky wad on his right side. Even the slightest movement sent a white hot surge of pain through his body. A drawn, pale hand lay next to his face, its nails filled with yellow clay. He was startled when the fingers flexed indicating life, then in his delirium, he laughed lightly at the realization that the placid appendage was attached to his own shoulder.

Another arm; however, hanging in a crotch of a nearby tree was not a portion of his body. It belonged to someone else and it was evident that the arm's former owner would no longer have need of it.

Cold, as deep as the deepest winter frost, tightened Chance's body and set his teeth to chattering. He fought to subdue the shaking for this response was aggravating the pain that pooled in the spot on his right side where the poncho's folds lay wrinkled and hard. Stones beneath his body cut into his garments and made him even more uncomfortable.

A crow cawed in the distance, the volume of its croaking partially subdued by the roar of the river passing over the detritus of the ruined bridge. Iron rails lay along the top of the embankment and several had been driven into the ground vertically by the force of the destroying explosion. Gray clad soldiers wrapped in the fog of early morning, strode amid the ruins using pry bars, to pull the spikes and throw the track into the roaring torrent that was the Big Black River.

Chance drifted in and out of consciousness as the sounds of the trestle's destruction continued. It was only hours later that he regained alertness and began shaking again. The wafting mist rising from the river had concealed him from the Confederates on the elevated road bed and while the fog was a savior, it had brought back the chill.

Stones grated underfoot behind where he lay as a person shrouded in fog approached. The daylight, if that's what it could be called, was blanketed in a veil that did not permit the sun to penetrate to the ground.

Suppose that the rebels were not gone? Suppose they were looking for wounded Yanks?

Perspiration beaded on Chance's face as the footfalls drew nearer.

Play dead, stop your breathing, he told himself.

His ears strained to pick up the measured steps that were approaching. Neunan tried hard to suppress the quickness of his breathing but the pain was unbearable and his inhalations came in staccato gasps.

The footsteps came closer winding their way down the embankment until the person stood over Neunan. Chance held his breath not knowing if the end would come with the crack of a pistol or the skull splintering blow from a rifle butt. Instead, a small hand slipped under his poncho to his open jacket and fumbled with the chain of his watch. The nimble fingers unhooked the keeper bar from his vest, then flexed into a closed fist. Chance heard heavy breathing emitting from above and he tried to interject his shorter ones between those he was hearing. His nose failed to draw in the expected smell of sweat, tobacco, or whiskey but instead his sense picked up a delicate fragrance.

"Hey, Ol' Mose, this one is alive."

Neunan lay motionless, suffocating, dying to expel the useless air from his lungs. Finally, in the seconds before he knew that his lungs were on the verge of bursting, he gasped. The morning air came sweet to his air passages.

"Soldier Boy, are you hurt bad?" Warm fingers touched his face, then slid down to the neck of his poncho and shook him.

Chance opened his eyes and squinted at the form crouching over him. "Please don't shake me so. It hurts so bad." His voice pleaded. "If you mean to kill me, then do it quick."

"You just lay still, Yank. We aren't going to hurt you anymore than you already are. We're friends and we'll take care of you." The voice was soft and laced with a southern accent. The wounded soldier focused his eyes on the slender figure dressed in an over sized tweed coat, canvas pants and knee boots. *Was this person a young boy? No, by God, it was a woman!*

More footsteps approached and a hulking form dropped to its knees beside Chance.

"How bad is it, Son?" A deeper, gruffer voice questioned.

"Knifed me. The Rebs knifed me in the side and it's pretty bad, I'm afraid." Chance swallowed once and continued. "I might die." He startled himself with the matter of fact manner in which he appraised his situation. "Where's the rest of the boys?"

"You mean your friends?"

"Yes."

"Why they run off or got blowed into a dozen tree tops. They ain't a live Yankee within fifteen miles of this tooty-toot trestle less'n its you. Ain't nobody crossin' the Big Black here in dis place in a month a Sundays. Them Rebs shore done a job on this here bridge."

"You mean the whole detail's gone?"

" Yep. They's either washed up in a drift downstream, runoff back ta Jackson, or like I said, hangin' like butcher meat in da trees."

"Hush up, Mose. You've told him enough. We've got to get him up and out of here before the fog lifts. The rebel cavalry is sure to come back down the tracks in good light to see what kind of hell they've raised." Soft finger tips touched Chance's forehead.

"Don't waste your strength trying to talk."

"I'm hurt most severe, Ma'am. This I know." Chance forced the statement from his lips.

A face emerged close to his from out of the mist. Large brown eyes looked into his fevered ones.

"Don't worry, Yank. Mose and I will care for you and get you back to your army."

Chance's eyes widened as he realized that the two who'd come to his aid were black.

XXXXXXXXXXXXXXXXXXXXXXXXXXXXXXXXXXXXXXXXXX

The wound was healing nicely. Much quicker than Chance had expected. It was no longer an inflamed, oozing opening between the ribs on his lower back. In the days of delirious fever following his rescue, he had lain in the darkened cabin awaiting the placement of the cool cloths on his forehead and body. His uniform and undergarments had been removed and he had been placed on a corn shuck mattress. Surprisingly, the bed clothes of his pallet were the nicest white, lace edged sheets he'd ever seen. On top of his aching body, stacks of quilts had been placed to break the fever that was ravishing his body. Neunan's constitution had been strong and his body had persevered. The herbal poultices which Mose applied to his injury had sped his recovery and the soldier would be forever grateful to the giant man. Mose's finest traits, and the man possessed several, were his patience and gentleness. With hands the size of hams, Mose applied the bandages with the tenderness of a young mother caressing her new born baby. Each time he uncovered the injury, he'd bring the bandage to his nose and smell it for tell tales signs of gangrene. Then he would lower the wrapping and declare that the stain on the cotton cloth smelled all right. In addition to his nursing skills, he was an expert woodsman. Using an antiquated musket and a fishing pole, he brought nourishment to the small cabin in the clearing. The man would roam through the timber and fallow fields and bring in edibles that only an expert outdoorsman could find. Bent and stooped from forty years as a field hand for Colonel Rooney Edwards, Mose was truly the salt of the earth. The middle aged slave had no book education but was still an intelligent man, one who knew the basics of survival and was half the reason that Chance Neunan was alive.

Andrea Edwards, for the house slaves often were given the plantation owner's surname, was the other reason the soldier had pulled through. She was beautiful and versed in the classics and all the other educational endeavors of her white mistress since she'd been raised in the Edwards girl's company. Rooney Edwards was breaking the state's slave laws by permitting his human property to learn to read, but he desired that his only daughter have a conversationalist and a friend in the sprawling plantation manor. Because of her upbringing and social standing in the black population, Mose always acquiesced to Andrea's wishes treating her with the respect a father would give a daughter and prizing her counsel on every issue.

Once the evening meal was consumed and Andrea busied herself with its cleanup, Mose would bring out his smoking material and go to an old battered knapsack for his Bible. He'd fill his pipe and sit in the cabin's doorway and commence to hum. Between puffs on his clay pipe, he'd resume the melody of some hymn he'd heard in the slave quarters before the war had scattered the occupants. Mose would sit and smoke and clutch the Bible in his gnarled hands as the sun slipped behind the tree tops.

"Miss Andrea, could you please read da good book to Ol' Mose afore it gets dark?" he'd ask. Andrea, as if dealing with a small child, would take the book from him and softly read passages in the dwindling light. He would sit and hum as the young woman read the sacred words that described the inner goodness of man and the need to accept all human kind as equals.

XXXXXXXXXXXXXXXXXXXXXXXXXXXXXXXXXXXXXXXXX

It was on the fifth day of Chance's recovery as the strength sapping fever retreated from his body that he became more conscious of his caretakers. When the young woman had knelt next to the pallet on which he lay, he'd raised a flame hot hand to her cheek and whispered, "What's your name?"

"You shouldn't try to talk, Chance."

A puzzled expression flicked across his features.

"You know my name?"

"Yes, we found it inked on the inside of the flap on your cartridge box." The young woman wrung out a cloth taken from a small wooden bucket and spread it above his brow.

"You and your friend, Mose, have me stumped. I've learned his name but not yours."

"My name is Andreline Edwards. I prefer to be called Andrea."

Neunan laid the back of his pale hand against the tawny color of the girl's cheek and whispered, "No you shouldn't be named Andrea, you should be named Angel, for that's what you are."

Then he closed his eyes and drifted into a slumber that was so necessary for his recovery.

XXXXXXXXXXXXXXXXXXXXXXXXXXXXXXXXXXXXXXXX

Chance awoke the next morning as the sun filtered through the gunny sacks at the shelter's only window. He was alone and while his vision was clear, he took the opportunity to survey the cabin's interior. He would learn later, that the dilapidated abode was that of a share cropper who'd farmed the sloping foot hills of Rooney Edwards' vast estate. The share cropper was long gone as were Edwards and his family.

Andrea had scrubbed the place clean and hung the field bags at the broken window. A fireplace stood at one end of the structure but was used sparingly because the smoke from a constant fire would alert marauders that the dwelling was occupied. Both Andrea and Mose profited from the Edwards' departure, she wearing the fine clothes left in the closets and he helping himself to the master's stock of tobacco and food stuffs. Their forays to the vacated manor explained the fancy bed clothes on Chance's pallet. Despite her privations, Andrea managed to keep herself well groomed and neat. Mose, on the other hand, had worn Rooney's finely made wool clothes to tatters as he perused the woods and fields guarding against intruders. In the booty the two pilfered were several dozen of the most delicate napkins but judging from the grease stains on the thighs of the older black's pants, he had not been taught the niceties of dining from Andrea.

The young woman told Chance that the three had made their way to the secluded cabin with the aid of a mule and wagon, also former Edwards' property. The mule was freed in the woods and the wagon shoved over a bluff into the river at a considerable distance from the cabin.

The two seemed to have thought of everything. Absolute silence, during the day, was the rule with no voices above a whisper. Mose had sawed through the floor boards in the corner of the cabin, dug a deep cavity beneath the floor sills and lined the excavation with straw. All types of supplies and food items were stored in this chamber and kept out of sight. Mose took the extra effort of darkening the edges of the sawed ends of the boards and lightly re-nailing them back in place.

Andrea, at Mose's insistence, filled two bags with dust, twigs and shards of bark which were to be scattered around the room to give the appearance of abandonment upon the approach of strangers. Prior to Chance's coming, Andrea had spent two different occasions hiding in the secret storage space as interlopers searched the cabin. Ol' Mose took to the woods and watched from a concealed position as the bush whackers tromped in and out of the door. He was prepared to give his life, if need be, to save Andrea.

In early conversations with the attractive young lady, Neunan learned of her pampered life in the mansion as a companion to Estell Edwards, Rooney's daughter. Mrs. Lillian Edwards saw to the instruction of manners for both girls and Andrea had blossomed into a lady far removed from the difficulties of life in the slave quarters.

She is quite stunning, Chance thought as he painted a visual image of Andrea in his mind. *Her features were delicate and soft. Her hair was straight and jet black yet carried a tint of auburn. Her skin was tawny, coffee colored which possibly reflected a mixing of the races. No doubt her beauty had not been missed by the plantation owner. Chance cringed at the thought of Andrea's slender limbs caught in the clutches of Rooney Edwards in his forced conquest. Had not the war intervened, she would have been snared by the devious designs of the white bigot that owned her.*

Chance returned his eyes to the shaft of bright sunlight streaming through a hole in the sack hanging at the window. Thousands of tiny dust flecks swirled in the spike of light and drifted to the cabin floor. A hint of an early spring was spreading over the Mississippi landscape with the tree twigs lifting up their yellow-green buds to the warmth of the sun. Wild song birds called to each other from the lower underbrush, ready to begin their mating rituals and the larger crows were incessantly cawing to one another.

Neunan lay on the pallet in his underwear bottoms, bare-chested and perspiring. Andrea had repaired his clothing and stored them in the space beneath the floor along with his other personal effects. The leather accoutrements were claimed by Mose to become part of his hunting equipment but the loss did not bother the young soldier. If it would help the older man with his guarding of the cabin, then Chance was glad to give up the items.

The cabin door creaked and Chance rose up on his elbows.

Andrea peeked from behind the portal and asked, "Awake?"

"Yes. You startled me," the young man answered.

"It's best to be on your guard, now." Andrea closed the door behind her. She stood with a bouquet of violets in her hands. Well worn men's trousers, a pair of riding boots and a loose fitting shirt comprised her wardrobe. Her dark hair was pulled back away from her face, a yellow ribbon clasping it tightly next to her head. The large brown eyes sparkled with happiness. Once she deposited the flowers in a rusty tin cup and added water from a jug she walked to Chance's side and knelt. Neunan was enthralled with the fluid grace in her movement.

"Are you hot?" She whispered as she placed a cool, long fingered hand on his forehead.

"Yes, but I think it's from the weather and not the fever."

"I think so too."

Before she could brush the soldier's hand away, he reached up and touched her face with the back of his hand and slid it downward to her chin. Andrea twisted sideways, her well formed breasts pushing against the fabric of her shirt front.

"Yankee Boy, you surely must be feeling better touching a little nigger gal as you've done."

Neunan was confused by the rejection. He'd learned from the weeks that she'd been nursing him that Andrea used the sobriquet, Yankee Boy, as a means of putting him in his place. But he decided that he would go on the attack to determine what she thought of him and if she harbored any feelings toward him.

"Hey, what's my name, again?" Chance caught her arm in a playful grasp but she slipped from his grip.

"Why Massa Chance, Suh," she giggled mockingly.

Neunan gave the beautiful girl a stern look. "Andrea, Andrea, what's to become of you and your people when all this madness ends? Stop that laughing, I'm being serious."

Andrea stood up and gazed down at Chance, fire in her eyes.

"President Lincoln has freed us. We expect all the rights of the whites. We, who are educated, are sick to death of this bowing and siring that we've endured for hundreds of years. We'll never go back to any kind of servitude. That day in the South is over."

Chance looked up into her defiant, beautiful face.

"When our armies leave it'll be most of the same and you know it."

"I'll stay here with others like me and create a New South that will accept my people as equals." Andrea walked to the center of the room and turned back quickly to look at Chance.

"How old are you?"

"Twenty one," Neunan lied. "How old are you?"

Andrea smiled coyly. "Unless you're my master and you aren't, I'm under no obligation to tell you."

Neunan laughed as he pulled himself up to a sitting position.

"I guess it'll be up to us, the war generation, to get this old country back on an even keel. Lord, we have folks back in Illinois who look down on niggers," Neunan stopped and cleared his throat, "Negroes as being completely worthless. They're more set against you people than some of the southerners are here. It's going to take a lot of educating in the North for the citizens to accept your race and permit you to reach the goals you're looking for."

"What of you, Chance. You're from the North, have you changed your opinion of us?"

"About you, Andrea? Yes, you're an example of what can come of your race once they've received an education."

The young woman's chest swelled. "Why must we all have a superior education to be even considered the equal of the white man? Why can't you people accept us for what we are, and what you whites are, members of the human race?" she continued in a condescending tone of voice. "Why even I, a Negress, have more education than you who speaks so highly of the quality."

"I'm sorry, Andrea. You know how much I owe you and Mose. If I've offended you and hurt you in any way I did not mean to."

Andrea sought to change the subject. "Want to get up?"

"Uhuh. I know that I'm pretty weak but if you'll help me, I'll give it a try."

"All right, put your arm around my neck."

The woman bent over Chance and slipped her hands around his waist. Neunan's pale left arm encircled her shoulder and as he stood, he pulled her face to him. She stiffened and drew away as his lips brushed her cheek.

"Yankee Boy, I know for a fact that you are feeling much, much, better. Now back off, Suh, or I'll put my thumb in your wound."

Neunan was aware of a steady pressure on his right rib cage where she'd tightened her grip. He released the young woman and lay back on his pallet gulping for breath. Andrea stood up shaking her hair and smoothing her shirt front. She looked down at Chance's pale face.

"So you feel that your opinion has changed, has it? You feel that you can equalize things by bedding us." Andrea's remark cut deep, reddening Chances face to his hairline.

"You're beautiful, Andrea," he blurted.

"Hush!" she snorted, her eyes enlarging. "You're not the first white boy to tell me that. Massa Edwards," Andrea stopped in mid-sentence.

"Massa Edwards what?"

Andrea regained her poise. "Master Rooney told me that several times mostly at night when he was going up the stairs to his bed chambers."

"And?"

"And you can go to hell, Yankee Boy!"

Chance smiled knowing that he'd finally gotten the better of the proud woman who always seemed so confident. "Did you ever let Massa Edwards show you just how beautiful that he felt you were?"

Andrea turned her back to Chance for a few moments, then turned around to confront him, her hands on her hips. "No! I never let him. I told him if he ever, ever, touched me that I would tell his wife. He threw a babbling fit and said he'd have me taken behind the slave quarters and whipped but he never did. He knew that I had him where he couldn't do much."

Neunan extended his good left hand recognizing the hurt in her face. "I'm sorry, Andrea. I should have stopped a few sentences ago. You've told me things that I didn't need to know. I'm ashamed of what I've done." Neunan looked into Andrea's eyes waiting for a sign of forgiveness but she remained stoic. "Now, would you help me up, please?"

XXXXXXXXXXXXXXXXXXXXXXXXXXXXXXXXXXXXXXXXXX

By the end of the next week, Chance felt as though he'd recovered ninety-nine percent of his strength. His atrophied muscles were firming and he no longer needed Andrea's assistance to move around inside the cabin's interior. He hated the day she found he was more healed than she thought. Her realization took away his opportunity to feel her warm and firm figure pressed against his body.

Andrea had come to him with a slab of wood that served as a tray on which a tin cup of hot tea and a bowl of corn meal mush sat. She placed the affair on his lap and exclaimed, "Boy, you sure need a hair cut and a beard trim. You looks just like a wooly man come outta da woods." She laughed impishly and gave him a swat with a dish cloth she'd had over her shoulder. "Eat up and I'll get the scissors."

The soldier finished his meal and placed the utensils on the floor before moving from the pallet to a rickety wooden chair. Andrea returned with the scissors, a comb and a scratched mirror. She studied

Chance's half naked body for a moment, examined his healed knife wound, then pinched his right bicep between her thumb and index finger. She feigned amazement, opening her eyes wide.

"Ooehy, Yankee Boy, I surely think that you could lift a cotton bale all by yourself with that."

Neunan grinned at her but she didn't acknowledge it. She commenced snipping and in no time a sizeable pile of hair had grown on the plank flooring around his bare feet. When she'd finished, Andrea laid the scissors on the pallet and held up the mirror for her patron to assess her handiwork. As Chance peered at himself in the reflecting glass, Andrea busied herself brushing the hair from his neck and shoulders. She contentedly hummed a tune that sounded to Neunan like 'Camptown Ladies'.

"Looks good, Lawdy, I didn't know that there was such a handsome devil in Mr. Lincoln's army." Chance paid himself the compliment.

His caramel skinned attendant was giggling as she brushed his dark hair from the coarse texture of her field hand's shirt.

"Good Lord, I'd like to think that clipping your hair would've made you weak like it did ol' Sampson in the Bible. Then I could put you down when you had a mind to take hold of me."

"You'd better watch out, Andrea. I'm feelin' stouter by the day."

"Well, you're only half done, young Chance Neunan. Next you're going outdoors and taking a bath and brushing your teeth."

"Am I that bad?'

"Yes, you are. There's a bucket of water out behind the cabin and some of Mrs. Edwards' fancy French soap."

"But I don't have a tooth brush?"

"Silly boy. You got to make do. You break off a twig and pound one end with a rock and you got a tooth brush. Here's a cinnamon stick to chew on when you're finished." Andrea crossed her arms over her breasts and added, "Oh, I declare, you white folks make my back side hurt some times."

XXXXXXXXXXXXXXXXXXXXXXXXXXXXXXXXXXXXXXXX

Outside, in the warming sunshine of spring, Chance bathed himself then stuffed his soiled, tattered underwear in a hollow log at the edge of the clearing. Andrea saw to his change of wardrobe by placing items on a bench by the cabin door. Neunan pulled on Master Rooney Edwards' underwear and his own army trousers. He felt in the pockets and found the family watch, coins, his knife and the Root revolver. Of course, his haversack containing the *carte de visites* of him and Becky Scott, and the letters had been destroyed in the blockhouse at the trestle. Andrea had stuffed his army brogans with cloth so that the wet shoes retained their shape and when he tried them on, they fit perfectly. Another item of clothing Chance enjoyed was the Rooney Edwards' silk shirt which Andrea handed him at the door. She closed her eyes and gently caressed the sienna tinted skin of her cheek with the garment savoring the softness of the fabric. "You'll have to wear this, Chance. Your army shirt was too badly cut up for me to mend so you get this Paris made shirt. I took it from the Edwards' armoire."

Neunan spent the remainder of the day sitting next to the ram shackled dwelling sunning and listening to the call of the song birds. Becky Scott and the farm on the Kaskaskia were mere memories now, so long ago that they seemed like misty apparitions. The momentous events he'd passed through in his life now seemed beyond comprehension.

What of Becky? He thought. *Would she be thinking of him as he was of her on this moment somewhere on her uncle's farm in Ohio. Perhaps she was making butter or shelling corn or helping her mother prepare a meal. Or possibly she was finishing a bath as he had done and was standing by a wooden tub beside the fireplace drying herself. Her dark hair would be in tangles, her skin glistening as white as alabaster as she patted herself dry.*

Chance's mind swirled as he visualized Becky's silky, young limbs and lovely face. *If I concentrate enough, right now, can I cause her to pause for even a portion of a second and form my image in her mind as I have hers? Perhaps, but only with a flicker of sadness. She would think of me as being dead. After all she had heard nothing of me in weeks. The numbing news from the military that I was missing would have plunged her and my mother into the depths of grief. How would Becky and Clair have reacted to that sad message?*

"Chance, Chance?" Andrea called softly from the window.

Neunan rose to his feet, brushed off the seat of his uniform pants and walked to the cabin's doorway. Upon entering, the young woman exclaimed, "That certainly is an improvement. A person can breathe around you again."

"The Union Apollo makes his grand entrance." Neunan swelled his chest and strutted for a few steps.

"Oh Shaw, Chance Neunan, you are so full of yourself." Andrea turned away to go to the tiny little fire she'd kindled in the stone fireplace.

"Hey, wait a minute, girl. What did you do to your hair?"

"Do you like it? Since I was cutting your locks, I thought that I'd snip off some of mine." She smiled at Chance awaiting his response.

"Yes, but so much?" Neunan's eyes swept over her figure and up to her delicately formed features that were no longer hidden by shoulder length tresses. She had bobbed her black hair to a point where nothing fell over the back of her neck and only a small wave covered the tops of each of her ears.

"By Golly, I do like it, Andrea. But should I avoid telling you that you're more beautiful than ever, or will that make you angry?"

"Well, you've said it and thank you. I thought when Mose and I took you off through the timber to your lines that this would be a more sensible hair style, or as the French say, *coiffure.*"

"Now sit yourself down and eat this." Andrea stood, a pleased little smile curving the corners of her mouth. She held a steaming tin plate filled with potatoes and meat. "Prancing around here like a young rooster, you are a case, Chance Neunan."

"Aren't we going to wait on Mose to come in?"

"No, eat now while the food is hot. He said that it's getting harder and harder to find things to eat and our supply under the house is about used up as well."

"Sounds like we'd better pack up and head for the Union lines if things are pressing on us to find food. I feel that I'm strong enough to make the journey now." Chance dug into the vittles.

"This is the last of Master Rooney's port wine. Somehow I'm not sad to see it gone. At least he won't have enjoyed it." The young woman used a stick to push errant ashes back into the dying fire. She turned back to Chance and asked, " Is the food all right?"

"The potatoes are barely cooked but, under the circumstances, I shouldn't complain."

The soldier wiped his mouth with his napkin.

"That's because I had a small fire for only a short time. Mose told me to be careful with the fireplace and the smoke. He says the woods are full of bushwhackers."

Chance drained his tin cup and set it back on the coarse wood of the table top. "This is fine. I don't have much of an appetite. I guess I'm anxious to get back to the army."

Andrea stood at Neunan's side and picked at the smaller portion she'd dished for herself until she was finished.

"You and Mose are coming back with me, aren't you? You'll have to guide me because I wouldn't be able to travel these woods without your help."

"We said we'd go with you, and we will."

"Good, I'll get Mose in the army as a wagoneer and get you hooked up with an organization that is helping the blacks although I think you'll be doing the assisting instead of the receiving after a few weeks. You are so blasted smart."

The coffee skinned young woman began to clear the table of the eating utensils. She reached across in front of Chance to pick up a spoon; when she did, her cotton shirt escaped the waist line of her trousers and inched up exposing the tawniness of her mid-section. Her eyes caught Neunan's admiring glance.

"Haven't you seen skin before?"

"Oh yes, but not as beautiful as the way you wear it."

"Shaw, Yankee Boy, I'll be glad to get shut of you. Honestly if we stayed another week here, you'd wear yourself out chasing me around. Then if I let you catch me all you'd have is a little black pickaninny."

"Oh, I don't think so, Andrea. You're like a cat wearing a velvet suit."

She ruffled his newly shorn hair in a playful way. "Where'd you say that you were from?"

"Illinois. Why?"

"That's the state the president is from?"

"Correct."

"What's it like up there?'

"It's beautiful and the dirt is so rich that you don't have to plant corn but every two years because you raise such big amounts."

No, I'm not asking about the farming."

"Oh, you want to know about your type of people."

"Yes, my type of people." Andrea's voice was flavored with a tone of disgust.

"I'm not sure if I want to get into that topic with you again."

"Why not, I deal with it every minute of my waking day."

Chance sighed, "Illinois is a big state and there are populations in all the bigger cities. Decatur has quite a few Negroes as does other lesser towns. I don't know of blacks in Moultrie County where I'm from but they're bound to settle there after we win this war. The Negroes are taking hold now and fighting alongside the white soldiers and they are being looked at in a different way. Oh, they'll be some bad whites that'll give you trouble but it won't be near as difficult up north as it is here for you."

Andrea didn't respond, she merely looked pensively at Chance.

BOOM! The loud report of a musket resonated from deep in the woods.

"Looks like quail for breakfast." Andrea said.

Pop! Pop! Pop! Pistol shots shattered the void of silence following the musket shot.

Chance sprang from his chair and went to the open cabin door.

"Bushwhackers!" Screamed Andrea her hands placed on each side of her face and terror written on her features.

XXXXXXXXXXXXXXXXXXXXXXXXXXXXXXXXXXXXXXXXX

Somehow, they managed to stamp out the little fire and pull up the boards covering their hiding place. They dropped down beneath the floor before the first riders entered the clearing where the cabin stood. Chance had kicked over the table and spread the debris from the sack on the flooring as the first horse whinnied outside.

In the mad scramble to reach the sanctuary, Neunan had tumbled into the pit on top of Andrea. She pushed hard against the earthen wall and wiggled to provide space for him. Chance shuffled the boards around above them until they fell into their proper place and rested level on the floor sills. *God, I hope they don't see the saw cuts on the ends of the boards as they search the place;* he thought.

Only the dimness of the cabin's interior could save them and every moment the mounted men spent outside in the failing light would make it more difficult for them to make a thorough search of the premises. The longer the irregulars lingered before entering lengthened the margin between life and death for Andrea and Chance.

Chance lay in the straw padded hole facing Andrea, their breaths coming in short intervals. In the gloom, he could make out the beads of perspiration on Andrea's upper lip and see the fear in her eyes. She lay rigidly against him with her arms drawn up to her chest.

The riders circled the cabin cautiously expecting resistance. Whispered conferences were held above the jingling of reins and the squeaking of saddle leather. After a period of silence, the door was kicked open and tramping boots pounded into the room. If Chance and the former house servant were found now, the hole beneath the floor would likely become their grave.

"See anythin'?" A high pitched voice whined.

"Naw, but the place's been lived in that's fer damned shore."

"Probably that nigger that we 'bout catched," rejoined the sing-song whiner.

"Well, I'll bet that burly sonna bitch of a slave never picked this bunch of posies," a rough voice added.

Footfalls scraped overhead and Chance could envision a tattered soldier examining the violets which had been picked in the forenoon.

"Could that 'lil Negra gal what was Rooney's house maid be livin' here?"

"It's possible. Say wouldn't she be a great roll in the hay?" Laughter ensued from above. An inaudible comment followed and more laughter.

Neunan felt Andrea tense and commence to tremble. He stroked her shoulder to calm her, his movement concealing his own fear.

"Say is there a root cellar under this place?"

The two prostrate figures in the humid darkness became more rigid. "Naw, Rooney never dug one." answered the whining voice.

"How'd you know that, J.B?"

"Cause I helped Rooney Edwards build this place when I was younger, that's how." There was a short pause and then a clarification. "Well, Rooney didn't do no actual work, hisself, he hired me an Elmer to do the buildin'."

"I thought Rooney rented this lil' farm out to a share cropper." A voice that hadn't been heard previously chimed in. "When Ol' Lady Edwards caught him bringin' some of the house girls here to break 'em in she made him give up this love nest. Or that's the way I heared it." The rider answering to the initials J.B. added. Another of the group hocked and spit onto the floor above the huddled pair.

" Ol' Rooney just couldn't wait 'til his wife and youngin' left to go up to Chattanooga to get outta the summer night vapors. When she got packed off, the old bastard had a regular harem goin' here."

More laughter followed by the sound of flatulence. Then more hilarity.

"I say we burn this rat trap down. We don't need to leave a hovel for all the runaway niggers to hide in."

"Hold on there, boys," retorted the man called J.B. "I know this old hut is in a mighty poor shape but if we torch her, Ol' Rooney will give us holy hell. We all know that he'll come outta this war needin' all his property and bein' better off than we will."

"That's the reason we outta burn it down. Some of these blue blood sons-a bitches need to be took down a notch or two," the would- be arsonist asserted.

Andrea's lips were trembling and Chance laid his finger tips on them.

"No, we ain't gonna destroy any of Rooney Edwards' property and that's final. Let's go find that old nigger who shot at us in the woods and if any of you fellers want to swing by here later and touch her off, that's between you and Rooney. I'll have no part in it."

A vicious little argument ensued, laced with so many obscenities that Chance lost count of them. Finally the group tirade ended abruptly with the assertion, "Let her stand!"

Chance and Andrea clung together listening as the rough interlopers stomped all the furniture into kindling and broke what little that was breakable. The sound of boots on the floor retreating to the cabin door and the moan of men gaining their saddles told the pair that the patrol was departing.

"Have they gone yet?" Andrea whispered.

The warmth of her breath caressed his hand. "Yes, I think so but let's play it safe and wait a little longer."

They lay together for a few more minutes, their bodies relaxing. After a time Chance changed positions and slid his left arm beneath Andrea's neck and placed his right hand over her hip feeling the firmness of her supple body beneath the coarse, canvas trousers she was wearing. Andrea raised her face to Chance and with their lips inches from each other she murmured, "We should leave here soon. I can whistle in Mose and we can set off for the Union army lines."

Neunan trailed his right hand up along her body until it rested against her cheek. "Yes, we've got to go."

"Perhaps we should stay a bit longer my little Yankee Boy and not take any chances." In the darkness of their place of concealment, Andrea could no longer contain herself and her lips found the young soldier's.

The kiss was soft and searching at first, then grew stronger, more insistent.

"We should stop, Chance."

"Shh, those ruffians might still be outside." Neunan's free hand roamed up the slender woman's side but returned to her outer thigh.

"You're no better than Rooney Edwards." she whispered, the words coming rapidly.

"I thought that you said Massa Edwards never had you."

"He didn't and no white man ever will." Andrea struggled against Chance but he pushed harder stifling her efforts to escape.

"Then how can you say that I'm no better if you haven't tried either one of us." Chance waited for Andrea's exasperated breathing to subside. "Besides its dark under here and you can't tell if I'm white or black. You see we're equal."

Andrea started to protest again but he stopped her with a kiss. His mouth wandered down her throat and his nostrils inhaled the fragrance of her skin. Neunan kissed her down her shirt front drawing in her spell that sent his desire into a white hot flame. She relaxed and commenced returning his kisses, responding to his caresses, sighing and softly moaning. The woman wove her fingers through his hair as she laughed lightly whispering, "Chance Neunan, you sure are making your point." She kissed him hard and flicked out a fire brand from between her teeth that sent Chance's head spinning.

"Damn, Andrea, I've got to make love to you. You've been in my mind since the first time I opened my eyes and looked into your lovely face."

Their kisses became wetter, deeper as they both struggled to remove their clothes.

XXXXXXXXXXXXXXXXXXXXXXXXXXXXXXXXXXXXXX

Andrea lay partially covered, her eyes closed to the creeping gray dawn that filtered around the piers on which the cabin sat. Chance watched as her breathing caused her exposed breast to rise and fall. Her cast off trousers lay beneath her and all that hid her velvet nakedness was a half buttoned shirt and stockings.

Neunan leaned close and kissed the point at the base of her throat where her clavicles joined beneath the smoothness of her skin. His finger tips traced a line down over the silkiness of her outer thigh.

Andrea stirred from her slumber, opening her long lashed eyes and smiled up into his face. Then she moved closer and placed both her hands behind Chance's neck and drew his head to hers. Their lips came together once more.

"Oh, my little Yankee Boy, you've given me a standard to judge other men by."

"I would hope there would not be any other men, Andrea." He removed a straw from the tangle of short hair above her ear and kissed the tip of her nose.

"We've got to get you up and dressed before the sun burns through the morning haze. God knows that I want to continue to lie here with you, Andrea but it's dangerous to stay." Chance held the beautiful woman's face in both his hands. "We've got to get away from this clearing and try to locate Mose."

She shivered and curled up next to Chance signaling that she did not wish to end their coupling even though her passion was spent. The soldier tucked at the back of his shirt which was hanging out of his trouser's waist band.

"Do you think we can find Mose?" Chance asked as he ignored Andrea's intent and found the woman's shoes and under garments.

"If he's not gone into deep hiding he should answer to my whistle."

Neunan started removing the floor boards and setting them aside. Once out of the hole, he found a gourd jug that had escaped the rampage of the marauders. This he filled from a wooden bucket at the corner of the house and returned to the doorway, Andrea stepped outside straightening her clothing. Chance handed her the drinking receptacle and brushed the straw from her back and buttocks. Then he took her by the shoulders and turned her to face him. His gaze moved from the top of her head to her rough brogans.

"I know that I've told you this a hundred times but I'll tell you once more, you are one beautiful female."

Chance and Andrea

The yellow-green budding twigs of the tree branches hung still and damp as the two wound their way through the woods. Over the eastern ridge line, the first orange of the coming day was making its appearance. A cardinal startled by their approach flashed crimson across the path that they were following. Blackberry sprouts, armed with infant thorns snagged at them, impeding their flight. Vines newly emerged from the warming soil clawed at their ankles as they circled around moss covered logs and sought out openings in the entanglement that was the primal forest.

Andrea, wearing heavy men's shoes was slowing the pace as the sun reached its apex.

"Lord, how far do the think the camp is?" She leaned against a spindly sapling gasping for breath.

A thin trickle of blood trailed down her cheek from a scratch at the corner of her right eye.

"We can rest hear for a little while but we can't tarry too long. If we're caught….." The soldier turned his attention to Andrea's wound and wiped away the blood with the cuff of Rooney Edward's silk shirt. The two stood leaning supporting each other, warming in the high noon sun. Then they continued their trek, down through the ravines and up the steep inclines only to come to another deep hollow. On several occasions, Andrea stopped and gave a whistle for Mose to respond to, but each time only the call of crows or the twitter of song birds broke the quiet of the deep forest. As the twilight neared, Andrea asked to stop once again where she removed two cold corn dodgers wrapped in a cloth from inside her shirt front. Once they'd eaten and had a swallow of water, Chance sat Andrea down, removed her heavy shoes and massaged her swollen feet and calves.

"Aren't you sorry that you lowered yourself last night when you made love to me?" Andrea looked away as Chance kneaded her calves.

"No, not at all. I'm to the point that I think that I'm in love with you."

"Don't say that." The slender woman kept her eyes averted from Chance's. He placed her legs across his thighs and leaned forward and kissed her. Andrea allowed him to press his lips on hers but she did not respond. Tears welled up and out of her anguished brown eyes.

"Chance, this can never be. We can not love one another, not in this time. Not now."

She wiped away the tears with the back of her hand. "Perhaps in fifty, no a hundred years what we have found in each other will be accepted. But not now."

"No, no that isn't true. Come with me back to Illinois, you'll see."

Andrea sobbed deeply, her shoulders quaking with every anguished sound that she made. Chance tried to comfort her but all his efforts fell short. Finally her crying lessened and ceased. Still, she refused to look at Neunan. Andrea tucked her hair behind her ears and continued to evade Chance's gaze.

"No it won't do." She bent forward, put on her socks, pulled the boots over her feet and rose.

Exasperated and confused, Chance looked up at Andrea not knowing what to say or do. In the midst of their fruitless conversation, Neunan had permitted his attention to waver from the dangers in their environment and now his senses returned to their usual sharpness. His nose detected a waft of wood smoke which was carried by the breeze into the entanglement where they were resting. Smoke meant people and people wearing the wrong uniforms were not the sort either of them wanted to become acquainted with.

"What's the matter, Chance?" Andrea observed the tension in the soldier's body.

"Stay here. Don't move. If you hear a commotion, hide."

"Tell me what's upsetting you." A look of bewilderment furrowed the former slave's brow.

"Smoke, can't you smell it?" Chance pulled himself up on his feet and walked into the undergrowth, following the scent of the fire. Cautiously, he moved through the foliage, placing each foot just so in order not to make any sound. He worked his way slowly, stopping to listen before moving on to another spot of concealment. Birds flitted across Chance's path increasing his level of alertness as the smoke grew thicker.

A thin spiral of gray-white vapor curled upward from within a thicket of wild cherries at the base of an ancient, white oak. He parted a tangled laurel vine hanging heavily from the lower branches of the oak and saw Mose for the first time. The patrol had caught him as they had vowed. The hulking man had been stripped and tied with telegraph wire to a stump, wood piled around him, and burned alive. Mose's appendages were burned to stubs and his skull showed through the charred skin that was still attached to the bone. Chance forced himself to look into the pitiful face of the man who had saved his life. As he gazed at the grotesque features his eyes discerned a bullet hole in Mose's forehead. He hoped that the projectile had crashed into the frontal lobe and stilled his excruciating torment before the flames did their dirty work.

Thank God, that there was some Christian among the rabble that took the old field hand. The shooter was possibly the only member of the shameful unit that realized the execution was brutal and inhumane How could these fiends do such a thing to another human being? To kill an adversary in the heat of battle was one thing, but to torment and torture the enemy in such a manner was unacceptable.

Neunan left his vantage point and knelt close to the body. He bowed his head and said a silent prayer for Mose. Quietly, he stood up and made his way back to Andrea's hiding place hoping against hope that she still would be there and waiting for him.

XXXXXXXXXXXXXXXXXXXXXXXXXXXXXXXXXXXXXXXX

"Andrea?" Chance called.

No response.

"Andrea?"

"Yes, over here." She emerged from behind an elm tree. She reacted to Chance's pallor. "What's the matter?"

"Mose."

"Did you find him?"

"They caught him, the bushwhackers or a Reb cavalry unit, it doesn't matter. He's dead."

"Can't we do something for him?" Andrea tried to brush passed Chance but he caught her by the crook of the arm.

"There's nothing we can do for him. He's dead and don't you ever ask me how he died. Not ever!"

The woman put her hands to her face and uttered a bleating little scream of anguish before beginning to sob. Neunan took her in his arms and pulled her to his chest where her tears soaked his shirt front.

"Mose was a fine man. You could look the world over and not find a better one, white or black or red or yellow. I know he's gone to a far, far, better place, now."

Chance stroked Andrea's shoulders. "Please don't cry anymore. You've cried a bucket full today and you're not cut out to be a crier. Please stop."

XXXXXXXXXXXXXXXXXXXXXXXXXXXXXXXXXXXXXXXX

How could civilized men turn to such barbarity? How could one human treat another with such banal insensitivity? These troubling thoughts surged through Chance's mind as he half carried, half dragged Andrea down into the hollows, across rushing creeks and up the next incline. The woman seemed to be in a state approaching full, knee buckling fatigue but somehow, she carried on. She grasped saplings and feebly assisted Chance as he heaved her weakened body up one summit after another. The soldier had given up his intentions of using stealth to travel through the vast wooded terrain; his quest was to reach the Union army camp before he too fell and could not get up. As they reached the crest of one of the highest elevations that had challenged them, Chance's left foot slipped in the heavy leaf fall of the past autumn and he fell heavily on his side. Andrea went down beside him and lay next to him, chest heaving. Their clothing was in tatters and covered with stick-tights.

The day, and what day was it? Chance had lost count, was quickly dying and a full moon was ascending in the east, mixing its blue-gray glow with the fading yellow. The pair had been without food for hours or in their muddled minds, was it days?

Andrea pushed herself up and sat on her bottom, combing her fingers through her hair.

"Tuckered out, aren't you?" Neunan asked weakly. Andrea moaned.

"I don't think I could take another step. My legs won't let me." Pain had crept into the former slave woman's voice.

Chance rolled on his back and tried to focus his eyes.

Andrea started to utter another description of how she felt when Neunan placed his hand on her arm.

"Shhh, hear that?"

"Hear what?"

"The drums. Down on the other side of the hill, I hear drums beating tattoo. An army camp is on the other side of the hill we're on!"

"Help me up. Let's go see." Andrea extended her hand.

Neither paid any attention to the whip-or-will that had started his repetitive call from the darkness of a tree line on a facing hill. All their senses were keyed on the white canvas half shelters roofs adorning the little huts that shimmered in the moonlight. On the cleared plain below them lay a brigade encampment.

Miraculously, they had staggered through the hostile valleys and ridges to a point approaching death to finally reach safety. Chance stepped close to Andrea and put his arms around her waist. Below, lay the Federal winter camp outside Ardmore, Tennessee

"Ready to go?" Chance gave her waist a little squeeze.

Andrea turned away and replied, "I'm not going."

Struck dumbfounded by her assertion, Chance released her and sought to see her face in the brightening moonlight. He saw her eyes glistening with tears and her cheeks shining from the moisture.

"Not going? This is the only way for you."

"No, it's the best way. Don't you see if I follow you down into that camp I'll just be another yaller gal that gets cast aside for someone else?"

"You don't understand, do you?" Chance spoke with ardor. "I love you. I've shown it and I want you to be with me forever."

Andrea shifted her weight from her left leg to her right and crossed her left arm over her chest.

"Do you, Chance? Or was it the set of circumstances we found ourselves in. We both had needs that have been put off by this God awful war." Her eyes looked past Neunan's. "We were convenient for each other. You took advantage of me and I of you. I thank you for your being there to share the passionate moments when I needed someone." In spite of her exhausted state and unkempt appearance, Andrea was still beautiful. She looked down at her feet before looking up into Chance's eyes and saying, "We can have no deep affection for each other; the times won't allow that."

"Where in the Great Jehovah will you go, Andrea? You can't live in the woods."

"I have contacts in Nashville. I was told by my mother's friends that she'd gone with a group of Master Edwards' slaves to the Union lines there."

Neunan attempted to make a final plea but Andrea placed her finger tips on his lips, silencing him.

"Like it or not, Chance, this is the course I'm taking."

"Andrea?"

"Hush yourself, Chance, we are different. I won't change my mind and it's no use for you to try any further."

She started to pull away but Neunan caught her and pulled her to him. Their lips met and Andrea melted into his embrace, their kisses coming rapidly. The moon beams threw light and shadow on their intertwined bodies as they both lost track of time.

"Go now, Chance."

"Can't you give me an address where I can reach you? Anything?"

"We will probably never see each other again, but I'll always keep you in my heart."

"Andrea…"

Then she stepped into the shadows and was swallowed by the darkness.

XXXXXXXXXXXXXXXXXXXXXXXXXXXXXXXXXXXXXXXXX

"Halt! Who goes there?" the sentry's voice challenged in the moonlight.

Chance dropped quickly to his knees and sought shelter behind a stump. Cautiously he rose on his haunches and peered at the guard who'd assumed the 'charge bayonet' position in the bluish half light cast by the moon. Sucking in a breath of moist air, Chance ventured a reply. "Chance Neunan, 41st Illinois Infantry!"

"Advance and be recognized," came the forceful command.

Chance heard the soldier's musket lock click. A dog started barking in the camp.

"All right, I'm comin' in. Don't you get an itch with that trigger finger of yours." Neunan gained his feet, raised his hands and started walking toward the shadowy sentinel.

"Halt! Private Eckols, call the Sergeant of the Guard!"

In moments, Chance was surrounded by half-dressed men who'd tossed aside their bed clothes and turned out to see the strange soldier. Word spread like a telegraph message from hut to hut at the commotion taking place on the outer perimeter of the encampment. Neunan was escorted to a smoldering fire and seated. Logs from wood piles hidden behind the pitiful little dwellings were procured and the embers were immediately kindled higher in order to verify his identity. The men mostly gaped at his bedraggled appearance and whispered back and forth among themselves. Some edged closer to study the tired figure as if he were an alien being having fallen from the sky. The collection of soldiers parted as a scruffy sergeant entered the circle and began the interrogation. Chance was so feebled by his ordeal that he could barely form words to answer the examiner's questions. Five minutes of talking seemed as if he'd talked for hours regarding the destruction of the railroad trestle on the Big Black and his miraculous recovery and escape. A surgeon was summoned, and by the light of a burning fire brand, the scar from the knife wound was examined. The doctor poked at it with an extended index finger and asked, " Does that hurt? Got any soreness of any kind?"

"No sir, it gives me no trouble. I've just come through 'bout jillion miles of timber and hog backs, the likes of which I've never seen before. Country so rough that you wonder how it could ever be settled." Neunan looked up at the staring, wide eyed throng that seemed to hang on every word. "What I could really, really use is a cup of coffee, a hot meal, and a place to sleep."

"We can take care of that." called a voice from the assembled men.

"You latch on to a couple of these men, get yourself fed and you come down to the surgeon's hut and I'll put you up for the night." The doctor stated as he took a pocket watch from his vest and studied it. "I'm sure that the Captain and even some higher ups beyond him will want to talk to you. Then if you can satisfy them with your answers they'll release you to your regiment. The 41st you say? They're located at the end of the valley and after what you've been through, it won't be much of a walk."

The red headed NCO who'd appeared when the sentry called out the Sergeant of the Guard eyed the group encircling Chance, made a selection and ordered, " Wallace!"

"Yes Sarge."

"Get this man a gum blanket and a regular wooly off the supply wagon and when he's had his fill of coffee and tack, you and Stevens show him down to the surgeon's quarters. I'll put a guard outside just in case this feller is pullin' a humbug on us. I don't expect he'll give us any trouble. I ain't never seed a man more tuckered out than he is."

XXXXXXXXXXXXXXXXXXXXXXXXXXXXXXXXXXXXXXXXXX

Seeing kindly and caring faces wearing the old uniform was like a tonic to Chance. His short night's sleep had been deep and restful. The breakfast of fried fat pork, hard crackers and coffee had rejuvenated his aching body to the point that his head was clear and he was completely coherent when a Major and a Captain questioned him from the 3rd Iowa. Partially content with the validity of Neunan's identity, the officers sent Chance, escorted by two guards up the brigade street to the site where the 41st was encamped.

Now he was once more among his own. Pete O'Donnel nearly crushed the life out of him with a massive bear hug and Tom Warner pounded his shoulder so hard Neunan suspected that the joint would never work correctly again. Chance's arrival created a tumultuous disturbance with men spilling out into the company street anxious to see the modern day Lazarus. Captain Rouse and Sergeant Wilson, both confirmed Neunan's identity to the guards from the Iowa unit and returned them with a letter certifying the fact. A new Lieutenant, named Brewer, had transferred into the 41st and did not take part in the process. One NCO whose hair and beard were streaked with gray shouldered his way through the excited throng and offered his hand to Chance.

"You ain't the only man in this regiment who's returned from the grave, Neunan."

Chance paused, attempting to recognize the gaunt soldier standing before him.

"Walt, Walt Bone. Is that you?"

" You bet your boots it is."

Chance let out a whoop and jacked the man's hand up and down like a pump handle.

XXXXXXXXXXXXXXXXXXXXXXXXXXXXXXXXXXXXXXXXXX

Later in the day, Neunan awoke in the tiny little hut the remaining three messmates had constructed in his absence. Sergeant Wilson had excused him from duty until he was examined by the regimental surgeon as he'd been in the Iowa camp. That process and getting refitted and re-issued were tasks which had to be looked to before he could be effectively considered as a soldier in the Federal service.

Pete O'Donnel pushed the flimsy door aside, stooped low and entered into the tight little confinement.

"Damn! It's cold out there. A man wouldn't think it'd be this cold in the middle of March in northern Mississippi. We all thought the move up from Jackson would be alright even though we hated to give up our comfortable winter digs. Now it looks like it warn't such a good idea. But what can you do? You go where the army sends you." Pete stamped his feet. "Did ya sleep good?"

"Yes, like a log."

"I can tell ya if you was a log outside earlier this mornin' you'd have frost on ya."

Chance grinned and yawned.

"Say, Pete, what's this I hear that the regiment's going home on furlough?"

"Yep, ol' Abe's given us a rest, that is them that re-enlist for the duration. The ones that don't, like the new recruits and the ones that want to serve out their time and be discharged ain't gonna get no time off. More than likely they'll be re-assigned to a different army corps while the bulk of the 41st is on leave. O'Donnel hung his musket on wooden pegs driven into the log wall behind his roughly made bedstead. "This has got to be the happiest days of this miserable war. By golly, Chance we'll get you over to the quartermaster and get you decked out to look like a soldier again. You can't take the oath lookin' like that. Then in a few days it's for home and a roll in the feather bed with that sweet girl of your'n."

Neunan's head swam with the information. Of course, he'd sign the papers that would send him back to his home even though neither Becky nor his parents would be there to greet him. He'd check with the Dixon's to see if the old man and his wife had an address for the Scotts in Ohio, and although Becky wasn't as important to him as she'd once been, he felt that he should attempt to make things right. He would stay at the farmhouse and visit his father's and Aunt Emma's graves in the late afternoon. He'd sit beside them on his gum blanket and watch the sun set on the far ridge on the west side of the river.

Chance rolled over on his side and faced the rough bark of the log wall next to his bed.

"What's the matter, Chance?' Is it something I've said?"

" No, it's nothing."

"Yes it is. Hey, hold on, I know what's eatin' you. It's that you haven't heard from that lil' gal of your'n since you got bushwhacked and cut up. We'll I can brighten yer day thar, soldier boy. Jest you look in that empty ammunition box thar under my bed and see if I didn't save the two letters that came whilest we thought you was dead."

Mound City, Illinois
February 3, 1864

CAIRO, ILLINOIS, AND THE NEARBY strategic navy repair and refitting base, Mound City, were quagmires of seeping mud and floodwaters. In February and March of any year, the Mississippi River where Cairo was situated roared out of its banks and spread across thousands of acres in Illinois, Missouri and Kentucky. Trees the size of small locomotives were ripped from the eroding river banks and sent sweeping downriver past the Union defensive works at Fort Defiance. Six miles up the Ohio to the east, a sodden installation in the hamlet of Mound City sat precariously on the wooded northwestern shore. It was here that the freshwater navy maintained its assemblage of blacksmith shops, warehouses, barracks, shipways, and hospitals. Before the tiny burg's citizens could comprehend the importance of the location, the military had rushed in and purchased or commandeered property. Forests were hacked down; saw mills erected and unseasoned, green lumber provided for the essential buildings. All were constructed without any pretense of longevity. The facilities were expendable and intended to last just long enough to serve until the end of the war. In the spring of the year, every inch of ground, like that at Cairo, which was not corduroyed or covered with boardwalks was a bottomless pit of shoe sucking mud. Luckily for patients and staff, the Mound City military hospitals were sited on higher ground which provided some respite from insects, fog and the encroaching water. It was here the wounded and sick were conveyed following the campaigns taking place in the rebellious states to the south.

The convalescents were under the care of the physicians of the United States Medical Corps assisted by the Sanitary Commission. The latter organization, a solely volunteer agency, provided comfort and care to the men beyond what was offered by the government.

It was on the slippery Kentucky River bank that Andrea first cast her eyes on Mound City. She, like so many of the black refugees, was enthralled with crossing over the Ohio in order to reach freedom. But Andrea was not destined to be swept up and placed in a contraband confinement enclosure to be released on the condition she perform set tasks for the government. No, she would make her own choices and not be bound by the decisions of others. She would dodge the guards at the wharf and land on the opposite shore free of any restraints or obligations.

Andrea watched the procession of army wagons rolling down the rutted, uneven road and squeezed in alongside a conveyance with the Fourteenth Army Corp emblem painted on its canvas cover. As she trudged along, she stole glances at the passengers making their way to the landing on the opposite side of the wheeled transports. Seeing a white haired colonel accompanied by two staff members, she quickly formulated a plan. Andrea paused, unbuttoned her shabby coat and stuffed her shirt front tightly into the waist of her trousers accentuating her femininity. Then she waited for the last wagon to pass and walked briskly up behind the trio.

"Would you gentlemen be making a crossing this morning?" She touched the older officer's arm.

"Be gone, slave woman, we've no time for you." A second lieutenant answered gruffly, pushing Andrea's hand away.

"No, Son, that will do." The colonel temporarily flustered by the young woman's forwardness had found his voice. "Let's see what this lady wants."

The group stopped and looked at Andrea, their eyes flitting past her tattered garb to take in the features of her beautiful face.

"What is it we can do for you, madam?"

"Thank you, gentlemen. I'm grateful to you for sparing time for me."

Andrea swallowed for affect before spinning the tale she'd concocted.

"Sirs, you see I must cross over to Mound City at this time. My husband and little girl were released from the contraband detention center in Nashville three days ago. For some reason I was not allowed to leave with them and I've been trying to catch up with my family but have been frustrated at every turn. I learned from a wagoneer coming south on the road yesterday that a black man and a little girl have camped out at yonder landing seeking information on a missing wife."

The second lieutenant stepped close to the elderly officer and muttered, "Sounds very strange to me, sir."

"Never mind, Lieutenant Brent. We shall assist this woman with her request. She's been through a lot, far more than we'd want our women to have to endure. It's obvious she's intelligent and being such, she will not be a burden on the relief people across the river."

"Thank you, Sir. It's just that the soldiers bother me so much and are always pestering me."

"I can certainly understand why." The older officer smiled. "And who is it we will be escorting?"

"Andrea Edwards, Sir, from Jackson, Mississippi."

"Well then, Andrea Edwards, we three shall act as your guard as you cross the Ohio. We will see that no one 'pesters' you."

XXXXXXXXXXXXXXXXXXXXXXXXXXXXXXXXXXXXXXXXXX

"Andrealine Edwards?"

"Yes sir."

"We are pleased to consider you for a position with the Sanitary Commission."

The elderly white man sitting at a low desk smiled broadly. He wore a white shirt with a sting tie and a dark frock coat. His appearance was ridiculously striking with a bald, shining head and a minimum of white hair commencing just above his oversized ears and billowing out into a full set of mutton chops.

"If you don't mind, I'd prefer to be addressed as Andrea. The name is shorter and less formal." Her eyes perused the neatly arranged desk until they came to rest on a low placard, "Mr. Masters."

"Yes, yes, understood. My associates here beside me are Mrs. Hortense Williams, whom I believe you know, and Mr. Abner Stephens." The leader of the selection committee looked down at an application form lying between his hands. Both of his assistants smiled wanly at Andrea.

"We are all amazed to see an application for employment filled out so neatly and with such exquisite penmanship, Miss Edwards. It is very, very, rare to discover such gifts in your race."

"Thank you, Sir. I was raised on a plantation in Mississippi as a companion to a white mistress who was my own age."

"Ah, that explains it. May I say, Miss, that you were most fortunate to have received an education."

"Yes, I realize that and I intend to do as much as I can to contribute to the betterment of my people." Andrea nervously stroked at wrinkles on the hips of her brown, full length dress.

"Admirable, indeed my dear, Andrea." Masters turned to the male standing at his left and asked, "Did you hear that, Abner? The young lady sounds as if she would be a prime candidate for your organization. That is if she keeps up her enthusiasm for her cause."

Stephens nodded in agreement.

"Now, Hortense would you add your observations of Miss Edwards' qualities. In short tell us and her why she should become a part of our relief work on a permanent basis."

The stern faced women cleared her throat before speaking. "Miss Edwards came to us starving and worn in a flood of blacks streaming north from the newly liberated states. Her clothes were in rags but in spite of that she was clean and carried herself with an air of authority. On the first day on which we of the staff became acquainted with her, she volunteered to assist in the feeding of the patients. Within the hour, she was ladling out soup from a large kettle to the needy men. She showed initiative from the start by recruiting two hospital stewards to carry the large kettle from the outside fire to the kitchen where the food could be served more quickly and efficiently. All she asked for on that first day was a bowl for herself when the feeding was finished. We didn't expect her to return on the next day but she did and on the next after that. Where she slept or how she'd found food beyond the little that we gave her was a mystery to us. On the fourth day we realized her value and placed her in the ladies' dormitory. That was three weeks ago." Mrs. Williams paused and added, "What we have standing before us in Andrea Edwards is an intelligent, diligent, clean and enterprising caregiver."

"Enterprising, you say? Give us an example please, Hortense?"

"Perhaps, I should have used a better word."

"Explain, please."

"Miss Edwards er, Andrea, saw the long hemmed dresses we nurses wear were always dragging in the mud and were a danger near the open cook fires that we are sometimes forced to use. She, against my instructions, hemmed her dress three inches higher and when her sister caregivers saw what she'd done, they followed suit."

"Yes a definite independent characteristic, I'd say." Masters' face grew stern. He directed his eyes to Andrea's feet but all he saw were the insteps of her army brogans.

"What then was the outcome of Miss Edwards' innovation?"

Nurse Williams pursed her lips and said as though she was reluctant to do so, "The action which she took was a splendid idea and an improvement we should have taken months ago."

"Do you have anything else you'd like to add, Hortense?"

"Yes, Andrea has been most influential in raising the morale of our wounded colored troops. As you are aware the hospital has received a few of the survivors from the Fort Pillow massacre. They came to us suffering from the most horrible wounds and dealing with nightmarish remembrances of what happened there. They literally escaped the clutches of the devil himself in the form of Nathan Bedford Forrest. You must know of the phenomenon known as the 'black sulks' that appears to attack colored folks who have passed through the worst of traumas?"

"Yes I have heard of it but refresh my memory, please."

"It is a condition which seems prevalent in the colored race where the people, in this case the soldiers, neither smile, nor speak, or eat for days while in recovery. Temporary nurse Edwards has made special efforts to console and comfort these men. She brings them sweets as their care allows, writes letters for them, and has brought many a poor boy away from death's door."

"Indeed, most excellent. Thank you, Hortense."

Masters pushed his chair backward away from his desk in order to open the front drawer. He withdrew a small wooden box and lifted its hinged lid. His pudgy fingers took out an oval, silver medal which he slid across the desk toward Andrea. On the face of the small metallic medallion were engraved the letters U.S.S.C. signifying the relief group's name; United States Sanitary Commission. Andrea picked it up and studied it, smiling as she did.

"There's more, Andrea." Masters handed the former slave a five dollar green back. "This is small compensation for all the good things you've brought to our efforts here. I fear, however, you may be stolen away from us by Mr. Stephens' developing bureau in the near future."

"And what organization would that be?" Andrea questioned.

Abner Stephens took a step that put him even with the corner of the desk. "Yes, young lady, there's no doubt in my mind that you would be perfect for our group. It is only in the formative stages at this time but it will come into being with the support of Congress. The relief movement, when it commences its work, will be known as the Freedmen's Bureau."

Moultrie County, March 17, 1864

BUCK JOHNSON THOUGHT HE'D DONE the right thing dispersing the money agent Lewis had given him as a retainer for services that his little gang of night riders had performed. He just should have used better judgment in the amounts distributed. Of course, as the newly appointed contact for the Knights of the Golden Circle, he awarded himself five hundred dollars and split the remainder in equal amounts to Bell and Sipes. Both he and Sipes had conducted themselves well with their money spending, buying only those items that they needed without attracting attention. Bell, on the other hand, engorged himself in a whirlwind of purchases. A new saddle, a silver Elgin pocket watch, several paid visits to Dotty Pike's and a brand new Colts' army revolver from Harden's Hardware Store drew the attention of Sheriff Sam Earp.

"Jesus Christ, Buck. That Earp was on me like flies on shit. He collared me and had me in his office in the courthouse so fast that my head was spinnin'." Willie Bell paced back and forth in the straw of the Johnson barn's runway. Worry furrowed the blond headed man's brow.

"Well just what in the hell did ya expect, you dumb shit?" Buck sat on top of one of the wooden mangers and watched the consternation spreading across Bell's features. " You were spendin' money like one of the DuPonts and everybody knows you don't have a pot to piss in. What did you tell Sam?"

Willie removed his battered hat and wiped the sweat band on the inside with his fingers. The temperature outside the building was setting on twenty five degrees and Bell was perspiring. "I told him that I'd come inta some funds left by my uncle who'd died in Vandalia."

"That's pretty thin milk, Son. Then what happened?"

"He said he'd check on that."

"He will. He's probably already sent a telegram to the county sheriff there and he'll be gettin' an answer back within the next couple of days."

"Jesus! What am I gonna do?"

"Get your sorry ass outta the country, that's what. Cut for Missouri. I'm told that a man could make a livelihood outta bushwhackin' in that state."

"But I don't wanna leave."

"It's for your own health. If the sheriff puts the squeeze on you again you'll squeal like a spring piglet."

"I won't talk, you know I'll not give away anybody."

"Yes you will and you know it. I've always suspected you of bein' the weakest of the three of us. If Lewis thinks you're about to give up the game I expect that he'll want you killed to shut you up."

Willie Bell's face blanched. "All right, I'll go but I think you've got the wrong opinion of me."

"That's a smart decision on your part, Willie." Buck slid off the manger and straightened himself. "I'll be takin' that piece you got shoved in the waist band of yer pants under yer coat."

"Why?"

"You bought it with Knights' money and it's their property. Now, hand it here." Johnson extended his hand palm up.

Bell hesitated, conjuring whether or not he should obey. Finally, he withdrew the big revolver and handed it butt first to Buck.

"I'll have you empty yer pockets too on that hog's head next to you, there."

"Jesus, Buck, you gotta leave me with some money to travel on." Bell protested.

Johnson picked up the small wad of greenbacks, counted out twenty-five dollars and handed that amount back to Bell.

"I'm advisin' you to go by yer home and load up with winter clothes and not say a word to yer folks about where yer off to. Understood?"

Bell didn't verbally respond, just shook his head in the affirmative, and walked passed Johnson to the barn door.

XXXXXXXXXXXXXXXXXXXXXXXXXXXXXXXXXXXXXXXXXX

"So you run Willie off?"

"Had to, he was drawin' too much attention to us, from the law. Do you know these two fellers I got with me here?"

"Well I recollect that I've seen the long haired man there at a farm auction over near the county line last fall." John Sipes stuck out his hand to introduce himself. "Howdy, I'm John Sipes."

"Howdy to you. The name's Ben Stuart and this here is my pard, Ivan Pollard. We got to know Buck there, when he visited over to Long Creek a few weeks ago."

"They're true blue in their beliefs, John. I'll be the first to certify them as honest in their sympathies." Johnson took up a stick and pushed a small log into a snapping fire that he'd kindled in a slough adjacent to the ice covered Kaskaskia. Above the assembled men, soft maple trees stripped bare of foliage waved in the chill wind of mid-March.

"Well, you fellers comin' as far as you have to join me and Buck is proof enough to me that you'll make good Knights of the Golden Circle society members." Sipes pulled his coat collar higher around his neck. "You ain't sendin' them back to Macon County, today, are you, Buck? For them to get back home has gotta be a half day's ride from here."

"No, the boy's are goin' inta Sullivan and gettin' a room at the boardin' house for a couple of days. They've cut loose from their families on Long Creek and now are gonna make war with us. They'll ride out to the home place and help me clean up the little cabin north of the house and stay there. The folks, if they ask about them, will get told that they're cattle buyers that I met in town."

"Sounds like a good plan, Buck. It's best the fellers not get seen too much there at the boarding house, else people will start askin' questions of them."

"Right. Now, the next step is to wait until we get word from Lewis."

Moultrie County Sheriff's Office, Sullivan, Illinois March 26, 1864

SAM EARP STRAIGHTENED THE GRAY shirt that he was wearing and checked to determine if he'd transferred his Moultrie County Sheriff's badge to his front, left breast pocket. He'd removed his dark, suit coat and hung it on a peg on the wall beside the office door. Deputy Hoskins had built a roaring fire in the stove and the room was unusually warm. Seeing that his apparel was in order, he directed his attention past the wide brimmed hat he'd placed on the edge of his desk to the stack of papers that seemed to grow larger with each passing day. He and his deputy had compiled a sizeable amount of details dealing with Copperhead activities in the area. This investigative work and information received from his cohort in Shelby County enabled Earp to pin point the predations of the secret group over the southern portion of his small jurisdiction.

At that very moment, Deputy Homer Hoskins was collecting evidence in relationship to missing sheep from a farm near Old Nelson. Earp doubted that the animals had been stolen by the night riders but instead had been driven off by packs of dogs that were known to frequent the area. The occurrence with the sheep was minor when compared to incidents such as the near sabotage of the rail line outside of Windsor and the drowning of Whitchurch at the Monroe Ford. These recent events coming on the same night were activities large enough and serious enough to get the sheriff's attention.

Sam stroked the ends of his mustache and twirled their waxed tips. He was aware of complaints that he was getting from some of his southern leaning constituents that Deputy Hoskins was being less that fair with their complaints. This element was suffering retaliatory strikes from a group calling itself 'the Union League' and the 'Butternuts' were becoming very vocal in their criticism of the Moultrie County law officials.

The Copperhead sons-a-bitches have brought it on themselves, Earp mused. *By God, if they wanted to show their disapproval of the war, then the cowardly dirt sills should've taken their whining families and moved south. I'm walkin' a tight rope between the two factions in this county but I'm not goin' to give in to the dark side as have those cowardly sheriffs in Edgar, Coles, and Clark Counties.*

The middle aged law officer paged through the papers until his eyes fixed on a yellow sheet carrying a cryptic message. It was a telegram from Sheriff B.G Brownlee in Vandalia. In its brevity the sheriff reported information that there were no known descendants of Willie Bell living in the county and there was no record of any inheritance distribution in the recorder's office to anyone named Bell. So Willie Bell, a local loafer, and a person never known to hold a steady job had been telling the biggest of lies to Earp regarding his source of income. Willie's parents had come to Earp's office seeking information on their son's whereabouts but Sam could tell them nothing. Not even that he'd grilled their son as to his adventures as a Copperhead night rider. It was common knowledge that Bell was thick with John Sipes and Cyrus Johnson, suspects that Earp was keeping his eyes on.

The heating stove popped as a green elm branch released it moisture in the flaming fire box. The sheriff eased his holstered revolver to a more comfortable spot on his hip and leaned back in his swivel chair He'd stopped in at the boarding house on the previous morning and asked to see the guest registration. Dotty Pike was never co-operative about releasing information but while the look of protestation spread across her features, she swung the ledger around on the desk and permitted the sheriff to examine the clients' names. Earp had an inner knowledge of her evening activities he could use to make her life miserable.

Two entries in the registration; Joseph Willings of Mt. Zion and Philip Hayes of Oakley drew the lawman's attention. Earp kept the index finger of his right hand on the last name listed as if he were holding down the man and trying to imagine the type of person he was. He doubted that the recorded names were the actual ones of the overnight guests. He didn't know why, perhaps it was a lawman's intuition that told him, but his suspicions were aroused.

"Did these two come in together this mornin'?"

"Yes, pretty much so."

"On the stage?"

"No, they asked where they could stable their horses and I sent them to McCary's."

"Says here that Willings claims to be a hardware salesman and this Hayes lists himself as a travelin' book subscriber."

"That's what they wrote down. I doubt if all that is true. I just take money and don't ask questions."

"What made you think they weren't in the profession that they said they were in?" Earp hadn't moved his finger from the ledger.

"If they was engaged in the type of work they claimed to be in, they'd needed big valises for their samples but all they had with them were little satchels. And on top of that they acted like their paper collars was too tight and their suits were,...well, not as expensive as you'd expect for men out representing a company." Dotty Pike knew full well what trouble she would be in if she held back information.

"It says here that they've paid for two nights lodging."

"Yes."

"Are they in their rooms now?"

"No, they left right after they put their stuff in their rooms. Neither one of them had their satchels with them. They headed southwest outta town."

"Get your keys; I'd like to take a look around upstairs to see what they're up to."

XXXXXXXXXXXXXXXXXXXXXXXXXXXXXXXXXXXXXXXX

"What's with the missin' sheep, Homer?" Sheriff Earp stood at the stove warming his hands.

The deputy shucked his heavy overcoat, removed his hat and hung both items on pegs next to Sam's by the office door.

"I took statements and looked around but couldn't find nothin'. The ground's froze hard and I didn't find any horse tracks so I figured that dogs had run them off. The owner, ol' man Standifer, said he'd heard a bunch of bleatin' in the night but he was too afraid to go outside to see what it was causin' all the commotion. He'd had the K inside the circle painted on the back side of his barn two months ago and that put the fear of God inta him."

"Yes," Earp paused and spit into the wood box and wiped his mouth on his shirt sleeve, "a single man with a damned paint brush and a bucket of paint ridin' around the country after dark can put the molasses in a man's union suit."

"What did you find out about the strangers over to Laury's boardin' house?" Hoskins joined his employer at the stove and thrust his hands over the heated iron.

"Plenty. I went through the rooms they'd rented and found suits they wore when they checked in yesterday still hangin' in the closets. Dotty must've not seen them too clear when they left yesterday to tell what kinda clothes they were wearin'."

"Anythin' else?"

"Yes, I found their satchels in the closet as well, mostly stuffed with old newspapers but in one of them I discovered wrappin' paper off a packet of Colt's revolver ammunition."

"Ain't huntin' season, is it?"

"No, it ain't. These two's up to no good. Let's you and me take a ride out to Archie Rhode's place when it gets a little warmer and see if he's seen the fellers ride past his farm. If he's seen them, then it's likely that they've got business with Buck Johnson."

A knock on the door broke Earp's train of thought and interrupted the conversation. A freckle faced boy whose cheeks and nose were flushed from the cold opened the door and announced loudly, "Sheriff, here's yer mail what's just come in on the stage and yer yesterday's Chicago newspaper too! The headline says that Nathan Bedford Forrest has took Paducah, Kentucky, and the whole state of Illinois is in an uproar! Governor Yates is callin' for added protection if that ol' rebel comes over the river."

Both law officers looked at one another. Earp took the bundle from the boy and stared at the newspaper.

"Best cancel that ride out to Archie's, Homer. Looks like we'd better stay close to the office to see if we're needed here." The sheriff slipped his suit coat on over his shirt and fumbled to repin his badge on his outer garment.

41st Army camp, Ardmore, Tennessee
March 17, 1864

CHANCE WAS AWARE OF A hospital steward placing cool, damp cotton cloths on his feverish forehead as he opened his eyes. Except for the attendant and him, the tiny hut was empty. Atop his body lay two wool, army blankets and his new frock coat. Neunan's mouth was dry and his lips cracked from the temperature that had surged through his body.

"Well, you're wakin' up. Me and the assistant surgeon thought that we might lose you but it appears you've whipped what ever it was that gripped you. How about a drink of water?"

"Where's Pete?" Chance mumbled.

"Your bunky? Oh, he's packed off with the re-enlisters and is headed north on the train to Nashville. The regiment is goin' up to Camp Yates in Springfield to commence their furloughs. You'd be with 'em if you hadn't took sick."

"How long have they been gone?" Chance took the tin cup from the man's hand and sipped from it.

"Three days at least. If the assistant surgeon gives you a clean bill of health this afternoon, he'll put you on the next train tomorrow with some other convalescents from the company. Maybe you'll catch up to them. You're on the rolls as re-enlisting and you might as well recover at home. Your furlough papers are stuffed in the inside pocket of your uniform coat, there. You didn't draw any accoutrements except for a waist belt and buckle. Oh yes, they added a knapsack over there in the corner. I guess the ordinance sergeant figured you were too sick to heft a musket and he didn't issue you one."

"Did you relieve me of my pistol and watch?"

"All over there with your extra shirt, socks and overcoat. The surgeon said it wouldn't do to have you rolling around in a fever with that stuff in your pockets."

"God, what happened to me?"

"The doctor says you were completely fatigued from your escape and that with some sort of *trauma*, your system encountered a shock that came near to killing you." The assistant wrung out an extra cloth and applied it to Chance's temple. "I hope you don't think that I'm prying but I couldn't help not seeing these two letters lying here on the floor by your bed."

"Oh, God." Chance's right hand went to his forehead as the information contained in the two missives came flooding back to him.

He'd opened the earliest dated correspondence, the one with the black banded envelope hoping against hope that it would not contain a message he could not bear.

Dearest Chance,   *February12, 1864*

 It seems that I'm continually writing to you with the blackest of news. Another tragedy has befallen you and our family. It is with the most heartfelt regret that I must tell you of your mother, Clair's passing. Our trek to Zanesville, Ohio, had just ended and we had not spent a week in our new location among our loved ones when she expired. Clair had taken a cold in the last few days of our journey and she hid its severity from us. Your mother was weakened by your father's death and as the fever rose in her body she professed to us she did not want to live without Mathias. We felt she clung to her life until she had seen that all of us had reached safety. She told us that she wished to see her brothers and their families for one last time and now she had done so. We are all feeling her loss and just looking at her vacant chair at mealtime brings a flood of tears to our eyes. I never told her your letters to me had been infrequent so as not to worry her further. I, myself, am concerned about you. You have not written to me and my anxiety grows with each passing day. Is there a reason you have not blessed my day with your loving words? Please write as soon as possible.

Your Love,
Becky

"I assume that you read them?"

"It was kinda boring just sitting here watching you breathe."

"That's all right. For all you've done for me, I can't be mad at you." Neunan closed his eyes and envisioned the words contained in the most recently dated letter.

Dear Chance,   *February 20, 1864*

I have received nothing from you although I have written two more letters. Is not my correspondence getting through to you? Here in Ohio, the winter has been mild and my father is making plans to go back to Illinois and put in a crop as soon as the weather breaks a little more. Perhaps Mr. Dixon will be able to help him with the planting. And of course, little Alfie is no longer little. He has grown three inches in height and put on twenty pounds. Ruthie Scott has written me recently. She has married Ad Reynolds and is living with him on a farm in Neoga. Addison was discharged from the cavalry at the hospital in Alton because of disability. She seems happy in her marriage and she writes often telling me of the joys of being paired with her love. Ruthie is optimistic about Ad's recovery but says that if he is too severely handicapped so he can't work, he'll consider applying for a pension from the government.

Chance, I am in such a quandary that you cannot believe. A certain Ohio Captain has been stopping by uncle's farm to see me. He is on convalescent leave for a wound he received in the fighting in western

Virginia. The man is a local farmer whose name is Ruben Stout and his intentions seem quite honorable. I have told him of your presence in my life but since I have no knowledge of your where- abouts or even if, God forbid, you are dead or a captive I don't know what else to do but to allow him to keep calling. I find myself treasuring his company and looking forward to his visits. Ruben is a fine man possessing good principles. Please, please, write me as soon as is humanly possible.

As ever,
Becky

In both letters, Becky had tried to let him down easy choosing words as delicately as possible in detailing his mother's death and describing the new man in her life. Chance swallowed and thought of her and the anguish she was passing through.

The war and his involvement in it were responsible for taking the lives of his father and mother as surely as if the two of them had been executed by a firing squad.

Johnson Farm, Moultrie County, Illinois
March 26, 1864

WIND WHIPPED THROUGH THE SKELETAL limbs of the giant mulberry tree that stood in the darkness in the Johnson family's front yard.

Buck had put his elderly parents to bed in their unheated bedroom a half hour earlier and now he pealed his ears listening for tell-tale snoring which would indicate they were asleep. He opened the door to the firebox on the stove and shoved in two additional logs and returned to his seat at the kitchen table. A myriad of swoons, huffs and wheezes drifted into the warmth of the eating area as Buck silently complimented himself on the half shot of whisky with which he'd laced both his parents' milk during the meal two hours earlier. Watching the clock, a family heirloom brought over from the old country, Johnson wiled away the time waiting for the arrival of Sipes and one very important guest. He wanted no interruptions to the conference from a drowsy family member. At the table lighted by a coal oil lamp turned low, Johnson had placed a map, pen and ink and two sheets of paper in case they were needed.

As the appointed time drew nearer, Buck brought out Willie Bell's new army revolver and nervously spun the cylinder over and over stopping the weapon's function by quickly bringing the hammer back to full cock.

Dammit, I should have made that little sniveling Willie give up the silver Elgin watch he'd bought with money that had come from the 'Knights' war chest. It had been purchased in his period of weakness and Johnson, as the leader of the group, should have confiscated the timepiece as he'd done the pistol. Then the watch would have been rightfully his and he wouldn't have had to be continually consulting the wall clock.

As the clock chimed eight times Buck rose from his chair, took up the lamp, went to the window and peered into the whirling March darkness outside. Then he raised the lamp up and down twice in quick succession. Johnson returned to the table, set down the illuminating device, took up the pistol and shoved its barrel into his waist band and waited. Within two minutes a slight tap on the kitchen's outer door gained entry for John Sipes and the agent named Lewis. Buck placed his index finger on his lips as a signal to be quiet then took each man by the hand and gave the secret handshake. Entering behind Sipes, Lewis had brushed past and placed a blanket wrapped bundle on the table before turning his attention to Johnson. Finished with the formalities, Buck gestured for all to be seated.

Buck and John Sipes folded their hands and waited for Lewis to speak. The leader seemed agitated and kept glancing into the shadowy corners of the room as if he expected more men to emerge from their depths "It's all clear, Lewis. We are alone except for my folks sleepin' in a back bedroom," Johnson spoke reassuringly. Buck failed to mention the other members of his group residing in the distant cabin. "You've met John, here?" He nodded toward his friend.

"Yes, we met at the edge of the timber." Lewis suppressed a shiver that started on his left shoulder. "Would you mind adding more wood to the fire? I'm nearly frozen through."

"Shore thing. John step out on the porch there and fetch in some logs from off the stack."

Sipes opened the door allowing an icy blast to flicker the flame in the lamp before closing the portal and rummaging about outside. Then he slipped back into the kitchen, opened the stove's firebox door, and filled it with logs. He paused momentarily to adjust the pipe damper before returning to an empty seat at the table.

"There is that better? Is everybody gettin' toasty?" Buck shot a crooked smile toward the rebel agent. "What's with the nerves, Lewis?"

The agent looked down at his folded hands. "I'm afraid that the opening phase of our extensive plan has gone awry."

"Oh, I don't believe your people have filled us in on this 'plan'." Johnson's voice was filled with sarcasm revealing his displeasure that he wasn't being kept informed of the society's more expansive designs.

"No, you have not received word of this operation at your level." Lewis paused contemplating how much he should reveal. "My superiors in Toronto have drawn up a plan that would put a Confederate raiding force in the heart of Illinois within the next few days."

Both Sipes' and Johnson's jaws dropped.

"I see the look of amazement on your faces. The strategy was to have Nathan Bedford Forrest raiding western Kentucky and capturing Paducah on the banks of the Ohio. Two days ago he and his command accomplished this task. He managed to burn several transports and barges east of the city and also capture a light gun boat which he utilized in the shelling of the river front. President Davis had, prior to the commencement of the campaign, given him discretionary orders to cross his troops over the river into Indiana and destroy the Union supplies at Jeffersonville if practicable. From that point he was to drive northward and cross the Wabash River into Illinois and push through any militia he might encounter on his way to Springfield. Can you imagine the howl that Lincoln would yelp when he realized the audaciousness of Forrest's invasion?"

Sipes spoke up. "It's true Buck, I read a copy of the Mattoon Gazette in Sullivan yesterday and the front page was filled with speculation of what was happenin' at Paducah."

"Precisely, Mr. Sipes. But the general's raid was meant to coincide with our operations in Mattoon."

"And that plan amounted to what?" Johnson was becoming more interested.

"Our operatives were to simultaneously attack the infantry units in Mattoon and Charleston and tie them up so as not to allow them to hinder Forrest's drive toward the state capitol. You and your men, Mr. Johnson, were to fire the warehouses filled with supplies and ordinance outside of Camp Terry on the night of March 27. You do have more members than Mr. Sipes in your party, don't you, Buck?"

"I can get all the help we'll need."

"I had written to our explosive experts in Canada to obtain a quantity of 'Greek fire' but their response came back there was none to be had. So your destruction of the storage facilities was to be carried out using conventional means."

"What's wrong with the plan then?" Sipes cocked his head.

"Why, I'm afraid that General Forrest has been too impatient to begin his conquest. With the prize that was to be had, he has moved into western Kentucky with too few men and the area his forces have invaded is much too large for him to occupy or hold. He has reached the zenith of his unit's penetration and cannot advance across the Ohio or secure the city of Paducah for any length of time. He won't be coming into Illinois or Indiana and will have to retreat from the captured territory or risk being cut off from his main base in central Tennessee."

"Where does that leave us?" Johnson leaned forward his eyes intent on Lewis' face. "Are we goin' ahead with our end of the operation?"

"What's your opinion?"

"I say that the Union military won't have any inklin' of our plans and them seein' Forrest retreatin' will give them a false sense of relief. They'll be off guard and it'll be perfect for a strike. Turn us loose and we'll handle the warehouses and when we get them blazin' good me and my boys will ride up the tracks to Charleston and pitch in with the friends of the cause. That is, if they decide to go ahead with their end of the plan of takin' on the troops there. We'll rattle Governor Yates and that bastard Lincoln's teeth."

"It could be very dangerous for you and your men if you choose that approach. If you link up with our operatives in Charleston, you'll be fighting in daylight and you could be recognized. If you're caught… well, you see my point."

"We'll do it!" Buck slapped the palm of his hand hard on the table top. "We been sittin' on our asses too damned long."

Lewis shook his head sideways revealing his displeasure at Johnson's audacity.

"We'll be tipping the society's hand once we drop our cover and initiate conflict in the open and in full daylight. You're aware of that?"

"You're damned right, I am. I figure that we can raise some hell with the Charleston boys, then light out for the timber and lay low for awhile. Sheriff O'Hair can handle his problem any way he chooses."

"Then get word to Sheriff O'Hair at the Coles County Courthouse that you'll be making an appearance to support him and how many men you'll have." Lewis rose and pushed the blanket wrapped bundle across the table to a position in front of Johnson. "Here's a little something in the way of thanks for the services you've performed in the past for our cause." The agent tapped his finger tips to the front of his hat brim and opened the door.

"Good luck, gentlemen and good night." He did not linger to watch as Buck started to untie the string from around the parcel.

"Whooee, would you look at this, Johnny boy!"

"I'll be damned! This is the first Spencer repeater that I've seen."

Illinois Prairie east of Charleston
March 28, 1864

THE SPRING HAD COME IN a strange manner to East Central Illinois in the third year of the war. Usually the rains turned the vast flatness into lakes that filled the topography between the oak savannas sprinkled on the prairie. The wetness of the thaw would rise out of the ground and mix with what deluges fell from the sky causing the inhabitants to muse of the biblical times of Noah. But this was not the case in the spring of 1864. The frost had left the ground at the end of February and the torrents of rainfall had not materialized. Yet the soil as it always is in spring was soft, mushy, and nearly bottomless.

Mud, yellow and heavy, clung to the bottoms of Neunan's trouser legs. It was everywhere thickly coating the bottoms of the pedestrians' trousers and collecting on the creaking wheels of produce wagons loading at the depot. Charleston, Illinois, lay sprawled like an inert amoeba astride a timbered ridge which swept down to the Embarras River situated to the southeast. The town was gaining a sense of respectability as a budding metropolis even though it still retained a number of rough hewn buildings and clapboard sided mercantile enterprises.

Charleston's main claim to fame was being the governmental seat of Coles County and the site of the Senatorial Debates of 1858; which pitted Stephen Douglas against the current president of the country. The town square was deeply rutted, daubed with horse dung, and enclosed a two story stone courthouse. The city's train station had been thoughtfully situated at the northeast edge of the city saving the downtown from the stench of the numerous cattle and hog pens located on the premises. These yards emitted the musty odor of rotting straw and manure which assailed the waking men's nostrils.

Chance rubbed his eyes and looked around as more soldiers stirred from their blankets, coughed, stretched and wandered off to the far sides of the animals' confinements to relieve themselves. The early morning sun bore down with an intensity that was severe for that time of year in the Illinois springtime. It had broken above a distant tree line as an orange orb radiating unseasonable heat that quickly melted the icy puddles which formed during the previous evening.

The young soldier watched the ice topped depressions from his comfortable straw pile beneath the depot's loading platform. As the sun conquered the ice, tiny rivulets escaped and trickled into larger wagon tracks which gave way to even larger depressions. Roosters crowed, dogs barked and privy doors opened and closed within the waking town. Breakfast fires poured gray smoke up through the chimneys of the shake shingled dwellings of the citizenry.

Funny, thought Chance, *how he could be so uncomfortable and keep falling back to sleep.* The sun was sending narrow shafts of light through the spacing in the platform boards overhead and onto his curled body.

Convalescents had disembarked from the railroad cars in the early morning darkness. They had tumbled out, sore and sleepy, limping and coughing, and formed ranks by lantern light. Following role call, the tired soldiers had been dismissed to find whatever sleeping quarters that were available. Hardly a man among them returned to the cars on the siding. The seven hour train ordeal had been enough for most everyone and the majority deemed the rudest sleeping locations better than the torture seats in the car's interiors. A number of the soldiers sought out dry fence corners and bedded down while others like Neunan slid under the loading docks to escape the cold and frost.

The town was temporarily filled by the soldiers belonging to the 54th Illinois Infantry who were assembling following the completion of their furlough. Those men who were recovering wounded from this unit struck off in the darkness to locate their friends. A few swung their knapsacks on their backs and started on the half mile walk to the center of town and the only inn located there. They had no inkling all the rooms were filled with officers from the 54th and lawmakers who'd come to hear Representative Franklin Sims speak in the city.

Chance waited his turn in line at the horse trough and observed groups of men scurrying like sand crabs to shady spots to escape the sun. All looked battle worn even though they wore articles of new clothing and carried new equipment. Behind Neunan on the depot's delivery platform stood the men's stacked muskets, haversacks and knapsacks, the tarred items oozing their usual black pitch in the relentless sun. *Some idiot of an officer,* Chance thought to himself, *stacking muskets exposed to heat like this. The gleaming rifles would be impossible to hold in another hour. You could always tell the sensibility of a commanding officer by such little things and old soldiers like Chance could distinguish imperfections in leadership immediately. But then what could one expect? The officer himself was a wounded man ordered to take command of a surly, rag tag group. The officer's charges were intent on making connections with their old regiments before being mustered out because of disabilities, or placed back in the ranks on active duty.*

"What's yer name, boy?" A first sergeant stood beside Neunan, folding a sodden red handkerchief which he placed in his right front pant's pocket.

"Chance Neunan, 41st Illinois."

The sergeant's four button jacket was flecked with chaff and his light blue shirt was damp around the collar from either the oppressive heat or his dip in the horse tank. He reached for a smoldering cigar he'd placed on top of a nearby fence post and took a long drag that set the tip to glowing.

"Sergeant Merrit's the name, from Paradise. That's the next stop on the rail line after Mattoon." The NCO extended his hand. "Kinda lost like the rest of us, ain't ya?"

Chance nodded. "I got left in winter camp at Ardmore on the Tennessee border. I missed the troop train north by three days due to a flare up of a fever I'd come down with earlier. I've been tryin' to catch up with the boys ever since but haven't gained any ground on them."

"They've probably already formed up and been dismissed at Camp Yates in Springfield for the start of their thirty day leave." Merrit brushed some of the straw off his tunic's front. "Not to worry there, Neunan, most everybody that's been wounded and is tryin' to make connections will be given credit for the days missed. Alls you'll have to do is to report in at Yates and you'll be credited for those late days back."

"That's good to know. I've been worried sick about bein' cut short on my leave."

Merrit drew again on his cigar and blew smoke from beneath his gray streaked walrus like mustache. "Where'd you get yer wound?'

"Got knifed while guardin' a rail trestle on the Big Black River in Mississippi."

The NCO felt inside the right side of his sack coat, found a scuffed wallet and withdrew it. He thumbed through its contents, looked up at Chance and said, "Would you want to walk down town and have some breakfast with me? I hope that you're not one of those fools that gambled away their leave money on the train. It don't matter if you were, I'll still buy."

"Sounds good to me, Sarge. I could use a hot meal."

It was after the two had indulged in a belly bursting meal of coffee, eggs, gravy and sausage that Chance had excused himself and wandered away to explore the city's business section. Merrit had poked a long, narrow cigar in Chance's mouth and lighted it before bidding his new acquaintance adieu and entering McDade's saloon. He told Neunan that he had a thirst for an elixir to finish off the enormous repast that they'd enjoyed.

Chance found a shady spot beneath a weathered awning and watched the late morning activities churning through the mud of the six acre town square. Fronting on the four sides of the courthouse was an array of general stores, saloons, the town's only hotel, post office, photography studio, harness shop, and a haberdashery advertising the latest in men's fashionable straw hats.

Neunan knew that he should have stayed at the train depot. Mattoon and Camp Terry were only thirteen miles further to the west and Windsor another hour beyond that. The all night ordeal on the rocking train from Paris, Tennessee, where he'd sat hunched against the side of the passenger car had sapped the strength out of his frail body. Rails and ties had evidently heaved upward due to spring thawing leaving the once well engineered rail line resembling a ride down a hill in a cider barrel. Cinders and lung searing smoke had poured into the coach's interiors attacking every orifice oozing mucus and tears as the rail transportation rattled north. Chance's attention wandered back to the safety of his overcoat which he'd left lying over his knapsack on the depot's platform, His gear was not far from the tripod of muskets watched over by a few sullen soldiers who'd been selected to stand guard. Neunan knew that his personal items were not secured but he didn't want to return to the tracks until nearer to the departure of the six p.m. train. He shoved his hands in his front pockets and drew on his cigar. For some reason, Chance suddenly became desirous of the company of a woman. Not necessarily in the carnal way but in a manner where he could hear one's voice or look at her softness in opposition to the sturdiness of a man. *A woman was god's gift to man. Holding Andrea in his arms in all her smooth, majestic loveliness was a treasured memory. Being with her was an experience he'd cherish for the remainder of his lifetime. Their tryst together should have taken place on a gigantic feather bed in a sun lit room where his eyes could have feasted on her tawny skin contrasting with the whiteness of the bed clothes. How much better it would have been for the two of them to have exhausted their passion in a civilized setting rather than in the darkness of a straw floored storage cellar. Andrea, what had become of her after they had parted? Was she a painted lady servicing the high officers in the camps around Nashville or had she achieved her desire to serve her people in their struggles to throw away the chains which had entrapped them for so long?*

Chance's pulse quickened as he thought of her. He removed his pocket watch and glanced at the dial. It was nearing 9:30 a.m. and there were many hours to spend before the west bound train pulled out of the depot for Mattoon.

"Hey soldier boy, you looking' for a little fun?" The inquiry came so close to his face that Chance imagined flecks of spittle spattering against his jaw. The question exuded from a breath that was onion and whisky tinged.

Neunan turned and studied the speaker who had interrupted his pleasant thought.

"Could be, I, er."

"Name ain't important, Yank. How much you willin' to cut for?" The owner of the alcohol etched breath appeared to be in his late fifties and supported a stained, duck suit with a frame that exhibited the effects of heavy imbibing. Like Chance's, the trouser cuffs of the suit's pants he was wearing were caked with mud.

Queer that the man should call me Yank, thought Neunan but he was in territory that was known for its strong southern sympathies so he allowed the sobriquet to pass.

The unidentified man stood inspecting his potential client and the size of wallet that he might be carrying.

Neunan rolled the cigar to the other side of his mouth. "Depends on the cut of the meat."

"It's fresh and hain't been bruised."

Soldiers kept passing; some stepping off the boardwalk into the mud while others barged between Chance and the man with whom he was negotiating. Most were members of the 54th regiment, bedecked in new frock coats and polished brass, all evidences of re-equipping.

The soldiers were feeling their oats during the last days of the furlough and were bullying the town's people over the most trivial thing. A few drinks in the late afternoon by either or both parties could turn these confrontations into some real nastiness.

"Want ta step inta the alley and finish our business? I'm gettin' tired of havin' my feet tromped on by these…," The civilian paused; "soldiers."

Suspicion furrowed Neunan's brow. *A short step out of view of the street, a blade between the ribs, and he'd be left dead on his feet, bleeding down inside his trousers, sliding down a back alley doorway.* Chance's hand brushed the Colt in his front pant's pocket.

"No need to be afraid, Mister, and no need to bring out any kinda weapon, either. This is a fair and square deal we got goin."

God, Chance didn't know why he'd listened to the disheveled man or why he'd slipped him a dollar for the address. He might be going to his doom but the lure of a woman and the brief companionship she would give him drove him on. A niece from Mt, Vernon, the suspicious man had said, down on her luck and forced to turn to the profession older than history itself.

Hell, she's probably the guy's mother, Neunan mused as he reached the gray house's entry gate and walked up the flagstone walk to the weathered, white door. The two story dwelling's front was festooned with dried ivy which partially concealed the structures need for paint. A gauzy curtain closed as his foot stepped on the porch.

"Sellin' or buyin' something, Sonny?"

A large, hard faced woman leered at the young soldier, filling the open doorway with her bulk.

"Jessie sent me Ma'am. Says that Miss LaVerne is expectin' me."

A feinted flash of recognition swept across the woman's countenance.

"Cousin Willie, I wasn't lookin' for you today!"

The woman stepped outside and wrapped both her massive arms about Chance squeezing him into her enormous breasts.

"What the hell?" Came Neunan's muffled question as he was pulled through the doorway and into the parlor.

"Aw shut up, ya idiot. We got to make some effort to appear legitimate in this damned neighborhood, else Sheriff O'Hair will run us outta town." The husky woman released him and closed the door.

"That Jessie has got to have shelled peas for brains sendin' you down here in the middle of the mornin'."

Neunan regained his composure and straightened his waist belt.

"Looks to me like the neighbors are goin' to think you're having a hell of a family reunion goin' on if your business picks up." Chance grinned as he finished the sentence.

"Business hain't been good a'tol. You'd think we was runnin' a funeral parlor 'stead of a cat house. Damned soldiers are bullyin' the town folks and our boys in blue ain't in the mind for pleasurin' with all the friction that's goin' on. Some of the soldier boys have been assaulted at night when they come here from uptown. Say, I'll betcha that's why ol' Jessie sent you down to us in broad daylight. Son, you done run the blockade and didn't get touched."

Neunan shuddered inwardly. To think that he had been used in the grand spirit of finding out if customers could be sent to the 'house' without being beaten up on their trek gave him cause for concern.

"I don't relish bein' one of your and Jessie's guinea pigs, Ma'am."

"Don't take it so personal, Honey. Maybe we can knock a little off yer visit."

"Yeah, What's it goin' to cost me to meet this Miss LaVerne?" *I hope to God that you aren't her.* Chance thought to himself as he glanced around the room for a possible escape route in case one was needed.

"Ten greenbacks."

The heavy set woman heard the soldier snort through his nose.

"No five, since you was the trail blazer."

XXXXXXXXXXXXXXXXXXXXXXXXXXXXXXXXXXXXXXXX

LaVerne was a much better looking specimen than he'd anticipated. Long, white limbs, deep blue eyes, and an overly rouged face, partly to cover the dark rings beneath her eyes and skin imperfections and partly as an indicator of her profession met the young soldier's gaze.

The woman minced no words as to what she was about to offer the young soldier.

"Belly or Back?"

An innocent inquiry from a virgin new to prostitution. Chance smirked to himself as he turned away to remove his mud encrusted shoes.

"You in a hurry, LaVerne?"

"I guess not. It's still mornin' isn't it? I just figured you had other appointments. Most soldiers do."

She lay on her stomach, her filmy nightgown swirling around her long legs. The sun flooded in through a half-raised window blind beside the four poster bed. A worn diary lay on a night stand next to her stack of pillows along with combs, hair pins, and other feminine necessities. A high backed chair piled with petticoats, a corset, and a rumpled but fine dress completed the room's furnishings.

Chance pulled off his uniform coat and hung it on the bedpost.

Miss, er,uh, the lady downstairs…"

"You mean, Lard?"

"Yes, Miss Laird."

LaVerne laughed. Not a hard laugh, not a musical one either, just a laugh.

"No, soldier, Lard is her nick name. Her surname is Black, Celia Black."

Chance laughed at his ignorance. "Well, anyway, she was telling me that there's hard feelings between the townspeople and the soldiers."

LaVerne sat up allowing one of her legs to hang over the edge of the mattress. Her movement caused her gown to hike up exposing a strong, round thigh with a small blue bruise on it. She tossed her banana curls back out away from her eyes.

"Yes, there's been beatin' given on both sides. It affects us here at the house too, don't think it don't. The soldier boys come here all mean and pissy and wail on us. You've met Jessie, right? He's our house security, if you can imagine that. Last week, he got the holy hell beat outta him by two big toughs from the 54th Illinois."

LaVerne stopped talking and looked at Neunan who was standing at the foot of the bed wearing his long underwear bottoms and his socks.

"You want to do business or talk soldier?"

"I thought perhaps that we could do both."

"You ain't one of them Pinkerton fellows snoopin' around, are you?"

Neunan laughed at her supposition.

He lay down beside the girl and drew her to him.

"No kissin'. I don't do mouth kissin'."

"We don't have to do any of that. I've got to catch a train to Mattoon at six this evening and that's all I've got to worry about. We can just lie here and talk if you want."

"I don't mind, but Lard will probably run you off for tryin' to stretch your five dollars."

"Lard told me your usual fee was ten dollars."

Laverne laughed and said, "Shit, Boy, she tells all the soldiers that." Then her blue eyes linked with his as she pulled a string at the top of her gown and a milky, white breast tipped by a pink roundel pushed from the bodice fabric.

"Still want to talk?" she murmured.

XXXXXXXXXXXXXXXXXXXXXXXXXXXXXXXXXXXXXXXXXX

The 54th Illinois Volunteer Infantry had brought the problem to a head within the city. Not that the regiment was unlike so many which passed through Charleston on the way south and to the warfront. It was just that a number of the 54th's officers and enlisted men had enemies within the city and as the war continued the animosity and hatred between the family members they'd left at home and the Copperhead element had reached a point of no return. The townspeople, leaning toward the southern cause in their heritage and sympathies, had just had a gut full of being bullied. On many occasions, they'd been coerced into dropping to their knees in the muddy streets and pledging allegiance to the government of the United States. The citizens were flat out sick of being chided as being secessionists and watching as their wives and daughters were belittled. Sheriff John O'Hair had sided with the townsfolk that had elected him so much so that the Mattoon paper had branded him and his Edgar County cousin who served in a similar capacity as Copperheads. O'Hair had appealed to the commander of the regiment to rein in his soldiers before serious consequences resulted but his requests fell on deaf ears. To add to the explosive situation, strangers openly wearing sidearms on the outside of their clothing had converged on the city.

Rumors were rife about the town. A suspected upheaval was coming and the citizens were relishing its appearance as a means of bringing down vengeance on their military tormentors.

LaVerne lay beneath Chance, perspiration beading on her brow, eyes closed, long lashes lying on flushed cheeks. She had made Neunan forget about the conversation that he wanted to initiate and instead had seduced him with her charms. The two had slept an exhausted sleep in the warmth of the room and the tangle of bed clothes.

Chance watched the rise and fall of her stomach and contemplated waking her to say goodbye but he didn't. In the career that LaVerne had chosen, he knew she needed all the rest that she could get. He eased out of the bed and began to dress taking care to avoid any noise that would disturb her.

A spattering sound originating from the direction of the courthouse square caused the young woman to roll over and ask, "What on earth is that?"

Chance knew immediately what the sounds were. He'd heard them at Shiloh, at Corinth, Vicksburg. "Pistol shots! Those are pistol shots coming from uptown somewhere. I've got to get dressed and head for the train station!"

"LaVerne! LaVerne!" Lard was screaming from downstairs. "It's started! It's started! Get dressed! Get dressed! We'll go to the cellar! Hurry!"

"Dammit! Why couldn't all this have happened after I'd gotten off to Camp Terry? Just my luck!" Neunan had on his coat and was hopping on one foot trying to put on his right shoe.

"You take care Soldier Boy and if you're makin' for the depot, don't go the way you come here. Take Elm Street. It's a straight shot to the railroad yard."

XXXXXXXXXXXXXXXXXXXXXXXXXXXXXXXXXXXXXXXX

Chance disregarded the directions that LaVerne had provided and headed instead to the town square. If Union soldiers needed help he wanted to provide what assistance he could. It was very likely that a number of the troops were unarmed having left their muskets stacked on the loading dock of the depot. The first three blocks were covered quickly but as he neared the downtown area, Neunan commenced to cut through back yards, climbing over board fences and ducking under drooping clothes lines. He chose any route he could that would keep him off the streets converging onto the square.

With his chest heaving and perspiration stinging his eyes, Chance neared the center of town and the courthouse area. Gray wisps of gunpowder smoke lay heavy along the base of the scrawny, naked trees clinging to life along the boardwalks. Somehow the situation in the city's business district was not as dire as he'd expected. Still, the first fuselage had dropped unsuspecting men on the courthouse steps and the rutted mire that passed for thoroughfares.

Neunan found the alley where he'd started the morning and eased along one of the businesses' outside walls, Root revolver, cocked and ready. Not a breeze stirred the puddles in the moist earth of the alleyway. Suddenly, the scattering firing ceased and the business section became as quiet as a tomb. From somewhere on a side street, two dogs began to howl. He caught his breath and exhaled and repeated the procedure again in an attempt to slow his racing heart. The passageway he'd entered opened between buildings and out onto the main street. To step brazenly onto the boardwalk could invite a crashing and sudden death. The blue of his uniform would make a beautiful target against the yellow mud covering the roadway. He had to cross the square at some point in order to move north, to what he hoped would be the safety of the railroad station. Neunan dropped to his knees, removed his kepi and peered cautiously around the edge of the building beside which he was positioned. A soldier lay crumpled in the sloppy mélange of mud and horse manure less than ten feet away, a crimson stain forming on his breast, the shiny brass fifty-four numbers glinting on the crown of his spattered kepi. Other bodies lay in contorted positions on the board walk and in the yard of the court building.

Spang! Splinters and dust exploded near Chance's head. He flopped on his stomach the wood particles billowing into his eyes. Another projectile smacked into the weatherboarding where his head had been seconds before.

Damn! Thought Neunan as he slid backward from his exposed position. *Is there one shooter or are there two?*

The building against which he'd taken shelter had no foundation as such, only piers that supported the floor sills. Chance sat shaking, propped against the weather beaten siding of a business establishment. He clutched his small revolver in his left hand and tried to control the trembling that was convulsing his muscles. No more shots came his way and he determined that his hiding place put him out of the view of his attacker. After a few minutes, the young soldier decided to work himself under the building and crawl up to the underneath side of the boardwalk to access a view of the street. His breath came in gasps because of his cardiac excitement and physical exertion. In the semi-light, his gaze moved from one possible hiding place to the next until a movement from behind a parked wagon drew his attention.

Yes, there was his assailant. He had adjusted something he was holding, possibly levering a new round into his carbine and this had revealed his hiding place. The sniper's ability with his weapon was obvious judging from the number of bodies lying in the street and on the boardwalk. The Copperhead has an advantage over me with that fast firing gun, Chance told himself.

Neunan pulled himself further forward into the narrow space beneath the boardwalk and watched for a few more moments. He came to the conclusion that a clear shot was not possible unless he drew his assailant into the open and out from behind the wagon box. He kept his eyes fixed on the conveyance as he began to grope through the debris that had accumulated in his place of concealment. His perspiring fingers handled three empty bottles before his grasp closed on a three foot long piece of two inch by two inch lumber. When the wood was in his grip, he studied what fortune had provided and devised a plan. Chance laid his pistol aside and struggled to remove his uniform coat and after some difficulty, managed to get it off and buttoned around the slender piece of wood. Then he shinnied backward until he could place the pseudo dummy upright against the outer side of the building. Neunan returned to his former position and extended his left leg until the toe of his shoe was resting within inches of the board bearing his frock coat. He'd positioned the coat so that when he nudged the board supporting it with his foot, the device would tumble into the alley opening. It was then, Chance hoped his antagonist would rise and show himself in an attempt to get off a shot. If the man behind the wagon didn't take the bait, then he and Neunan would have reached a stalemate. This subterfuge would have to work or his antagonist could call in help, then flank and kill him in the narrow alley passageway. Chance was nervously aware that he was in a battle for his life.

Splang! Another projectile tore through the weather boarding where the shooter had last seen the soldier.

Chance pulled himself up to his viewing slit between the ground and the bottom sill of the walkway. He rested his revolver barrel on a termite chewed sill and cocked the side hammer of the Colt Root. He checked the distance again to see if he could topple the coat into the alley with his foot. He could but there would be only one attempt to lure out the man from his hiding place. Then, if the affair was a failure, he'd have to crawfish backward from under the store and try to escape down the narrow passageway between the buildings.

Chance checked to see if the percussion cap was snug on the pistol's nipple, wiped the perspiration from his eyes with the back of his hand, and sighted down the groove cut in the firearm's top strap.

"Here she goes!" he shouted.

Raking down the weatherboarding as it fell, the plank bounced upward upon striking the ground. The coat's left sleeve flailed out as it started to descend. Wood splinters flew from the board as the sniper's bullet ripped into the bait.

The side hammered Root exploded at the same time.

Clawing at his checkered shirt front, the shooter staggered to the wagon's end gate and stood swaying. Shock and amazement crept over his features as he permitted his fingers to relax on the wrist of the Spencer carbine. He never acknowledged that the rifle he'd been holding had fallen into the muck at his feet. As though he were unbuttoning his shirt in front of a mirror in his bedroom, the ashen faced man opened the garment and stared at a small blue hole that was gushing blood from his sternum.

God, the tottering man was Buck Johnson! Neunan could not forget the face of the snarling bully he hadn't seen in over two years. But there was no mistaking the identity of the dying man that had torn at Chance's face in the shadows outside the school at Whitley's Point.

Neunan was oblivious to the report of his weapon for a second time or of the halo of powder smoke that arose around his face in the filtered light under the store. As though in a sepia toned dream; the soldier watched Johnson's body lurch sideways and flop into the rutted slop of the Charleston street. The young man would never acknowledge what he had seen or done and even though he'd be asked innumerable times, in years afterward, regarding the disappearance of the Copperhead, Neunan would remain tight lipped. Zack and Elva Johnson would only know their son had left one day in late March of 1864, and never returned.

XXXXXXXXXXXXXXXXXXXXXXXXXXXXXXXXXXXXXXXXX

The St. Louis, Alton and Terra Haute station master helped Neunan alight from the passenger train and onto the depot's passenger platform. Chance was stiff, sore and dirty as a sack of potatoes. His passage out of Charleston, through Mattoon and into the little hamlet of Windsor on the Shelby-Moultrie County border had taken two days. Outside of Camp Terry, the smoking ruins of supply warehouses lay blackened and reeking of scorched bacon and burnt cloth. The journey west out of the danger zone had only been permitted by the military officials after Colonel Mitchell of the embattled 54th Illinois had rallied and driven Sheriff O'Hair and his Copperheads out of the Coles County seat.

"No sir, son, You'll not find anythin' open at this time a night here in little ol' Windsor. We're under martial law and nobody's to be out after eight o'clock fer nothin'."

Chance eased the knapsack straps off his shoulders and let the pack fall to his feet. Then he peered through the bay window in the telegraph agent's office and read the large clock hanging on the waiting room wall.

"I've still got a half hour."

"What did you have in mind doin'?"

"I wanted to rent a horse and leave for the family farm over on the south side of the county line on the Kaskaskia."

"Didn't intend on havin' to cross the river at the Monroe Ford did ya?"

"No."

"That's good. A night crossin' at the ford is dangerous. Had a feller named Whitchurch get drowned at that place last July."

"I'll not have to cross the river to get to where I'm goin'."

"All well and good, but the Provost Marshal, he's got a temporary office set up in the Methodist Church, won't allow Cletus Grim to let no horses out 'til daylight."

"Why's that?"

"It's the martial law that's been imposed. We had a whole regiment in here yesterday, the 41st Illinois, chasin' after an army of fifteen hundred Copperheads. I never heard of such hog wash. Only an idiot would believe we had such a passel of Secesh around here. The soldier boys were in a bad mood having been put back on duty afore they got released fer their furlough. Colonel Pugh's got them off on a march to Ramsey, south and west of here searchin' fer ghosts. They'll not find a thing."

"Where does that leave me, then?"

"If I was you, I'd head on over to the provost's office and get yer orders straightened out, then get up to the Black Horse Inn and get a room fer the night. Then tomorrow you can start fresh in daylight."

"You've got a pretty good clothing store as I recall next to the boardin' house, don't you?"

"Yes, we sure do. But get things straightened out before dark. Yer subject to bein' shot if you're caught on the street after eight o'clock."

The rail official picked up a small wooden box and placed it on a stack of other such items near a wide door which Neunan assumed opened into a storage room.

"Say, son, you look pretty used up. Did you get inta that fight up the track at Charleston?"

"No, I was safe at the west edge of town at the depot when all that fightin' was taking place." Chance lied.

"You didn't see the Honorable Franklin Sims then at the courthouse?" Disgust flavored the station master's inquiry.

"Nope, I stayed away from downtown."

"The paper says that our respected Peace Democrat sensed there was a fracas brewing and took off for the tall timber before it started."

XXXXXXXXXXXXXXXXXXXXXXXXXXXXXXXXXXXXXXXX

Four o'clock of the next day found Chance astride a rented roan with two white forelegs traveling on the grass siding next to a deeply rutted road heading north. He'd expected to get an earlier start from the Windsor boarding house but he'd overslept and had missed the two meals that were included in the daily room rate. Neunan had to settle for a mess of stewed apples and cured ham sided with a chunk of white bread for the only meal he would consume that day. The female proprietor had set her black house lady to brushing his uniform free of dried mud and applying a liberal amount of the cleaning fluid, naphtha, for a fifty cent fee. The wool garments should have been aired out in order to clear away the fumes but though she'd pinned his clothing on a back porch clothesline, the misty weather hadn't allowed the fabric to expunge itself. So he was forced to watch as the owner of Bender's Shoes and Apparel turned up his nose as he assisted him with the selection of a shirt, socks, and trousers. A sturdy, unlined, canvas coat completed Chance's traveling trousseau.

"Better have this here hat, Mister. She's a lot better suited for prairie travel than that little soldier cap."

"How much?"

Neunan slid his finger tips over the brim seeking to determine if the quality of the wool was good.

"You'll not find a hat this fine anywhere this side of Decatur. I'll take five for it."

"I'll give you four."

"Done! And I'll wrap up yer soldier suit in a brown paper bundle to keep the weather offen it."

The horse, named Ollie, was a gelding with a pleasant disposition or so Cletus Grim claimed, and could be deposited at McCary's stable in Sullivan on the next day. Grim informed Chance he and McCary had an agreement that would save the owners from having to exchange rider less horses and lose money. Chance didn't care one whit about the arrangement since going into Sullivan to leave the animal would force him to ford the river. Instead he'd turn Ollie loose and let him find his way back to his own livery barn. Grim watched the soldier tie his uniform bundle behind the saddle and walk around the animal examining him.

"You just wanted to rent him didn't ya? You're lookin' him over like you want to buy him."

"I'm just tryin' to see if he's fit that's all."

"He is. I wouldn't be afraid to start off for St.Louis on him." Grim stepped forward and yanked up the saddle cinch. Neunan mounted and accepted the reins from the stable owner.

"Good day, there, fellers. I just got a telegram from over ta Shelbyville that three companies of the 41st is comin' east on a troop train and due to stop here." The station master whom Chance had met the previous night was waving a yellow piece of paper. "They'll be here in a half hour or so. I'm headin' over to the Provost Marshal's office to deliver the message."

"Good day to you gentlemen," said Chance as he kicked Ollie in the ribs and cantered away down the muddy street.

Not one bit of good can come of me sticking around and getting impressed back into duty with the regiment. I've got a furlough to take. Neunan thought as he cleared the last little dwelling at the north edge of the town.

XXXXXXXXXXXXXXXXXXXXXXXXXXXXXXXXXXXXXXXXXX

An early April moon had risen and was bathing the farm lane leading up to the Winford Dixon farmhouse. Cletus Grim's assessment of his rental property had been pure hum-bug. Ollie, the horse, was nearing exhaustion from his eight miles of exertion across the rolling prairie. The hour was late; possibly, ten o'clock and Chance knew he'd be waking Winford and Violet from their sleep as he reined in his tired mount. Several sharp raps on the front door rattled the glass but brought no response from the house's interior. He lowered his head and squinted through the gauze curtain at the door and spied a flicker of light that indicated that a lamp was turned low in the parlor. Bed springs creaked as bare feet hit the floor and padded to some other point in the darkened house. The initial signs of arousal ceased and a period of silence ensued. Then Chance's hearing picked up the familiar sound of the click of a revolver being cocked.

"Mr. Dixon? Winford?" he called out.

More silence. "Yes, a quaking aged voice answered.

'It's me, Chance Neunan."

Quiet.

"Open up, Winford. It is me. Mathias Neunan's son."

The floor groaned behind the locked door.

There was no response from the home's interior although he could still see the burning lamp.

Chance hadn't heard the stealthy approach of the owner until he felt a cold hard object poked into his flesh under his right ear.

"What'cha want, Mister?"

Neunan started to turn toward the voice.

"Don't turn any further. You got a loaded pistol shoved up under yer ear and you'd better fess up."

"That's you isn't it, Winford?"

"That's my name but I can't see as how you could be Chance Neunan since he got killed in Mississippi two months ago."

"You got a match, Sir?"

"You got any company with you?"

"Nope."

"You ain't lyin' to me?"

"Why would I? I am who I say I am."

A sulphur tipped match rasped against a porch post and burst into flame illuminating the two.

"Now, you can turn around just a little."

The small flame was thrust closer to Chance's face.

"Lord, God! You are Chance Neunan! Mother, turn up the lamp! Chance Neunan is here on the porch."

The pistol swung away and the match was dropped as Neunan was clasped in a rib cracking bear hug. "I knew they couldn't kill you."

" You men get on in here . You can do your celebratin' in the house." Mrs. Dixon stood clothed in a gown in the doorway, the lamp held high.

"Thank you Ma'am. You can't guess how happy I am to be back among people who are my neighbors. I've come to get some answers to a lot of questions which I have."

XXXXXXXXXXXXXXXXXXXXXXXXXXXXXXXXXXXXXXX

Both Dixon's had excused themselves and left Chance at the kitchen table. He sat finishing one of Winford's prized cheroots and sipping on a glass of the old man's sour mash. Laying heavily creased and soiled before him was a letter whose handwriting appeared very familiar to him. He picked up the missive and reread the weeks old news- some of which astonished him.

Dear Winford and Violet,   *March 11, 1864*

Your kind words were received last week. We, in no way, expected to hear of our families' loss of the farmhouse and outbuildings . The whole affair has set us back to the point that we will not consider returning to the Kaskaskia to put in a crop this spring. Of course, we know the identity of the leader of the night riders who is responsible for our grief and father says that, in time, he will be dealt with by the good Union folks in the area. We were happy to learn that Sheriff Earp had men stationed at the Neunan farm under Homer Hoskins' direction and thwarted the Copperheads' effort to burn down that place as well. I have good news which will balance the bad. I am pleased to announce to you both that I have become engaged to Captain Ruben Stout of the 24ᵗʰ Ohio Infantry and we will be united in marriage next week. We had wanted a June wedding but with the calamity of the loss of the farm buildings and my fiancé's having to report for duty soon, we thought this early date best. It seems that I have endured unbearable events and happenings beyond my years but having my Ruben at my side has enabled me to find happiness amid all the gloom. Out future will lie in our success, after the war, in what we will glean from the hundred acres that my husband owns here in Ohio. The loyal citizens in the Buck Eye state have had to deal with the likes of Clement Vallandiham until he was arrested last May by the Union army. He was the leader of this area's tribe of dissenters but his work was less cruel and people did not have to fear for their lives as you do in central Illinois. My parents are so devastated by their plight with the homestead that they doubt that they will ever return to the Kaskaskia. I shall close for now and wish you health and relief from the awful things going on in your area.

Sincerely yours,
Soon to be Mrs. Becky Stout

Chance never felt more alone in his life as he did at that time. Outside, the gray of the dawn was approaching but in the small kitchen, Neunan could not relate in a cheery manner to the new day. The passing of his parents and his best friend, Andy Crowder, as well as the loss of his first love, Becky, dropped a deep depressive weight onto his fatigued shoulders. He'd learned from Mr. Dixon everyone suspected that Buck Johnson was the nemesis behind all the raiding and burning. But Neunan had not told the aged farmer the part he played in Johnson's disappearance. Chance could vouch for Buck's death in the shootout on the street in Charleston but could not fathom why the Copperhead's name had not been reported in the newspaper casualty lists. There had to be a reason the Copperhead's corpse not having been identified and listed with the fatalities compiled by the military authorities.. Was it possible that members of Johnson's unit had spirited his body out of town and buried the cadaver in some remote spot never to be mentioned again?

Chance did not relish what he'd done on the 28th of March. Taking another's life strikes deep in the core of a man's morality but the young soldier reasoned that stretching the night rider under a gum blanket saved the lives and property of many of his family's friends.

Chance raised his arms, yawned and stretched. The residual stale taste from the cigars coating the lining of his mouth reminded him of how little sleep he'd had during the night. He rose from the table, turned down the wick on the lamp, set his gray hat on his head and found the door that opened out onto the barn lot. He'd curl up in the hay mow for a few hours before he'd mount Ollie and go over to the home place and visit the graves of his father and aunt.

XXXXXXXXXXXXXXXXXXXXXXXXXXXXXXXXXXXXXXXXX

The days seemed to speed by faster as Chance neared the midpoint of his furlough. He would have been lying if he'd told a visitor he was not anxious to return to the regiment. In just two more weeks he'd board the train at Windsor to return to the marshalling point in Springfield and join his friends. A great emptiness had enveloped him during the past week and he wanted to be back in a world where he did not have to dwell on things which disturbed him. His melancholy was deep and in each of the quickening days he fought to suppress it. Winford Dixon brought over a nice wad of greenbacks which Job Scott deemed was Chance's share of the items sold when the Scotts and Clair Neunan embarked for Ohio. Uncle Job, ever the optimistic one, had never given up on the return of his nephew and his uncle's foresight with a portion of the proceeds from the sale of the unneeded household goods and stock provided Chance with a temporary nest egg. Using the money, Chance's first set of goals besides making the farmhouse livable, included paying off any outstanding taxes on the farm property and securing the services of a stone cutter to identify his father's and Aunt Emma's graves. The horse which he'd rented in Windsor had been set free to find its way back across the prairie to the livery barn. Chance quickly became aware that there was little to nothing left in the cellar to eat and that he needed a means of transportation to access his needs. So, at the conclusion of the week, he went to see the Dixons about the loan of a horse. The old farmer cheerfully agreed to allow Chance to borrow 'Sis' one half of his draft team that was broken for the saddle. The wizened old man even threw in a bag of oats and allowed that the mare, if tethered on the spring grass, would have enough to eat until it was time for the soldier to report back for duty.

On the next day in the early morning of bright sunshine, Chance crossed the river at the ford and struck out on the Sullivan road. He'd astutely kept his uniform bundled in its brown paper wrapping in a bedroom chest and chose instead to wear mufti to the hamlet. The purchase of staples and foodstuffs were foremost on his mind as well as a visit to the barbershop. The streets enclosing the town's square were their usual puddled mess and would remain that way until the heat of May dried them. Neunan entered several businesses selecting items of subsistence but meeting no one who recognized him. It was after he'd tied the cloth sacks which contained his purchases to his saddle and had his locks shorn that he walked over to the county courthouse and the office of Sheriff Sam Earp.

"Good mornin', gentlemen." he announced as he stepped through the doorway and removed his hat.

Sam Earp looked up from a stack of papers which lay in disarray atop his desk. The constable's gray eyes gave Chance a steely perusal.

"What can I do for ya, stranger?" Earp's eyes never diverted from Chance's.

"I'm not a stranger here, Sir."

Homer Hoskins, the county deputy, stood at the stove rubbing some type of grease onto a boot he'd removed from his left foot.

"You do look kinda familiar young feller." Hoskins said matter of factly.

"I should. I'm Mathias Neunan's son back home on leave."

Earp scooted his chair back from beneath the desk and stood up. He squinted his eyes and peered intently at Chance.

"We got word that Mathias' son was missin' and presumed dead."

"Well it isn't so. It's me, Chance, getting' rested and goin' back to fight."

"Welcome home, Son." The lawman leaned forward, extended his hand and Neunan took it.

Hoskins wiped his oily fingers on his pants leg before offering his.

"We're real sorry about what happened out at yer folk's place and yer uncle's farmstead gettin' burnt." Earp eased his tall frame back against the side of his desk. "Those black hearts seemed to spring outta the ground and go back to hell whenever they've finished their devilment. They escaped every trap we had set for them. It seemed like we were always chasin' ghosts."

Earp motioned for Chance to take a seat. The deputy returned to the waterproofing of his footwear next to the heating stove.

"From the letters I received from home I'd say that you and your deputy have had your hands full."

"Indeed we have. Nobody got out and out murdered that we could prove. We did have some deaths that were damned suspect but we couldn't determine if they was anythin' other than from accidental causes."

"Are you at liberty to say who you think has been behind all this Copperhead activity?"

"Not really. Our investigation is on goin'. I would like to hear your opinion on who the hell we oughta be lookin' to arrest."

"Buck Johnson for one and possibly Clem Woodruff who runs the saw mill."

"Whoa, thar, Mr. Neunan. You're pointin' a finger at two pretty respectable men in the community."
"Maybe so, sheriff, but you asked my opinion. Both of these fellows had some hard words with my dad and Uncle Job regarding the rebellion."

Homer Hoskins set the oiled boot next to the stove's ash door and hopping on one leg removed his other boot.

"Were you on leave comin' through Charleston when the Copperheads had the soldier massacre?" Earp's eyes switched from being soft to piercing as he fixed them on Chance's countenance.

"Yes. I was at the depot. All the shooting and killing took place downtown on the square but I didn't get into it. Why do you bring that up?"

"Because we got word that one of the men that you mentioned was workin' with the Copperhead mob there."

"Who?"

"I'll not say. The feller hasn't been home in three weeks and there's people inquirin' about him."

"Yes and John Sipes hain't been seen either." Hoskins stood examining the sole of his ungreased boot.

"That'll be enough, Homer."

"Sorry, Sam." The deputy apologized sheepishly.

"And now, Chance, if there's nothin' more we can do fer you, I'd like to get back to my paper work."

"No, nothing more, Sheriff. Please get word to me if Buck Johnson comes back to this area. I've got a few questions I'd like to put to him."

XXXXXXXXXXXXXXXXXXXXXXXXXXXXXXXXXXXXXXX

Following his visit to Sullivan and his conference with the local authorities, Neunan fell into a routine that provided a degree of rest and time to be pensive. Once he'd arisen, washed and consumed a meager breakfast, he'd see to his borrowed mount. That done, Chance would take up his fishing pole which he'd fashioned from a long, green maple sapling and walk the farm lane to the river bottom. He found solace at the riffle where Becky and her cousin, Ruthie, naked as woodland nymphs, had cavorted months before. Chance would spend the day casting his line into the shallows and watching the cork go bobbing downstream until it settled the baited hook into a deeper pool. The location and the cool water was the haunt of the sucker and the red horse and even though fish weren't caught at every try, Chance enjoyed the sport. Many times, the young soldier would doze off and only be wakened by a tug on the opposite end of his fishing line. At other times after he'd fallen asleep, a bird's call would arouse him from his slumber and he'd retrace his steps up the hill, past the two graves to the empty farm house.

Standing on the house's front porch leaning against one of the supports, he marveled at the blossoming of the vegetation he looked down on. Verdant patches of yellow green buds, interspersed with the flowers of red bud tree and wild crab apple told him of the advent of spring and the coming summer.

It's going to be difficult to leave this and return to the army and the suffocating humidity and heat of a campaign in Georgia. Neunan told himself. *The Federal forces were in a full blown advance under the command of General Sherman toward Atlanta. In ten days, he'd be a part of that rolling, blue colossus. Yes,* he told himself, *God willing, he would return to the regiment and fulfill his duty. There was nothing but the farm to hold onto now and he wanted his world to be right before he returned to the homestead and made it prosper. If he was fortunate to be spared and came back from the war with a whole body and a sound mind, he could find a new love to become attached to.* Chance knew that the direction that his future would take was beyond anything he could do and only divine providence would determine his destiny.

XXX

Chance sat himself down at his usual spot beside two large, moss covered boulders and cast out his baited hook. He'd been told by Winford Dixon that shelled corn soaked in lye soap water was a most palatable attraction for the hog nosed sucker in the fast flowing shallows. Neunan had tried the concoction and learned that the old settler was right but catching fish was only a bonus. The gurgling water and the warmth of the sun were like a tonic to the soldier's body and soul.

He unbuttoned his shirt, eased the suspenders off his shoulders and slipped his feet from his heavy brogans. In a matter of moments, Chance's eye lids became ladened, his head nodded and he leaned back against one of the rocks.

His ears did not pick up the sounds of the horse's approaching footfalls as the animal picked its way through the spreading bushes nearby. On picket duty months before, this would not have been the case. Every sound, the snap of a twig, the scraping of cloth against a bush, would have sent him into a full alert mode with every sense tuned. Now in the bosom of safety, the soldier's guard was relaxed and the survival instinct had become dulled. Neunan was at the mercy of whomever was attempting to locate him in his place of rest.

His sleep was so sound that he was not cognizant of the rider's stealthy tread through the fragments of last autumn's dried leaves.

It was only when he felt the softness of the skin on the back of a hand against his cheek that his eye lashes fluttered. Then his dark eyes opened and he gazed up into the liquid brown of the irises belonging to Andrea Edwards.

"Andrea, is it really you?" Chance murmured. His trembling hand reached upward and clasped her fingers and brought them to his lips. The woman knelt beside him, tears streaking down her smooth cheeks. She removed a battered gray hat from her head with her free hand allowing her black hair to fall around her shoulders.

"Yes, my Yankee Boy, it's me. I couldn't wait those hundred years."

Chance drew her face to his and found her lips with his hungry mouth. The kiss was both tender and sweet. But the longer their mouths touched the more ardent their desire became.

Andrea placed her hand on Chance's chest and drew away.

"Good," she said huskily, "I wanted to see if you still felt something for me. Your kiss tells me that you do." Andrea brushed away a lock of hair that had fallen over her right eye.

"God, Andrea, your being here is like a dream. I can't believe it."

The two came together once more and their passion flamed as Neunan kissed her throat, and then moved his lips to her left ear lobe. It was only when he'd slid his fingers beneath her shirt at the waist line that Andrea protested. She folded his fingers into his palm and pushed his hand away.

The young woman, with her eyes half closed, smiled at Chance. "Look at me, I'm a mess. I've been in the saddle for seven days riding up here from Cairo. I don't think that you want me in the condition that I'm in."

"Do you think that matters to me? You're as beautiful now as you were on the day I first saw you." He nuzzled his face into her shirt front. Then Neunan righted himself and his eyes questioned her before he spoke.

"You didn't come all this way alone, did you? Tell me you weren't that foolish."

"I brought a friend. I'm a big girl and I know the hazards of traveling." Andrea hiked up her left pant leg and revealed a sheathed dagger protruding from the top of her boot.

The sight of the ivory handled weapon juxtaposed against the dark smoothness of the woman's skin sent a twinge of excitement through Neunan.

"Andrea that wasn't real smart to come as far as you have with no more than that little toad sticker to protect you."

"It was enough. I didn't run into any trouble." She brought her mouth to his and they kissed longingly, her delicate skin against the stubble of his two day old beard.

"Let's take a dip? Whatta you say to that?" Chance stroked the side of her throat.

"But the water will be cold." Andrea protested.

"Come on. I've got a jillion things to tell you about since we've been apart." Chance was pulling the young woman to her feet.

"Are they memories of me?"

"Most of them."

The two quickly shed their clothing and plunged into the shallows of the riffle amid shrieks and laughter. The chill of the gurgling water could not cool the desire that each had for the other's body and in mere seconds, Andrea was facing Chance, her body pressed hard against his. She stood shivering, breast glistening with moisture and her dark nipples erect. Together they moved into deeper water and undulated in the movements of love. The bright sun bearing down through the budding trees splotched shadows on the caramel color of Andrea's skin and the whiteness of Chance's.

It was not until after they had consummated their passion in a body shuttering climax that they swayed against one another and sought the river's bank.

As guiltless as two new born babes, they lay side by side on their clothing and told each other of the adventures they'd passed through.

"And Becky Scott, what of her? I recall your letters that I read in our hideaway cabin that she had a special place in your heart."

"Not anymore. She's moved with her family to Ohio, found a new love and married. She is no longer in my dreams. Oh, like every man who's ever loved, you always remember the first, but only in a blurred image."

At the conclusion of Chance's revelation, Andrea sat up and began fastening up her hair. She fumbled through her the pockets of her dampened trousers and withdrew a crumpled yellow ribbon and tied her long tresses behind her head. There is always something appealing to a man about the way a woman gathers her hair and secures it away from her face. Neunan silently thanked the beautiful nymph seated nude before him for the heightened pleasure her presence gave him.

"Very interesting, Chance. I guess that I never knew about the way men thought of their first loves." She lay down beside Neunan and snuggled against him.

"There, I've brought you up to date on all the experiences I've been through. Now tell me of yours."

Andrea Edwards didn't speak for a few moments, collecting her thoughts and categorizing the events. She moved away from his pale form and readjusted herself, her body uncoiling like amber syrup until she nestled her damp head on his stomach and looked up at the sky. Andrea raised her left leg into the air, pointing her toes at an open patch of blue above her. She slowly rotated her ankle as she ruminated.

"After I left you outside the army camp in early March, I continued north, subsisting on the charity of the freed slaves which I encountered. I avoided large groups of them so I wouldn't be placed in a contraband camp and by doing this, I could go where ever I pleased. Eventually I passed deeper and further through the rear lines of the Union Army and reached Cairo, Illinois. I don't mind telling you that my journey was far from an easy one. Days went by in a blur with me putting one foot in front of the other not knowing where I was going. All I knew was that I wanted to go north. Much of the time I walked but at other occasions, I managed to get up beside the drivers of empty army wagons. Most of them were kind to me but there were some who were looking for more than conversation. I was reaching exhaustion when I found the headquarters of the Sanitary Commission and asked for work in the hospitals in Mound City. I spent three weeks there doing some of the most heart wrenching work that one human could ask of another. It wasn't long before the organization's administrator concluded that I had intelligence and skills beyond those of a common Negress. Thank God, he was an honorable man and did not try to take advantage of me. From there I progressed and made acquaintances and connections which eventually placed me in a committee involved in the formative stages of developing the Freedmen's Bureau. That's a black relief group being proposed by some influential white abolitionists and Frederick Douglass. If this organization receives approval from the government it will be funded and become a branch of the War Department."

"And?"

"I've been placed in a position that will allow me to oversee the educational curriculums and construction of schools for my people in the 'New South' after this miserable war ends. You see, I'm between assignments and decided to take a diversion to try to find you. I wanted to see if you retained feelings for me."

"You've found out haven't you? You'll stay with me this time and not go on to this,… this position?"

"No, Chance. I leave for Decatur tomorrow afternoon to catch the night cars for Chicago."

Neunan groaned and placed his forearm across his eyes.

"I see that just as before, in the howling forest that we escaped through, that I can't change your mind."

Andrea sat up, leaning on her left hand.

"No. This is an opportunity for me to help my brothers and sisters who have been less fortunate than I to become educated or to learn a trade. This will enable them and the generations that follow to contribute in the new society."

"Why, why, do you do this to me? You've rejected me before and I thought I had lost you forever. Now you've come back into my life and hurt me again. Why do you torment me, Andrea?" Chance took away his arm and looked up into her beautiful eyes.

"I had to see you. I don't think I could have lived another week without gazing at you, touching you, feeling your lips against my skin." Andrea's eyes filled with tears.

The soldier pulled her to him and stroking her shoulder, he whispered, "Don't cry. Don't cry. It hurts me to see you cry."

Up the river, past its first sweeping ox bow curve, the rumble of an approaching storm reached the couples' ears. Neither had been aware of its coming so enraptured with the other that they were caught unaware. Both glanced through the tree branches to see the rolling thunderheads building higher and higher above them.

"Would you look at that?" Chance was on his knees gathering his clothing and laughing as he did. Andrea had slipped a shirt over her shoulders and was just as frantically picking up her garments. "Get some pants on and ride your horse up the hill to the house. I'll run along side. Maybe we can make shelter before the storm hits."

XXXXXXXXXXXXXXXXXXXXXXXXXXXXXXXXXXXXXXXX

Andrea was finishing her dressing watching from the front porch as Chance sprinted from the barn amid the gushing downpour. She caught him as he topped the uppermost porch step and tugged him to her. She was laughing hysterically at his sodden appearance.

"Yankee Boy, you shore can run fast for a white man. Get yourself in the house and I'll find something to dry you off with."

"And you sure are beautiful for a black woman." His hands grasped her slender waist and his lips found hers in a hungry kiss.

They half stumbled, half fell through the door and found the feather pallet that Violet Dixon had loaned Chance. They lay side by side in the dim of the room's interior listening to the thunder and the rain rattling on the shake shingled roof. After a time Chance spoke, asking; "You certainly have your future set, don't you?"

"Yes, at least the short term portion of it."

"What do you mean by that?"

"I don't believe that my position with the Bureau will be a job that will last forever. That wouldn't be right. When things are established, I intend to step aside and allow a gifted and intelligent black man from the emancipated states to take over. It should be interesting to see how the former masters have to deal with powerful Negroes. This is something they've never had to do and it will irk them no end."

"When you step down, then what? Will I come back into the picture?"

"Ooh, you are a persistent one, Chance Neunan. You know I think such a thing will never work between the races."

"That's what you say but you're talking like a slave girl and not like the intelligent, crafty woman that you are. I know we can find a place where we can live out our lives as husband and wife."

"Where do think in this whole world that there would be such a place?"

"California, that's where. If we don't find happiness there, we'll move into Mexico. There are places that will accept mixed marriages."

"You're a dreamer, Chance."

"So, I am but we're young and smart and the whole world is waiting for our entrance once this war is finished."

Andrea took Chance's face in her hands and kissed him tenderly. "I'll think very hard on what you've said."

Chance swallowed, and then whispered, "I'm so in love with you that I can't find the words that will express my feelings. Just remember that if you return to me, and I'll wait two years but no more, I won't let you leave again. It will be forever."

XXXXXXXXXXXXXXXXXXXXXXXXXXXXXXXXXXXXXXX

In the late evening as the rain drops dripped onto the porch steps outside the open door, Neunan rose, dressed and found wood for the fireplace. Andrea completed her dressing as well, then busied herself with making coffee, slicing some smoked ham she'd located in the pantry and putting corn dodgers on the three legged griddle by the cheery fire. She and Chance sat on the floor and shared their meal and embellished the stories they'd related to each other in the afternoon.

"I've never heard a man confess to killing another until this evening." The former slave sat with her hands clasped and studied Chance's face.

"I'm not proud of what I did but it came down to either him or me. It bothers me at times to think of having committed this most unforgivable sin but he was an evil man who took up the wrong cause and contributed to the death of my father. While Buck Johnson never touched my Dad, his actions were as lethal as if he had stabbed him with a knife."

"I won't ask you anymore about this affair in …what was the name of the town where the riot occurred?"

"Charleston. It's about thirty miles from here. Do you think differently of me for what I've done?"

"No. I suppose that all who fight in wars must do such things. It's just I've never heard anyone admit to being responsible for such a deed." Andrea Edwards took Chance's hand in hers and patted it.

"I've told you a great deal about my parents, Andrea. Can you tell me something about your mother and father?"

"I don't know much about my Daddy except that he was a big field hand named, Able. Master Edwards sold him off shortly after I was born. Some trouble between my Daddy and the overseer."

"He must've had an independent streak in him like his daughter."

Neunan rose, found a candle, lit it, placed it on a wooden box and returned to his place beside the woman he loved. The flickering light cast a warm amber glow over their two bodies. Andrea waited until her lover had settled himself before continuing.

"Yes, I suppose he could be credited with instilling the ambition I have."

"And your mother? Where is she?"

"She ran off with the rest of the slaves when the Yankee army passed near the Edward's plantation. Didn't even try to get word she was leaving." The dark skinned woman's eyes glistened in the candle light. "No matter. I hadn't seen much of her in later years. Mrs. Edwards forbade her coming around. The Mistress didn't want the house servants to mingle with the field workers and catch any *nigger*"... Andrea paused, "diseases."

It was Chance's turn to comfort the woman who had ridden two hundred miles to find him.

A steady rain had set in outside and drops were falling down the chimney hissing into particles of steam. Chance went to the door and closed it, then turned to see Andrea removing her clothing by the light of the candle. They spent the rainy night entwined in each others arms comforted by the warmth of their bodies and the fire in the stone fireplace. Their love making was tender and gentle, both finding a rapture that they had not previously known.

XXXXXXXXXXXXXXXXXXXXXXXXXXXXXXXXXXXXXXXX

The day dawned bright and clear, the sun's rays drying the dampened spring soil and turning the rain drops on the low bushes into globules of sparkling glass. Birds flitted and sang their ever present optimism outside the farmhouse windows. Chance awoke first and touched Andrea's face with his fingertips. She stirred, then opened her eyes and smiled at him. Neither said a word but turned to opposite sides of the pallet and stood up. They dressed and commenced their toilet never speaking. Chance went to the barn, fed and watered Andrea's horse and brought it to the house's front porch. Andrea had prepared a small breakfast of coffee, molasses and corn cake and bid him to take a seat at the makeshift table.

They ate looking at each other, their silence only accentuating the hurt which they held in their hearts. Both knew once more they would part but that if there was a God, he would reunite them after the war had ended and Andrea's work was finished.

"It's time to go, Chance." Andrea's eyes gushed as she stood. Her shoulders trembled as she leaned into Neunan's chest. His kisses to her forehead did little to stifle her sobs.

The young soldier helped her up into the saddle before he stepped back and locked his eyes on her face.

"It's time for both of us to go, my love. I'm leaving today as well. I'm going back to the regiment early to get a head start on ending this infernal war."

"Take the utmost care, Chance." Andrea extended her hand downward and Neunan brought her fingers to his lips.

"How will I find you, Andrea?"

"I left the Chicago address of the Freedmen's Bureau on the box that was our table. Please write to me."

"What if I lose the paper? I must know where you are."

"Don't worry, if you do, I'll find you. I think I'd make a wonderful Pinkerton agent with the detective work I used to locate you here in Illinois." The dark skinned woman's mouth turned up ever so slightly.

Chance didn't want to release her hand but when his grip lessened, she drew it away.

"God, you're beautiful! I want to remember you just as you are, sitting on your horse like a royal princess looking down at the man who loves her so fully and completely."

Andrea's lips parted in a smile as she wiped away a remnant of a tear with her shirt sleeve. She loosened her animal's reins with her left hand and turned its head away from the porch. Then she gigged its ribs with her boot heel and the horse responded by bounding up the gravelly incline which led to the high road and the route to Sullivan.

Chance watched her go, disappearing up the trace, passing in the corridor through the budding trees and resuming a journey that one day he hoped would circle back to him. He stood, his eyes affixed to Andrea's form until the trees along the lane swallowed her. Neunan, entered the house, found the folded paper containing the address and secured it inside his wallet. Then he went to the barn, saddled Sis and returned to the porch where he tethered the horse to a bush growing next to the steps. Changing his clothes, Chance returned to the porch and basked for a time in the morning sun before buttoning his uniform frock coat. He retrieved his knapsack from inside the farmhouse door, slung one of its straps over his shoulder and locked the portal behind him. He allowed his gaze to wander over the structures, the house, the barn; the fencing around the garden and all that was familiar and dear to him. Neunan blinked twice, took a breath and stepping off the porch, mounted his borrowed horse and started up the lane to the high road which would branch off to Windsor. From overhead a defiant scream caused Chance to look up. A red tailed hawk circled in slow pirouettes in the azure, blue sky above him. The appearance of the majestic bird and the undaunted spirit it exhibited was taken as an omen by young Neunan. He would survive and return to the farmstead if God permitted him the strength to do so and then he'd search until he found Andrea Edwards

The End

About the Author

Eᴅ LᴇCʀᴏɴᴇ ʜᴀs ᴘʀᴇᴠɪᴏᴜsʟʏ ᴘᴜʙʟɪsʜᴇᴅ two books of short stories; *The Grave on the Point* and *Beyond the Point*. Both books feature characters or plots set in the Midwest.

LeCrone graduated from Eastern Illinois University, married his high school sweetheart and fathered two beautiful daughters. A summer residency at The National Gallery of Art in Washington, a master's degree, and thirty three years of teaching followed before he retired. Hobbies which include Civil War artifact collecting, reading, black powder marksmanship, and gardening all honed his desire to produce his current book. He and his wife make their home on wooded acreage in rural, McHenry County, Illinois.

Epilogue

THIS BOOK IS A WORK of historical fiction although real personages and events are utilized within the text in order to provide a sense of time. The main characters are purely imaginary and no comparison to people either living or dead should be made.

Mathias Neunan is loosely based on the life of my great granduncle, Mathias LeCrone, who managed to fight in the war with Mexico and later in the early stages of the Civil War. Sergeant John Scott, who was portrayed as the uncle of Chance and Becky, was an actual soldier who was hanged by the Confederate authorities in Atlanta, Georgia, as one of the conspirators in the Great Locomotive Chase. Sergeant Henry Strieter, the flag bearer of the 41st Illinois, who carried the national colors in the action on the Pearl River, too, was also a non fictional person who was awarded the Medal of Honor for his valor.

General John McClernand, commander of the XIII Corps at Vicksburg, was removed from his position prior to the Confederate capitulation. Neunan's brigade was badly handled in a suicidal engagement in late July, on the Pearl River but General McClernand was not responsible for the debacle. In the Illinois general's defense, it should be pointed out that he, like other politically appointed officers, was held in low regard by West Point trained commanders. Grant and Sherman were often miffed at the ineptness of the appointees and made no attempt to conceal their attitudes. General McClernand returned to Springfield following his demotion, and resumed his law practice. He had married his deceased wife's younger sister during the formative stages of the Vicksburg campaign and his relief from commanding the XIII Corps on June 18, 1863, permitted him to return to his re-constituted household. McClernand eventually was recalled to duty and placed once again in command of the XIII Corps for a short period in 1864. He resigned in December of that year and took no part with his former charges as they joined the push by General Canby to capture Fort Morgan and Mobile, Alabama, in the final days of the war.

General Jacob Lauman, responsible for an ill advised attack on the Pearl River in July of 1863, was brought before a court of inquiry and cashiered from the service.

All the Regiments, Brigades, Corps, and Divisions did exist and their placements on the dates used in the text are as accurate as possible.

Colonel Issac Pugh of Decatur, commander of the 41st Illinois, never attained advancement in rank despite his sturdy leadership. He survived the war. The 41st was so decimated in number that it was consolidated with its sister regiment, the 53rd on December, 23, 1864, in Savannah, Georgia, at the conclusion of Sherman's March to the Sea.

Copperhead Sheriff John O'Hair escaped capture in the days following the riot in Charleston, Illinois, on March 28, 1864. He and an associate fled to Canada and remained there for a year before returning to Coles County where he was never prosecuted. Twenty-eight participants in the riot were arrested for their involvement in the incident and sixteen were sent to Fort Delaware by the military to await trial. The men languished there for seven months until they were released and sent home after the signing of an oath of allegiance to the federal government. A civilian criminal court was ordered to try two others accused of murder who took part in the riot, they being; John Redmon and George Rardin. Their defense team asked for and received a change of venue from Charleston to Shelbyville in Shelby County and then to the courthouse located at Effingham in Effingham County. On December 7, 1864, the charges against the two men were dropped and they were freed. In the case of the soldier of fortune, Englishman, George St. Leger Grenfell, who was to be executed for his role in the plot which attempted to free the rebel prisoners in Chicago, clemency was granted and his sentence was commuted to life at Fort Jefferson in the Dry Tortugas. Grenfell, and one of the Lincoln assassination conspirators, Dr. Samuel Mudd, served admirably during a yellow fever outbreak which swept through the inmates there. Escape, however, was always prevalent in the Englishman's mind. On a windswept, dark night, Grenfell and three others carried their ball and chain to a commandeered boat and went to sea. It was assumed by the prison authorities that the escapees' destination was Key West, Florida. The four, their boat, and their restrictive leg devices were never seen again.

Other names utilized in the text are the actual names of soldiers drawn from the regimental service rolls. Sheriff Sam Earp was the elected law enforcement official in Moultrie County until 1862. He was succeeded by a man named Ingram who completed his term of office in1866. The author reserves the right under the guise of poetic license to embellish the text by using the more flamboyant Earp name.

Freedmen's Bureau: Established on March 3, 1865. This agency was under the direction of the War Department and was headed by Union General O.O.Howard. It addressed all matters and concerns of the refugees and freedmen in the states under reconstruction. Its major accomplishments were in the area of schools, churches and education. The Bureau was disbanded once Union occupying forces were withdrawn from the southern states.

United States Sanitary Commission: Founded 1861-1866. A civilian, volunteer organization which staffed field hospitals, raised money, provided supplies and worked to educate the military and the government regarding health and sanitation. Leading advocates in the commission were; Dorothea Dix, Clara Barton, Elizabeth Blackwell, Mary Livermore, Louisa May Alcott, and Mary Ann Bickerdyke.

Camp Goode, located in Mattoon, Illinois, was renamed and known as Camp Terry after September18, 1862.

Historical points such as the village of Old Nelson, the Old Nelson Ford, the Monroe Ford, and the Sheep Ford, all in Moultrie County, Illinois, now lie beneath the waters of Lake Shelbyville.

Endorsements

Story teller Ed LeCrone has created a first rate story from a few little known events of the great American tragedy, The Civil War. By choosing a small community in central Illinois, Sullivan in Moultrie County, LeCrone has successfully drawn upon the local history of that era (because of the knowledge he gleaned while growing up there) and combined it with little known events of the Civil War era that could only have happened to the people from that area. He has woven these national events with the regional in a masterful manner. By using letters to and from the soldier, Chance Neunan, and his sweetheart back home, the story of the fighting which occurred near Vicksburg and Jackson, Mississippi, are accurately covered. The author connects the wounded main character, Neunan, to a recuperative leave which returns him to Illinois and into the middle of a Copperhead, antigovernment and antiwar riot in nearby Charleston.

By following the story line of *Fire on the Prairie*, the reader will become engrossed in the day by day events of military life as well as the civilian life at what could easily be referred to as the frontier of civilization. With, perhaps, a slight touch of Ambrose Bierce and also the macabre of Edgar Allen Poe, LeCrone has told a story well and, in all honesty, makes you wonder a bit about a possible sequel for further adventures of this young and adventurous soldier.

- Frank R. Crawford, author of *Proud to Say I Am a Union Soldier*, 2007.

While I have misgivings regarding historical novels where the use of actual occurrences serves simply as a backdrop to meet the needs of the author, I quickly discovered otherwise in the case of Ed LeCrone's *Fire on the Prairie*. It was but a few pages into the book that I began to rethink my earlier objections to such novels and found myself caught up in a rather surprising and entertaining story. I came to appreciate Ed's careful weaving of the basic storyline and sub-lines as he allowed his characters to flow in and out of factual events.

My basic objections to historical novels still stand but an exception in the case of *Fire on the Prairie* should be made. I can say honestly that I enjoyed Ed LeCrone's latest work.

-Dave Noe, co-author of *Firearms from Europe*, 1999.

LeCrone gives the reader a little bit of everything in *Fire on the Prairie*; war, love espionage and murder. Set during the American Civil War; LeCrone artfully weaves a tale of the challenges that were endured by folks at home on the farm in Moultrie County, Illinois, as well as those of our soldiers on faraway battlefields in Dixie. This historic novel keeps the reader on edge as our hero, a soldier boy in blue fights Rebels, Copperheads, and family tragedy while at the same time trying to find love. The ending is not to be missed...

-Ed Urban, publisher of *The History of the 36th Illinois Volunteer Infantry*

LaVergne, TN USA
18 May 2010
183144LV00003B/8/P